MY KINDA

Night

USA TODAY BESTSELLING AUTHOR
LACEY BLACK

My Kinda Night
Summer Sisters Book 2

Copyright © 2017 Lacey Black
Cover Design: Y'all. That Graphic
Editing by Kara Hildebrand
Format by Integrity Formatting

Published in the United States of America.
All rights reserved.

ISBN-13: 978-1-951829-21-6

MY KINDA

Night

1

Payton

It's a Summer sister tradition that on the first Saturday of each month, the six of us get together. We take turns picking the location or activity, anything from margaritas and a movie to wine and painting classes at the small gallery uptown. One thing, though, is as certain as the sun rising over the Chesapeake Bay every morning; there will be alcohol involved.

Always.

Tonight, it's another stupid painting class. Create and Paint, that's what this class is called. I prefer to call it "Painting sucks, let's get drunk!" while I chug my fruity Moscato because that's the only wine worth drinking. Abby whips out red every once in a while and I swear to God Almighty that I'm going to shrivel up and die like those nasty, sour grapes used to create red wine.

I'm the oldest of six Summer girls. Of course, I'm the boss, the leader, and the best at everything (except painting, obviously). As

I approach my thirty-third birthday in a couple of weeks at the end of January, I also realize that spending time with my sisters as much as I do is going to become more of a challenge.

Jaime is three years younger than me. She's the sister who ran away to college and never came back. Well, at least until her fiancé left her the week before the wedding. She moved home, had to move in with our dad and grandparents, and worked for me at Blossoms and Blooms for a short period of time.

Then she met Ryan. Watching those two discover their love for each other was like watching soft porn. Sparks and hormones flew like fireworks every time those two were within a fifty-foot radius of each other.

AJ is the third sister at twenty-eight, or Alison Jane as her birth certificate states. Though, we've called her by her nickname for as long as I can remember. She's the eighth grade math teacher at Jupiter Bay Junior High, home of the Hawks, where she's taught ever since receiving her teaching degree. She has also enrolled in online classes for her Master's degree. As of January twentieth, AJ will be a night student.

After AJ comes Meghan. She's twenty-six and a hygienist at the local dental office. How someone can work inside another's mouth all day and not get grossed out is beyond me. But she does it. Daily. Meg is also engaged to Josh, a man who treats her like the princess she is. Meg and Josh became engaged in December during a romantic trip to New York City for their anniversary. He went all out: Empire State Building, fancy dinner, down on one knee. It was perfect, just like they are.

Rounding out the Summer sisters are the twins, Lexi and Abby. Lexi, short for Alexis, gives me a run for my money in the boss department and is a hairdresser uptown. She's married to her high school sweetheart, Chris, who rarely attends any of our family functions. He's busy trying to take over the financial world, and believes that the only way to achieve that is to work nonstop. I don't think it's all roses and fairytales at the Jacobson house.

Abby, or Abigail, was born mere minutes before Lexi, but is as different as can be. She's reserved, quiet, and shy in ways that the rest of us aren't. Abby is an English Literature major and works as an editor for a major publishing house out of California. She's on her computer all day, and rarely ventures out of her little apartment. It's my goal in this new year to get her out and into the dating world, especially in light of the fact that her love for her best friend is unrequited. Levi is a great friend, but doesn't see the wonderful woman before him. He's too busy sticking his penis inside of every woman in the state of Virginia. (I say that lovingly.)

Let's not forget our father, Brian, and our grandparents, Orval and Emma. Inappropriate doesn't quite adequately describe the older couple who helped raise all six of us after our mom died. I was seventeen when she succumbed to ovarian cancer, leaving my father behind to get six girls through the teenage years. Enter the grandparents. I've got stories for miles, but we'll get to those later.

Born and raised in Jupiter Bay, a small town of about eight thousand along the Chesapeake Bay, I've become accustomed to the small town lifestyle. I own the local flower shop, where I devote every ounce of my soul to making it a success. I'm not gonna lie, I had my doubts there at the beginning. I didn't know anything about running a business, but was determined to make it work. It's a lot of work, especially with a small staff of one other employee to keep overhead down, but I'm successful. And proud of it!

And that brings us to tonight. It's the first Saturday of the New Year and we're busy celebrating with sandcastles and wine. Hops and Grapes, a local retailer for microbrews and wines made on the east coast, is the place for tonight's Paint and Create class. Right now, my beach scene resembles something a kindergartener would draw with finger paints.

"Mix together a little white with the brown until you get the light sandy color you're looking for. Dab your brush in the water and then in the paint, and make long strokes across the canvas."

Giggles erupt beside me. "She said long strokes," Lexi whispers not so quietly.

"I get to make long strokes. Ryan is impressively large in the man-junk area," Jaime says, gulping the last of her wine.

"Yes, we know. You tell us every chance you get." This from Abby.

"Yeah, it's starting to get annoying. If I had an impressive man-sword waiting for me at home every night, I'd never leave the house," AJ adds.

"Not worth it. I'll take my rabbit over a man any day. That baby has seven speeds and a rotating head," I grumble, making a mess out of my sandy beach.

"Stop being so grumpy. Maybe if you actually had the real deal for a while, you wouldn't be so damn cynical all the time," Jaime says from across the table. She never takes her eyes off her canvas as she makes smooth, straight brushstrokes.

My face burns and I pray the vultures I share genes with don't notice. Of course I don't get so lucky. I've always said if it weren't for bad luck, I wouldn't have any luck at all. Trying to concentrate on my masterpiece, I keep my eyes down and focused on the sandcastle in the corner of the scene.

"I think there's more to the story! Do you see her blushing?" Meghan's laughter flits from the opposite end of the table. How in the hell she can see my face is beyond me. It's probably that sister-radar all of us possess. It's so damn annoying.

"I am not." It's a weak defense, I know, but it's all I've got.

"Deny it all you want, big sister, but your face is definitely blushing," Lexi adds.

"Ladies, when you get your sandcastle the way you want it, we'll add a few details and highlights before moving on to the water." The woman instructing our class has worn a constant smile the entire hour we've been here, and frankly, I'm starting to think she hit the sauce way before our arrival tonight.

"Why does my sand look like cellulite?" AJ asks. "I give up. I'm just drinking from here on out."

Jaime glances over at our sister's painting. "My God, that's horrible. Thank God you're not the art teacher!"

"Cheers," AJ replies, raising her glass and tapping it against Jaime's.

"Any wedding plans yet, Meg?" Abby asks, wetting her brush before swiping it through the paint. Always the perfect student, that one.

"Not yet. We're thinking fall, though." Meghan's face lights up at the mere thought of her pending nuptials to Josh.

"That'll be the perfect time." Abby's able to keep her smile happy when she's in discussion, but I've seen the desolation in it too. Even tonight, I see something in her eyes that makes me sad. I'm sure her best friend is the root of her anguish, but I won't call her out on it tonight. That's a conversation to have at another time (with less alcohol).

By the time our three-hour torture session is up, each of us has painted waves rolling onto the beach, with a shovel, pail, and sandcastle. We pose as a group for pictures, each of us proudly displaying the fruits of our labor. My sisters each discuss where they're going to hang their newest creation, while I contemplate which closet I'll throw it in.

"Yours is great," Abby says with a big smile.

"Helen Keller could have done a better job," I retort with a snort of laughter.

As we say good night and thank the instructor, we all walk out together into the crisp early-January night. Not surprisingly, Josh and Ryan are waiting. Jaime and Meg practically run towards their men, each one jumping into their arms as if it's been days since they've seen each other instead of a few hours. Longing rips through my chest and settles into my stomach, heavy and unrelenting. I try to push those pesky feelings aside, but sometimes, it's just no use. They plant in my chest and brain and dig in deep.

"Good night," Abby says, pulling me into a hug.

"You going out tonight?" I ask, recalling her mention of Levi's gig earlier in the evening.

"No, I'm going to take my new painting home and hang it on the wall."

"Wow, don't overdo it now on a Saturday night, Abs. Too much excitement will cause wrinkles."

"I just, I don't really go to his gigs anymore."

"Why?" I ask, though already knowing the answer.

She shrugs her shoulders and gives me a small smile. "Just not feeling up to it."

I let it go. I already know she doesn't go anymore is because it's too painful to watch him leave with some skanky bimbo with a dress size bigger than her IQ. Levi may very well never know what he's missing with Abby, but the romantic in me is still hopeful of him getting his shit together and realizing he loves her.

Hey, I may be cynical as hell in the love department, but I'm still a woman. And this woman wants only the best and a happily ever after for every one of her sisters.

As for me? Well, I've decided that my happily ever after will be in the form of cats. I'll be the little old lady wearing hair curlers and her bathrobe around town, picking up every stray feline she can find.

And you know what? That's okay. Not everyone is cut out for the spouse, house, and perfect postcard life. Despite what they tell you in the romance novels or in Disney movies, there isn't someone out there for everyone. Sometimes, a person is just supposed to be alone.

That's my destiny.

Dean

2

Sundays are always the same. Wake up, get dressed, make coffee, and breakfast. Grocery shopping, lunch at the café with my mom, and then whatever afternoon activity my five-year-old daughter deems necessary. Followed by dinner, bath, a story or two, and bedtime. That's my life.

She's my life.

I've become accustomed to going with the flow. When you're a single dad, you learn to bend your knees in just about every little detail of life. Schedules change, things happen, or more often than not, things don't happen. It's a part of life for everyone, but none more than when you're a singular parental unit taking care of a child.

My schedule isn't my own. I know that, understand, and accept it. It's been that way from day one. From the moment that tiny, wrinkly little girl was placed in my arms, I've been a goner, a victim of eternal love.

If only I could say the same about Brooke, my ex.

I have exactly seven minutes left before my daughter wakes up, and I'm not about to let unpleasant thoughts of my past damper my morning. As soon as Bri wakes up, my day officially begins. Never mind that I've already finished two loads of laundry, emptied the dishwasher, worked out, and showered, all before seven. Sleep is something I gave up years ago, and if I'm being honest with myself, I lost it long before Bri came into my life. I was in no way a partier in college, but I could stay up all night studying or getting lost in whatever book series I was reading. College was more about making good grades and securing a well-paying job than anything else for me. In fact, I think the only party I went to in those four years at university was when I went inside one to deliver a pizza.

My mother was a single parent and barely made ends meet. She worked her ass off at two jobs so that I could have the necessary basics that most other kids receive day in and day out. She did the best she could, even if we had to do without, and I'm forever grateful for her sacrifice.

I make sure the house is ready for the hurricane that comes with a five-year-old. The toys are picked up and neatly stacked in the storage bins, but I smile knowing that it'll only last just a bit longer. As soon as she's up, Bri will be all over this place, playing with every toy she can find.

When the clock finally hits seven, I set my coffee cup down and head towards her room. The pink walls are bright as the sunlight reflecting off the Bay filters through white curtains. She helped me pick out everything in her room a year ago when I purchased this house and we made the move to Jupiter Bay. It wasn't a far move, nor a difficult one to make. Especially in light that we were only heading one town over from Ridgewood, the place where I was born and raised. And it's also still close enough to my mom, who helps when she can with Bri.

She's sleeping on her stomach, with her rear up and her knees tucked beneath her. She's slept this exact same way since she was an infant. Another smile spreads across my face, especially when I gently shake the sleeping girl.

"Sweetie, time to get up," I say soothingly.

"No," she grumbles, turning and facing away from me.

"'Fraid so. Let's get up and have breakfast. We have to meet grandma in a few hours."

"I don't wanna." Her surly attitude doesn't surprise me in the least. Waking up in the morning is her least favorite thing to do. She's more of a night owl the way her mother was. Sometimes it's difficult to get her in bed at a decent hour.

"Too bad," I say with a laugh. Grabbing the Frozen blanket, I pull it off her and scoop up her small body. "Come on, sweetie. Let's go to the bathroom and then get breakfast."

I deposit my daughter in the bathroom and proceed to the kitchen. The griddle is hot and ready to make pancakes. I pour a few onto the pan just as Sleeping Beauty enters the room.

"I'm tired, Daddy. I want to go back to bed."

"You know you can't, honey. You need to eat so we can get dressed and get groceries."

"Can I have mac and cheese when we have lunch with Mimi?" Mimi is the name she started using for my mom when she was learning to talk.

Flipping over the pancake, I ask, "Don't you eat mac and cheese every day?"

"Yes, because it's yummy."

"It is yummy, but I'd love you to have something other than mac and cheese today," I say as I pull the first three pancakes off the griddle. "Grab the syrup. You can have these," I add as I set the pancakes on her plate.

Pouring more batter on the griddle, I watch out of the corner of my eye as she douses her food in sticky syrup. Looks like we're taking another bath this morning. Smiling at myself, I flip three more and my stomach growls while I watch them cook. Fortunately, that's the good thing about pancakes: they're quick. Placing the food on another plate, I join my daughter at the table.

The rest of our morning progresses as we get ready, grocery shop, run back home to put them away, and finally head up to the café to meet Mom. She's already waiting at a booth when we enter.

"Mimi!" Bri yells in the busy café as she runs towards my smiling mom.

"Good morning, sunshine. How was your morning?"

"Good. Daddy said crap when we were in the store. He got all the way to the front and remembered some'ting in the back." Without a care in the world, Bri grabs the cup of crayons the waitresses always deliver to the table for her to color on the white paper placemat.

"Bri, we don't say bad words, even if you're repeating something Daddy said. Got it?" I say in my best 'stern daddy' voice.

"Got it," she replies sweetly with that smile that melts my heart. It's no wonder she's spoiled rotten. I'm helpless against those big brown doe eyes and that smile.

Mom smiles broadly at me. "She's got quite the memory," she says humorously.

"Yeah, it's great. She doesn't hear me when I'm in the kitchen and she's watching TV in the next room, but the moment I mumble a curse word under my breath, she has the hearing of an owl."

"All kids, honey. All kids have that. It's called selective hearing, and you had it too when you were younger."

The perky waitress brings out our usual two glasses of ice tea and a lidded cup of apple juice. "Good morning, Brielle. What are you going to draw today?"

"A zebra and an elephant!" Bri replies, scribbling pink frantically on the paper.

Jenna sets two menus on the table as she says, "That will be a fabulous picture."

"You can have it when I'm done." Scribble, scribble, scribble.

"I would love it. I'll put it on my fridge next to the picture of the goat."

Jenna winks at me. "I'll let you look at the menu and be back in a flash to take your orders."

"Mac and cheese!" Bri yells.

"Indoor voice, please. And we've already discussed this. Your choices are cheeseburger, chicken fingers, or spaghetti."

"Sketty, please," she answers without looking up from her masterpiece.

"You should ask her out," Mom says. It takes me a moment to catch up and realize what she's said.

"What? Who?" I lower my voice in an attempt to not be overheard by little ears.

"Jenna. She likes you."

"She's too young."

"No such thing, honey."

"Not true. There's definitely a too young category, Mom. Especially for a man who just crossed into his thirties."

"Fine, whatever. She's probably mid-twenties, which is not too young for you."

I consider her words for a few moments, but quickly toss them out. She's cute, funny, friendly, and always pleasant to Bri, but even with all of those attributes on her side, I'm just not into her.

Fact of the matter, I've found myself *into* only one woman lately. I've spent six months fantasizing about someone who is as hot and cold as they come. Friends one moment and ripping each other's clothes off the next. Truth is she's the only woman to get my heart racing in a long damn time, if you know what I mean. And can I really call her a friend? It's not like we hang out. Ever. It's a weird situation, and one I'm not ready to dissect at the moment, especially with my Mom.

"She's a sweet girl, but I'm just not interested." Her brown eyes are focused on mine, assessing and reading me like a book.

"Fine. If not her, then who?"

Before I can reply, Jenna returns to take our orders. I order the spaghetti for Bri, a Ruben for myself, and Mom orders a turkey club. Since our conversation, I pay a little more attention to Jenna. Her smiles hold a little flirtation and her eyes linger a little longer than expected in casual conversation. My mind wanders to the possibilities a relationship with the friendly blond might entail, but the daydreams are brushed aside by the memory of a brunette with deep green eyes and a smart mouth. She monopolizes way too much of my thoughts and even more of my dreams.

Damn, is she front and center in those. And usually naked.

A few random nights with her did nothing to quench the desire sparked to life by her. In fact, I'm not sure I'll ever be sated. Not after that first night, nor the few that followed. But rules are rules, even if I'm not the one to set them. There are certain relationships that are to be strictly platonic.

Ours is one of them.

Jenna leaves our table to take care of another. I relax in the booth, my arm extended across the backrest. We both watch Bri color for a few minutes before I initiate the topic of work.

"So, I've thought about what you said and I've decided to go." I don't have to refresh her memory because I'm positive she knows exactly what I'm referring to. It's not like we have a lot of topics hanging open and unresolved.

"I think that's wise. You need to for work, and we'll be fine."

Exhaling deeply, I give her my full attention. "I know. It's just a bad time at work, and it'll take a lot of coordination with you to help with Bri."

"I've already told you that I'll adjust my schedule, Dean. You need this conference for work as part of your continued education. I'll stay at your house with Bri, get her off to school, and then head to work myself. She'll still go to Miss Nancy's after school and I'll get her when I get off work. It's for, what, three days? I think I can manage for thirty-six hours. We'll be fine."

And they will be, I know it. It's just that I've never left Bri for that length of time. The occasional sleepover with my mom is one thing, but three whole nights? When that's all you've done for just over five years, it's hard to let someone else take the wheel for a few days.

But she's also right that it's required of me for my job. I've put it off three times now, and I'm unable to get out of not going any more. My boss and one of the owners of the firm gave me strict orders to attend this conference or else. And since I require my job to, you know, buy groceries and pay my mortgage, I guess it's off to Richmond I go.

"I know, Mom. I just hate the thought of leaving her."

Jenna delivers our food and all conversations turn to Bri and her animal drawings. She's obsessed with everything animals from barnyard to the ones in the wild. Her room might be pink but there's animal posters covering parts of the walls and an array of stuffed dogs, cats, horses, cows, monkeys, and even a zebra on her bed.

"When do you leave?" Mom asks when the plates are being collected.

"Just over two weeks. It's a Wednesday through Friday conference," I say as I grab the check in the center of the table. "This one's on me."

"You got it last week," she chastises with a frown.

Mom found a steady, decent paying job several years back, and while I know she can easily pick up the check at lunch, I still prefer to get it. Call me chivalrous or old fashioned, but I just think the man–or in my case, son–should pay.

"You can get next week if you're quick enough," I retort with a grin.

"I thought I raised you better than to be a wisenheimer. At least let me cover the tip," Mom says as she pulls two fives from her purse.

"Fine," I say before turning towards Bri. "Time to go, pumpkin."

"Grab your jacket, Bri, and I'll help you get it on while Daddy goes up and pays the check."

"'Kay, Mimi. Can we go to the park?" I hear my daughter ask as I head up to the counter.

Glancing over my shoulder I watch my mom take Bri by the hand and head outside to wait for me. The café is always busy for Sunday lunch, and today is no different. As I collect my change and head towards the door, a familiar face is walking through. I stop in my tracks at the first sight I've had of her in several weeks. She's stunning in a light blue sweater that hugs her glorious chest, tight dark jeans covering my favorite pair of legs, and tan ankle boots that I wouldn't mind seeing wrapped around my neck.

She's a vision.

And when those dark green eyes lock on mine, I'm a goner. Completely smitten and she doesn't even know it. My chest burns as oxygen fails to move through my lungs. Her smile starts hesitant but spreads sincerely to light up her heart-shaped face. There's warmth and familiarity reflecting in her eyes until a woman walks in and stands beside her.

She instantly closes me off, shutting down the flutter of happiness I saw starting to settle on her face. She warmly greets her companion, a woman whose resemblance is uncanny. A sister, probably.

Instead of letting this moment turn uncomfortable, I offer them both cordial greetings and head towards the door. Before I can breach the threshold, however, I can't help but turn back and glance over my shoulder. She's there, standing beside a table filling up with people I can see as her family, but her eyes are on me. They lock for several heart-pounding seconds before the corner of her mouth turns upward. I can't stop my own smile from cresting my lips.

Winking at the woman that I often run into in my dreams–and those day ones when I'm alone in the shower–I turn and step out into the sunlight. Jupiter Bay is a small town, and I'm never prepared for the way my body reacts to seeing her. My libido fires to life and my blood starts to hum. I'm always caught off guard when I run into her, but I'm left yearning for more. She gave me a taste, and I'm left wanting. More of everything.

More Payton Summer.

Payton

"Who was that?" AJ asks as we take a seat beside each other at the largest table in the café.

"Who?" I ask casually.

"Seriously? Who? Ummm, the hottie with his eyes on you. Don't pretend you didn't notice. Grandma has twenty-eighty vision and *she* could even see those invisible sparks."

"What hottie? What did I miss?" Grandma says from behind, startling me in my chair.

"Some guy was checking Payton out," AJ tells her in a singsong voice.

"Ahhh, Payters. Do you want me to go get his number for you?" Grandma asks, taking a seat at the end of the table beside Grandpa. Of course, she says it loud enough to catch the attention of everyone at the table. I can feel the heat creep up my neck and land squarely in my cheeks.

"No, Grandma, I don't need his number," I reply while reaching for the glass of ice water in front of me.

"Back in our day, we didn't have those phones. When we liked someone, we had to ask their parents if we could court their daughter," Grandpa adds.

"Psssh! The only courting you did was in the backseat of that old station wagon," Grandma hollers over the noise in the café. Pretty much all commotion and activity inside the restaurant stops instantly. Cue that blush again.

"I loved that ol' car," Grandpa says with a chuckle.

"Anyway, if you're too shy, Payters, I'll go flag down the hottie and get his phone number for you." All eyes turn towards me.

"No, thank you, Grandma. I'm good."

"There's no substitute for the real thing, Pay. No amount of toys can satisfy a woman the way a man can."

"Jesus, we haven't even taken our seats yet and we're already talking about penises?" Ryan says, holding out an empty seat across from me for my sister Jaime.

"Or lack thereof," AJ says. "Grandma was getting ready to school Payton on the differences between a vibrator and the real deal. Apparently, Grandma's an expert."

"I am an expert. I've been playing with one since I was old enough to drive a car. I've seen my fair share of meat sausages, girls. Big ones, little ones that curved to the side. Once, I even saw a black one that was bigger than my forearm."

And cue the choking on my water. AJ tries to pound on my back, but she's too busy laughing to really help in the matter. Ryan is trying to hide his laughter behind his menu and poor Abby looks like she'd rather melt into the floor and disappear. Everyone else is fighting their own battle with laughter. The only person not surprised by Grandma's blunt comment is Grandpa. In fact, he seems completely unfazed at all the penis talk–especially since a good chunk of it wasn't pertaining to his.

"Can we talk about something other than penises in a family-friendly café?" I beg.

"Like that man who was making moon-eyes at you?"

"You didn't even see him. How do you know he was making any kinda eyes at me?"

"I know these things, Payter Potater. I'm *Grandma.*"

She says it like that's supposed to be a good enough reason, and because I don't have the energy or the desire to fight her on it, I let it go. Of course, she thinks she's right and that's why I'm not fighting back. The fact is, I don't want to draw more attention to the man who makes my pulse quicken and my panties melt. I've spent four amazing nights with him in the last six months, but no more.

I can't.

We practically work together in a sense, and it's a line I can't cross. My business means everything to me, therefore you don't diddle where you eat. Or in my case, you don't diddle where you work–again. That one time was a mistake. An amazing, fantastic, orgasmic mistake. One I won't make again. I still have a hard time looking at that stainless steel workstation without recalling the feel of that cold metal against my bare chest while he made me scream his name not once, but twice.

And let's not forget the fact that my front windows are all open to the street. Thank God he had enough sense to turn off the lights in the front of the flower shop before sliding his dick inside me from behind.

I shudder at the memory.

I swore that would be our last time. Hell, I said that after the first night. And the time after that. Next thing I knew, we'd spent four different nights together. Besides that one night at my business, one that spilled over to my place later, we'd always met up at my house. Hell, I don't even know where he lives. All I know is that we're linked professionally, and therefore, shouldn't have engaged in sex. Not once, and definitely not four times.

"You feeling okay? You're all flushed?" Jaime asks from across the table.

"Fine," I reply, sipping more water.

"Don't let her bother you. She only wants to help."

"I know. I just wish she'd lay off me finding a man, you know? Not everyone is cut out for coupledom."

She stares at me hard. "That's bullshit and you know it. I'm the poster child for wanting to stay single forever, Pay. And look at me now," she says as she glances over at her boyfriend. They both smile before Ryan places a kiss on her lips. They're always kissing and feeling each other up. I guess if I had that new, crazy love feeling, I'd be all lovey dovey, touchy feely too.

But I'm not.

Thank God.

"Hey, Jaime, how did it go with Ryan's family at Christmas?" Meghan asks.

"Fine," she replies quickly. Too quickly.

Lexi must pick up on it too because her eyes narrow into little slits as she zeros in on her target. "There's a story. I can tell."

"No, no story. How are the wedding plans coming, Meg?" she asks, going for the redirect.

"No you don't! What happened?" Lexi insists. When she sinks her teeth into something, she's not about to ease up.

Jaime's eyes close before she glances over at Ryan. He's smiling like the cat that ate the canary, which basically just confirms that there's a story there.

"Fine," she mumbles, conceding. "Everything was great at first. I loved helping his mother cook and his sister was friendly and easy to talk to. We hit it off quickly. On Christmas Eve, I ran upstairs to shower, and well, Ryan ended up needing a shower at the same time."

Ryan snorts beside her. "Babe, I didn't need a shower."

"Anyway," she interrupts, drawing out that one word. "We were, you know, together in the shower, when his mom came into our room to bring an extra blanket for the bed since it gets cold at night in New York. She heard my scream in the shower and thought I hurt myself. She can running in and…"

"And Mom caught me in the upswing during some of my best moves. I've never killed a hard-on so quick in my life."

"That's saying something considering you two have been busted getting freaky more times than all of us combined," I retort with a laugh.

"My boobs were pressed against the Plexiglas shower door, Payton. It doesn't get any more humiliating than that."

"What about the time you were busted by Barney the cop while having sex in that field entrance?" Lexi asks.

"Or what about the time you had a screaming competition with your neighbors at the Bed and Breakfast, only to find out it was Grandma and Grandpa?" Meghan asks through her own laughter.

"Oh God, those were so humiliating too."

"Are you and 'Oh God' fooling around under the table over there?" Grandma yells towards Jaime, loud enough to catch the attention of those around us. Her face burns with mortification.

"No!"

"One of these days, I'd love for you to say, 'Yes. Yes, I am stroking him under the table.'"

"Oh God, Payton! I could never do that," she replies, shock mixed with her laughter.

"No, I bet you wouldn't, but Lexi would. Too bad she's stuck with Chris the Dud." I gape at my sister, shocked that those words actually came out of my mouth. I've thought Chris was all wrong for my sister, basically as long as I've known him, but I've never actually said it out loud.

"It's okay," Jaime whispers, glancing over at Lexi. "She didn't hear you."

I sigh in relief. Even if I'm not a Chris fan, he's still my sister's husband. He tries really hard to provide for her financially, but not on a personal level the way you'd expect a spouse to. Case in point, the one thing she wants in this world is a baby. She went last month for testing at a big hospital and her results came back clear. There seems to be no problems with her ovulation or her parts. Chris, on the other hand, won't go get tested. He keeps putting her off, saying it'll happen naturally if it's meant to be.

Shouldn't a husband *want* to go get tested to find out if there's something that can be done to help the process along? Especially because that's what she wants most in this world?

Something nags at the back of my head. Why wouldn't he get checked out? Does he not want a child as desperately as his wife? Maybe he's embarrassed. I've read articles where the man feels inadequate when found to have a problem with his sperm count. I mean, aren't all men supposed to be able to produce an heir? Therefore when unable to get the job done, they feel less manly. Or some shit like that.

Whatever.

All I know is that my sister wants a baby, but for some reason, he's either not ready or willing to make that happen.

And that really pisses me off.

I glance over at Lex, not surprised to see the seat beside her occupied by someone other than her husband. In fact, Chris is absent more than he is in attendance when it comes to family functions. It doesn't matter if it's a night or weekend, either. He's always working, wining and dining prospective clients or his existing clients, trying to get more business from them. As a young financial advisor at Edward Jones, he's always looking for ways to get his foot in the door before those of the two senior advisors in the office.

"You okay, sweetie?" I'm startled from my own thoughts by my dad, Brian, who bends down and places a kiss on my cheek.

"I'm good, Dad. How are you?"

"Can't complain," he answers and takes the final open seat next to Josh. They immediately begin talking.

My dad seems to be smiling a little more than in the past. Losing my mom to ovarian cancer when I was seventeen left a big hole in our family, including my dad. He devoted his entire life to raising his six girls, but even then, it was tough. He had to work full-time to be able to support us, and thankfully, my grandparents were around to help out. Otherwise, I'm sure it would have fallen heavily on my shoulders.

In the fifteen years since Mom passed, I've never seen him so much as look at another woman, let alone take one out to dinner. I'm sure he's lonely; hell, how could he not be? But he never lets on that his life is anything less than full. At least on the outside. But deep down, I see his sadness. I couldn't imagine losing the love of my life at such a young age. The thought alone leaves me sweaty in the pit area.

"Payters, I think you should sign up for online dating," Grandma says after our orders are taken. Everyone stops and stares at me. Again.

"What is this, pick on Payton day?"

"Never. I think it would be a great way to meet men your own age."

Fidgeting uncomfortably in my seat, I say, "I don't need to meet men. I meet plenty of men all the time."

"I'm not talking about the ones coming in to buy flowers. I'm talking about the available ones that are looking to play hide the salami with my gorgeous granddaughter."

"Could you not talk about the salami and my daughter in the same sentence, Emma?" Dad chastises before chugging his tea.

"Fine. Payton, what you need is a good ol' fashioned round of bumping uglies," Grandma rephrases happily.

The entire table groans.

When the silence descends on the table, Abby speaks up quietly. "I've thought about online dating."

Her confession catches me, along with the rest of my sisters off guard. "Really?" I ask, trying to mask my surprise.

"Yeah. I mean, it's hard for me to get out and meet people when you're trapped in front of your computer screen fourteen hours a day with work. I thought I'd see what it was all about, you know?" She wrings her hands together and worries her bottom lip with her teeth.

"I don't really like the idea," Dad says. "There are all kinds of weirdos out there, Abby."

"It's just something I've been considering lately. I don't know why I said it out loud. It's not like I've decided anything," she adds, turning her attention to a cracker packet from the basket on the table. The way she stares at it you'd think it was the most fascinating cracker packet in the entire world.

"Well, if that's what you want, we support you," Meghan chimes in. "Just promise us you'll be careful."

The rest of lunch progresses with minimal talk of online dating, fertility pillows, and sex. Even though they're completely inappropriate most of the time, I can't help but adore the way Grandpa rubs the top of Grandma's hand. They're totally touchy feely, often bordering on that fine line between loving and PDA. Oh, who am I kidding? They usually jump straight over that line and dive headfirst into groping.

What would it be like to love someone so completely that you'd risk public indecency on a regular basis because you just can't help yourself? To find that one person who makes you laugh and causes your body to sing at the same time? Someone who'll never make you cry?

Long ago, I thought maybe I had found that someone. Not all frogs transform into a prince. Some are just frogs through and through. And not every love is a great romance.

My mind instantly bypasses Cole and jumps straight to the man who triggers many dirty thoughts. He might have left his shirt behind after our first night together, but he took something when he left. In just a few encounters, he bulldozed through the reinforced walls I built surrounding my heart to protect it from getting hurt by those who claim to love you. He unknowingly broke through my tough exterior and started to make me like him.

Bastard.

4

Dean

"Dean, we have you all set up to leave on Tuesday evening. The conference begins at eight A.M. sharp Wednesday, and with the time it would take to travel to Richmond, we've decided to include an extra night at the hotel so you can arrive the night before."

My heart skitters in my chest. Shit, now I have to leave even earlier. "Thank you, sir. I'll have to make sure my mom is available to help with my daughter for the extra night. If it doesn't work, I'll leave early enough the morning of to arrive in plenty of time for the first conference on Wednesday."

Mr. Corbin looks annoyed at my response. He's definitely more accustomed to a "yes, sir" answer when he gives an order. "Well, keep me posted."

"Will do, sir."

We finish up our brief meeting. Most of my clients I rescheduled or will be taking care of their needs prior to leaving on this three-now four-day adventure, but there are a few that Mr. Corbin will have to be ready to assist if the need should arise. It never fails that while you're gone, someone forgets to pay their quarterly business taxes or submit for an extension by the mandated deadline. No matter how much planning you do, financial emergencies always arise.

Our receptionist, Cora, delivers a sandwich from the corner deli when she returns from her lunch break. The new year brings the busy season for anyone in accounting, which is why I'm surprised Mr. Corbin is sending me to this conference. Reviewing updated tax laws can wait until summer when things aren't so hectic that I have to eat a lunch meat sandwich at my desk an hour after I was supposed to.

Grabbing my phone, I dial Mom's cell. I'm not sure how busy she'll be, but I'm prepared to leave a message. Wouldn't be the first time she's unavailable to take a personal call in the middle of the workday. So I'm pleasantly surprised when she answers on the second ring.

"Hello?"

"Hey, Mom. How's it going?"

"Oh, not too bad. Just finishing up a late lunch," she answers. I can hear a bag crinkling through the phone.

"Me too. Listen, there's a slight change in plans. The conference starts at eight sharp Wednesday, which means they want to send me the night before."

"Probably a good idea. I don't mind coming over Tuesday after work. I can help get dinner started so you can eat with Bri before you head out."

"Thanks, Mom."

"No worries, son. That's what I'm here for. I've already talked to Angel and she's flexible with my hours during that time. She knows that I'm playing Daddy for the week."

I recall all those years my mom was Mom *and* Dad to me. And now here I am, playing a dual role for my own daughter. This is definitely not how I saw my life turning out.

"You're still picking her up from Nancy's today, right?"

"Of course I am. I wouldn't miss my standing Wednesday afternoons with my granddaughter."

We talk for another few minutes before signing off. Mom works in a small family-owned jewelry store for a third generation jeweler. Angel Anthony has been in charge of the company her grandfather started back in nineteen sixty-five for fifteen years already, and the business is flourishing. She's compassionate and fair as an employer, and Mom loves her.

Since Mom gets off early on Wednesdays, which just happens to be my late night at work, she picks up my daughter and takes her back to my place, where they cook dinner together. By the time I get home, dinner smells delicious, and they got to spend a little time together. It works for us, but I'm not oblivious to the fact that my mom is a huge help when it comes to raising my daughter.

The afternoon progresses slowly in a flurry of numbers and reports. My days are filled with client appointments, preparing income taxes for individuals and businesses alike. The basic taxes are few and far between. Most of those standard, easy taxes go to quick service agencies like Hewett Jackson or H&R Block. The ones that come to an accountant's office are businesses or those individuals with lots of deductions and filing long form.

That's where we come in.

There are four of us at this agency, and since there's limited accountants in town, we're busting-ass busy. There's another smaller firm of two CPAs, as well as an older woman who's been at it for almost forty years. At thirty-one, I'm the youngest at Corbin and Denton, but not new to the business. Back home in Ridgewood, I was young, hungry, and eager to play with numbers all day, and happily started at the bottom. Right out of college, I worked for the man who mentored me. Since Ridgewood is a small town of about six thousand, I knew the Brady family growing up. I interned there during the summers, making copies and doing just about everything I could to learn the ins and outs of the business.

That's also how I met Brooke.

Even though I will never regret my relationship with her, after all she gave me my daughter, but she's a subtle reminder of why you don't date your clients.

As I glance down at my next few appointments, I see the one name I've come to crave. It's not an appointment, per se, but a scheduling note that her fourth quarter income and employment taxes are due in my office. That means that after she closes up shop, she'll be stopping by my office–and on my late night, too. My day suddenly just got a whole lot better.

I get to see the woman who invades my dream, my shower fantasies, and those rare daydreams where I get a few moments of peace.

I get to see Payton Summer.

Payton

I'm losing my mind. I've been running around like a chicken with my head cut off for the last two days, and today isn't any better. As enthralled as I am that my business took off, it's days like these that I wonder if I'll ever be able to catch up and breathe.

The shop is a mess, the workstation's covered in greenery, and the display case empty. All a good sign, right?

Right.

Rachel has been busy, working more than her normal hours. She's been taking orders and helping the walk-in customers, while I make the arrangements and deliver them, if required. I wish I could say it's just the peak busy season, but it's mid-January, so that's not it. Maybe my business is finally taking off, full steam ahead.

It's quite possibly time for me to look into hiring more help. My first order of business will be to find out if Rachel is interested in working full-time. If she is, then I could probably get away with hiring another part-time employee to help with deliveries and extra floor coverage. If she's not interested, then I'm looking for a full-time employee.

Either way, the extra help is necessary for my business, and my sanity.

Believe it or not, Grandma has been coming in and helping lately. When she gets bored watching General Hospital on the Soap Opera Network, she meanders on up to Blossoms and Blooms and helps out. Mostly she just talks to the customers and gets in the way. She can't use the cash register, can't make arrangements, and is a little crazy behind the wheel. So really she's just there to take orders and gossip with my customers. (Like she is now.) But for some crazy reason, they all love her, so I don't complain.

"Remember that trade show I registered for last year?" I ask when I see the note written on the calendar by the register.

"That flower show in Richmond? You signed up last fall, right?"

"Yeah, well, it's supposed to be in a week and a half. I think I'm going to see if I can get my registration back."

Grandma stops in her tracks and stares at me. "Why?"

I exhale deeply. "Because we're so busy and it's not fair to Rachel to have to cover for three days by herself."

"I'll be here to help her," she says, "We'll be fine." She sounds so confident, like it's a no brainer for me to leave the business I built over the last three years to my part-time employee and my eighty-year-old grandma. No worries at all.

"It might not be the right time," I tell her, my words holding no conviction. Honestly, I really want to go to this show, but I just don't see how when the shop has been as busy as it has been.

"If not now, then when? This show is every January, right? Well, your next opportunity is next year. Go, Payton. It's a great opportunity for you to learn new things and incorporate them into your business." She walks up and stands directly in front of me.

"I want you to go. We'll make sure your business is still standing while you're gone."

Swallowing hard, I look down at the little spitfire woman. "God, I hope so. You really think it would be alright?"

"I know it will be. Go. You deserve this. You deserve a little time away, even if it is work related."

I offer her a watery smile, which she returns with her own wrinkly grin. There are huge advantages in attending this show. I was lucky to even get tickets. Florists from New York and Chicago always attend, display their latest creations, and teach a few tricks during expert how-to sessions. It's an amazing opportunity to talk shop with fellow florists and pitch new ideas over coffee. Honestly, I can't wait. "Okay. I'll go."

We silently get back to work, me closing down the shop while Grandma straightens up. "You know what they say about tulips, don't you, Payters?"

"What's that, Grandma?"

"Two lips. Like the female flower. Or as your Grandpa likes to call it, the vajayjay."

"Grandma," I chastise, thankful that we're alone at this particular moment. She's busy sweeping up flower stems and greenery snips, or at least I thought she was.

"Delicate, soft, and fragrant as a flower."

"Please stop talking," I beg as I close out the register and the credit card machine.

"If you don't want to talk about the female anatomy, then what can I help with, Pay?"

"Nothing. Thanks for helping me catch up," I reply, grabbing an empty moneybag and inserting today's deposit.

"You're all done for the night?" she asks, returning the broom to the small closet in the back storage room.

"I wish," I snort. "I've got about an hour's worth of work ordering supplies. Then I need to drop off the quarterly income and employment tax documents to Corbin and Denton." Glancing down at my watch, I realize how late it is. The last customer didn't leave until five thirty since they were finalizing flowers for a loved one's funeral. "Shit, I'll never make it."

"What's the matter?"

"They close at six. I'll never get over there in time. I'll have to drop it all off in the morning and pray my accountant has enough time to get it taken care of."

"Let me help. I'm heading home now to help Grandpa with a little problem he sent me a text about a few minutes ago." She looks down and gapes at her phone.

"Is Grandpa okay?"

"Oh, he's fine, dear." She smirks. "At least he will be when I get home and can give him some tender loving care. It happens every time he takes one of those little blue pills."

Please don't say any more. Please don't.

"Can I drop that off before I head home?"

Glancing down at the folder that needs to be at the accountant's office by six, I concede to let her help once more today. Even if I leave right now and run over there, I still have to come back and get more work done. If I can stay here and get to it, I might be able to make it home before reruns of *Full House* start on Nick.

"Fine. Take this envelope to Corbin and Denton. One of the secretaries or assistants is usually there. Just hand them the envelope."

"Who do I leave it for?" she asks, reaching for the packet of papers.

My heart speeds up and tap dances in my chest just thinking about him. The way he looks sitting behind his large mahogany desk. His perfect hair the color of smooth caramel, his eyes hidden behind glasses so deep brown that they almost look black. Until you're close–close enough to feel his breath on your face–where you can see the brown ring around his iris. The way his lips feel against mine, a dance so slow and sweet that I'm left breathless and yearning.

"Earth to Payton," Grandma says, waving her hands in front of my face.

"Oh, sorry."

"You feeling all right? You're all flush and panting." She places the back of her wrinkled hand on my forehead.

"I'm fine. Just getting tired already," I reply, taking a step back and busying my hands with the remaining paperwork. "His name is Dean McIntire, and he should be there."

"I better get going so I make it before they close." She quickly gathers up her jacket and the paperwork and heads towards the back door. "Oh, and Payton?" I stop in my tracks as she glances over her boney shoulder. "The occasional orgasm might help alleviate that blush."

Before I can even react, she's out the door, whistling a tune that sounds like Justin Timberlake.

My cell phone rings as I'm locking the back door. With the deposit bag tucked beneath my arm, I dig into my purse for the phone. Once I grab it, I start to walk towards my car, which is parked in a small lot used by a few businesses on my block. The name on the screen causes me to stop in my tracks.

Dean.

Part of me wants to ignore the call, knowing that I'm not strong enough to say no if he were calling for personal reasons. I should have said no the first time we met up, and definitely shouldn't have agreed to the three meetings that followed over the course of two months. We both realized that a relationship wasn't in our best interest, and even though the chemistry is plausible and visible, it just isn't meant to be.

"Hello?" I ask, worried he'll hear the nervousness in that one word.

"Hi, Payton. It's Dean. Do you have a minute?" he asks. Something in his own voice catches my attention. Apprehension.

Slipping into my car and dropping my bags on the passenger seat, I work the key into the ignition and start up the car. "Yeah, I'm just leaving the shop. What's up?"

"Is this a joke?" he asks, completely catching me off guard.

"A joke? What are you talking about?" I ask, cranking the heater up to warm my vehicle.

"There are some…discrepancies in your statements that you dropped off this evening. I was glancing over it before I headed home so that I was prepared to get it all filed tomorrow morning, but some of the numbers are definitely…off."

"Off? What does that mean?"

"Well, if I were to submit it the way it is, you'd probably be audited for tax fraud."

My heart jumps and hammers in my chest. "What?" I whisper.

"Yeah, I'll be honest, it looks like someone added a bunch of zeros to some of the income and expense lines. None of the totals add up."

"That can't be right. They were fine when I printed them off this afternoon." My brain is working overtime to try to figure out exactly what I did wrong. Could I have accidentally hit extra numbers when I was inputting the data? No, there's no way. QuickBooks figures all of those out for me.

"Well, I'm looking at a quarterly income of fourteen million dollars, and an expense of eight hundred thousand."

Holy. Shit. "What? That's not right!"

"I figured as much," he says with a chuckle. "We need to figure this out sooner rather than later, Payton."

"I've got my laptop with me that has my accounting software on it. Are you at the office?"

"Yeah, I'll be here."

"I'm on my way." I don't say anymore before signing off.

Sitting in the parking lot, I'm stunned by the crazy phone call. I haven't heard from Dean in weeks, but my body instantly reacts to his voice the way it did all those months ago last fall. How in the world did my numbers come out so high? Fourteen million in income? I freaking wish! Unless those flowers are tipped in real gold, that would be a hell of a lot of blooms leaving my store in the fourth quarter. Yes, we had a great three months with Thanksgiving and Christmas, but not anywhere near a million dollars, let alone fourteen.

"What in the hell is going on?" I ask, throwing my car in reverse and carefully pulling out of my parking space. Mine's the only car left in the lot at six-thirty at night.

I drive in silence towards Corbin and Denton. Their office is located at the far north side of Jupiter Bay in a newer complex that houses a dental and a physician's office. Considering that it's after five, the lights in the offices are off.

The front door is unlocked as I make my way towards the stairs. The accounting office is located on the second floor of the building, along with one for a small attorney's practice. I find myself practically sprinting up the stairs, taking them two at a time until I reach the top. The door directly to my right catches my attention. It's the only one with light filtering through the glass.

Eager to figure out what's going on, I try the door. It's unlocked. I'm greeted by the sight of Dean McIntire, casually leaning against the tall receptionist counter. His light brown hair is slightly askew, as if he's recently ran his hands through it. His eyes are hidden behind a pair of dark wired glasses, but I can feel them on me nonetheless. My body temperature rises about ten degrees in the span of three seconds. It's crazy, the way my body reacts to his presence. It was like that the first time he walked into the office and introduced himself as my new accountant.

"Hi," I croak through a dry throat.

He doesn't say a word, but I feel his eyes devour me from head to toe, leaving no part of me untouched by his gaze. I'm sure he can see my heart leaping in my chest and the way my body involuntarily sways in his direction. It's a natural reaction, as normal as breathing.

"Hi." Dean pushes off the desk where he's perched and stalks towards me. Yes, stalks. That's the only way to describe his movement. It's fluid and dangerous and makes my panties wetter with each step he takes towards me.

Goose bumps rise on my heated flesh as he stands directly before me, close enough that I could wrap my arms around his neck and pull him into a kiss. If I wanted to, that is. Which I don't. (This is where my pants would catch fire.) Dean leans forward, his arm skimming across my upper arm. Even through my coat, I can feel the heat of his flesh. I'm just about to ask what he's doing when he flips the lock on the door. The sound of it engaging echoes throughout the empty office. It reminds me of the slamming of prison doors, except being locked in a room with Dean McIntire is nothing like prison. It's more like a fantasy.

"You okay?" he whispers, his warm breath caressing my cheek.

"Yes." My voice is hoarse and doesn't even sound like my own.

"Are you sure? I'm not sure you're breathing right now." He raises that uber sexy eyebrow and gives me a half smirk. His eyes, hidden behind glasses, are smoldering and his lips plump, perfect for kissing. I've thought of that look several times over the last few months, especially when I was alone in my bed.

"Fine." I croak. Seriously, whose voice is that?

"Good," he says with the slightest rise of the corner of his lip. "Let's go to my office and figure this out."

He steps aside, waiting for me to take the lead. I know where his office is located; I've been there a few times since he took over my account last spring. What I wasn't expecting was the warm hand on my lower back as we walk down the hallway. Since it's a smaller office with only four accountants, we find ourselves at his open office door before I'm ready. Yet, I'm pleasantly surprised when he doesn't remove his hand from the small of my back. Wait. No, I want him to remove it. Don't I?

Aww, hell. I'm so screwed. Figuratively speaking, that is. Because I'm definitely *not* being screwed right now, as much as I wouldn't mind feeling the coarseness of his legs rubbing against my thighs.

Pay-ton. Get a grip, geez.

Dean leads me towards a small table and chairs in the corner of his office. I notice the envelope and subsequent paperwork sitting neatly in the middle of the round table. He pulls out a chair, still keeping his hand on my lower back. Shudders of pleasure ripple through my taut body. The sudden desire to hop on the tabletop and spread my legs is overwhelming. Images of our tryst in my own business parade through my mind like some X-rated movie.

"You okay?" he asks, his eyes scanning me, clearly amused by my suddenly flushed face.

"Fine. What did you find?" I ask, clearing my throat as I slip out of my jacket and getting down to business.

"This," he says, taking a seat beside me and reaching for the stack of papers. I notice right away that with him beside me, I catch faint whiffs of his cologne. It's rich and intoxicating, and I involuntarily find myself leaning towards him. Again.

The papers he slides in front of me pull my attention. Instantly, I see what his phone call was referring to. It wasn't me accidentally hitting extra buttons when inputting the information. This error is definitely human made, but more particularly, a certain human. I can tell by the way the extra zeros added to a few lines are shaky and hurried. What the hell?

Grandma.

"What did she do?" I wonder aloud.

"You know who did this?" he asks.

Gazing up, I'm drawn to worry evident in his deep brown eyes; so dark, they're muddied with concern and compassion. The glasses that I've only seen him wear when he's working are perched high up on his nose. A strong jaw frames his tanned face, and his lips are parted, little puffs of breath seeping from his open mouth.

"Yeah, I know who did this. This trickery has my elderly grandma's signature all over it."

Dean leans back in his seat, taking in my statement. "Why would she do this? Doesn't she understand how much trouble you could have gotten into if I hadn't been paying attention to the numbers?"

"I'm sure she knows you'd be thorough in checking the paperwork. And I haven't exactly figured out why she did this, but don't worry, I will. Can we make the changes to this and clear up the mess?"

"Yeah, she actually wrote it in pencil so we could probably just erase it, but I'd prefer to reprint clean copies."

Reaching into my bag, I pull out my laptop. I set it on the table and boot it up. While I'm waiting for it to start, Dean brings over a USB cord that connects to his printer. He watches as my home screen appears, displaying a picture of my five sisters and me at the beach this past summer.

"I was going to ask if they were your friends, but the resemblance is uncanny," he says, a small smile plays on his lips.

"Yeah, five sisters."

"No brothers?"

"Nope. I think Mom and Dad stopped trying after five and six were twin girls," I reply with a chuckle. Pointing to the screen, I introduce him to my sisters. "Jaime, AJ, Meghan, Lexi, and Abby."

"I've seen a few of them around town. I didn't realize they were your sisters, though I probably should have noticed the resemblance."

Absently, I touch the screen before clicking on the accounting program I use. It only takes a few moments before it's up and I'm able to reprint my report. Dean grabs the papers from the printer and brings them over to me. I watch him work for a few moments, silently observing the way he pushes up his glasses and the way little wrinkles appear between his brows while he's concentrating.

"I think we're all set," he says, dropping his pen on the tabletop.

"Excellent." Quickly, I shut down my computer and pack it back in my bag.

My original Wednesday night plan was my favorite takeout of Chicago style hotdogs and curly fries, and maybe reruns on television. Now, my vivid imagination is conjuring up *other* things that I wouldn't mind doing tonight. Namely Dean McIntire.

But that's not going to happen. He's the one who insisted we keep our relationship professional, and I wholly agree. I'm not looking for anything more than a few fun nights, and even though I'm not sure what he's looking for, I'm sure it doesn't match my thoughts.

"Thank you for stopping by and helping get this mess straightened out."

"Oh, no problem. I'm glad it wasn't something more serious than it was."

He laughs. "Yeah, I'm not sure her motives for the added digits, so you'll have to let me know if you find out."

Throwing my computer bag over my shoulder, I reply, "You can bet your ass I'll be asking her about it."

My green eyes clash with his brown ones. An invisible electric current charges through the air. I can see his chest moving, drawing in deep breaths of air, while I'm wondering if I'm even breathing. He's breathtaking in his crisp white dress shirt and dark blue tie. Black trousers fit to perfection around his trim waist and nice ass. I never really had a type, but if I did, he'd be it. A little bit nerdy mixed with a lot of masculine. He's like gravity; my body is drawn to him.

He takes a step towards me, then another. Dean stands before me, close enough to touch. My mind is battling between what it *should* do and what it *will* do. I should thank him for his time and walk out the door. It's what I've been saying I'll do if I should ever hear from him again, but now confronted with the situation, I can't seem to make myself say the words.

Instead, I let my bag slide down my arm and drop on the floor. I take a half step forward until I'm practically plastered to his front. My heart pounds in my chest as lust and desire take over all rational thought. Because no matter what I say or how hard I try to convince myself, I just want him.

And I'm going to have him again.

At least for tonight.

Dean

6

The first thing I notice is her scent. Jasmine and roses. She's floral sweet; my favorite scent as of the last several months. I can't go anywhere and see flowers, let alone smell them, without thinking of Payton.

The next thing I notice is the way the swell of her breasts press against my chest as she moves in closer. Her bag is discarded on the floor, an inconvenience she's quickly ignoring. If only our clothes could be disposed of just as quickly.

When I discovered the extra zeros on Payton's documents, I quickly called home and told Mom that there was an issue. I know Bri is in good hands; probably already fed and heading towards the bath. My call to Mom was quick and the message was simple: I don't know how long I'll be.

No, this wasn't exactly my intention when I called her, but I'm not about to pass up one second alone with Payton. My daughter's taken care of and that's all that matters. Taking advantage of this unexpected time Payton's offering is a damn close second. Even if the night's cut short so we can get back to our own lives.

Looking down into her cloudy emerald green eyes, a bolt of lust slams into my gut and spreads throughout my bloodstream. "We seem to keep finding ourselves in this same predicament."

"Which one would that be?" she asks coyly, but she knows exactly what I'm talking about.

"I can't seem to stay away from you." My voice is deep and husky and laced with desire.

"I can't stay away from you either." Her confession is like a beautiful song, sweet and poignant.

When I lean forward, lining up our lips perfectly, I hesitate for a second, giving her a chance to back out. Her eyes are burning into mine, and I know without a doubt that she'll never walk away. She can't. Just like me. There's something incredibly strong that pulls us towards each other. I'm not about to question it, not with her body pressed against mine.

Slowly, I lower my lips to hers, savoring the first taste of her lips in so many long weeks. She's like a balm, an elixir to my soul, and I have no clue why or how that happened. She's more than a booty call or a one-night stand. Even that first night when I snuck out in the early hours of the morning to go get my daughter, I knew she was more.

My lips move on their own, coaxing her mouth open so I can get my first real hit of Payton. When my tongue slides into her mouth and touches hers, blood floods into my cock, which is pulsing and throbbing painfully in my pressed Dockers. My dick reacts this way every damn time she's around, let alone when I get to touch and taste her.

Her hands slide up my back, gripping at my dress shirt, pulling it from my pants. Without even realizing it, we're moving until her ass is pressed firmly against my desk. She lifts up and perches atop the hard wood (my desk, not what's happening in my pants).

Her long legs open and wrap around my waist. Despite both of us still wearing pants, there's no place I'd rather be.

Without breaking the kiss, my right hand reaches down and grabs her leg, lifting it up so that I can get closer. Closer to touching her. Closer to being inside her. Closer to making her come on my dick. My left hand slides up the back of her shirt. Her skin is so soft, so alluring, and so fucking smooth.

One-handedly, I unclasp her bra like a damned professional. Even I'm impressed with my skills right now, especially in light of the fact that she's got me a fraction of an inch away from being completely out of control.

As much as it pains me, I pull away from her lips. Something else calls to me. Payton keeps her leg high on my hip and her eyes locked on mine as I slide both hands from her waistband, pushing her sweater up as I go. Her bra is askew and hanging, barely covering up her ample breasts. My mouth waters for one little taste.

I quickly shove her sweater over her head and watch the bra straps fall down her arms. Her nipples are hard little buds and my brain practically short circuits. Keeping my eyes on hers, I lower my head and stick out my tongue. Her moans of pleasure fill my entire being as I swipe my tongue gently across one, then the second tight little bud. My second pass is more aggressive, however. Her hands thread in my hair as I latch on to one perfect nipple, licking, sucking, and teasing. Payton shifts forward further on my desk, grinding against my erection.

"Holy shit, that feels so good," she groans as I move to show the second one the same attention as the first.

"I love the way you taste. I could lick and suck on you all day."

Reaching behind her, I push aside all of the crap on my desk. My stapler, computer mouse, tape dispenser, and penholder go flying, landing somewhere behind my desk. I lay her back, taking in the absolute breathtaking view of a half-dressed Payton splayed across my desk top.

"Damn, you are fucking spectacular like this." Her chest rises and falls quickly and my hands tingle to touch her.

Keeping my eyes focused on hers, I reach down and pop the snap on her workpants. They're soft and khaki, and even though they look fabulous on her ass, they'll look even better thrown on my office floor. She helps lift her ass as I shimmy the pants down her legs. Jesus, her legs. They're mile-long and smooth as fucking silk. I want to lick and taste every square inch.

When her pants are gone, I quickly dispose of the light blue boy-cut cotton panties. There's no missing the dark wetness on the light material as I slide them down her legs. My already rock-hard cock is pretty much steel at this point; I'm so aroused that if she were to touch me, it all might be over with.

Now that I've gotten rid of those pesky clothes, I gaze down at her naked body. That little lilac tattoo, the one I love, is staring up at me, begging for me to lick it. So I do. I start at her belly button and work my way out to the purple and black ink, dragging my tongue along the delicate skin, swirling it over my favorite tattoo in the world. Payton writhes and moves beneath me, breathing hard in little pants.

Up next, I draw my tongue southward, heading straight to my favorite place to taste. I'm assaulted by the scent of her arousal, her wetness glistening along her sweet pussy. At first taste, my body almost erupts in my pants. She's delicious and mouthwatering, and fuck, if I don't crave her more than before.

I take my time, gently sliding my tongue along the seam of her. She groans loud enough to be heard in the lower level. Thank God it's after hours and we're locked in here. I flick my tongue across her swollen clit, working her closer and closer to an orgasm. Payton's always been the most responsive woman I've been with. No one has ever made me feel like King of the World the way she does every time we're together.

Perching her legs on my shoulders, I work her over with my mouth. I can feel her legs tensing, tightening around my neck. Using my two fingers, I move her lips apart and slide my tongue inside of her tightness. She's grinding against my face, riding my tongue like it's a prized bull at the rodeo. Only, I want to ride her longer than eight seconds. I can feel her internal muscles tightening around my tongue, and I know she's getting close.

"I want to feel you come on my tongue," I tell her before diving back in. Her only response is a loud groan.

Licking, sucking, fucking her with my tongue, it's enough to push her over the edge. Her orgasm rips through her body, her back arching up off my desk. It's a true sight to behold, one I'll never forget. The way she shudders beneath my hands, her juices coating my tongue and lips. Best. Feeling. Ever.

"I'm not done with you yet, sweetheart," I say as I stand up, unbuttoning my dress shirt as I go.

Loosening my tie, I slide the knotted silk over my head and drop it on the floor. My shirt and undershirt follow quickly. My cock is hard and heavy in my boxers, all but ready to come out and play. Payton's limp on my desk, but the moment my hands start to unbutton my pants, her eyes are wide and filling with desire once more. She's always had a minimum of two orgasms when we've been together. Never less. When you're a single father, you learn to appreciate the time you get with a naked woman, and I've become accustomed to pleasuring Payton. I don't care how long it takes, always at least two.

But our chemistry is so combustible, two, with her, is easy.

She whimpers as I drop my pants, boxers sliding down my legs with them. My body is aching with need for her, the tip of my cock wet with my own desire. I know what she wants, so I reach down and grab my shaft at the base. I've been blessed with a cock most men would kill for, but I've never been arrogant or conceited with it.

Until her.

Payton parts her legs further as her eyes watch me stroke myself. My body is so tight with want I'm afraid I just won't last, so I squeeze my dick tightly, pain spreading through my groin. My desire abates, but only temporary. I know the closer I get to sliding inside her ready body, the greater my need will grow.

"Tell me what you want, Payton," I say, low and husky.

"You. I need *you*."

I grab my wallet from my pants before stepping between her spread legs. Before Payton, I was more on the shy side. I didn't have a lot of experience to help build my confidence and prowess. I'm a geek to the core, a nerd who never partied or had girls falling all over him, and my sexual conquests before her is a number still reached by counting on one hand.

And then I met Payton.

Everyone before her faded, every time with her brand new. She calls to me like a siren, singing to my soul in a way no one has ever spoken before. Suddenly, I'm saying things I'd never say and doing things I'd never do. All because it excites her, and me.

So as I step between her thighs, I rip off the condom wrapper with my teeth and stroke myself once more. Another bead of liquid seeps from the tip of my cock. Before I slide on the condom, I find myself running my finger through the moisture. Her eyes widen with desire, dilated so darkly that I can't tell what the color of her beautiful eyes should originally be.

Her tongue slips out of her mouth and runs along her bottom lip, and instantly I know what I need to do. Stepping forward until my dick is nestled against her wet pussy, I slip my finger into her mouth. Her warm tongue instantly swipes along the pad of my finger, licking off the pre-cum. I groan as she licks me clean.

With a pop, I pull my finger from the warm recesses of her mouth and grab the condom. My hands have a slight tremble as I sheath my dick in the latex. I line myself up at her entrance, eager to slide home, but I hold back.

"Please," she begs, that one word never before sweeter.

Taking my dick in my hand once more, I slide it through the wetness of her pussy. "What do you want?"

"You know," she pants, moving her hips as if to entice me.

"I do know. I want to hear you say it." I fight to keep myself from giving in just yet.

"I need you to fuck me."

Her words are gasoline to an already burning fire. Without preamble, I flex my hips forward, burying half my dick inside of her warm pussy. She gasps as she stretches around me. Carefully, I pull back and inch forward slowly, giving her time to adjust to my size. It doesn't take her long until she's wiggling, moving in sync with my body.

Sex has never been like this before, at least not to the extent of how crazy-good it is with Payton. The way her body moves, like she's evoking every ounce of pleasure she can get from me. And damn, does she induce an insane amount of pleasure. Tidal waves of bliss course through my body, alive and unrestricted.

Lying on my desk, she's a vision I'm sure to never forget. I can't help but watch the gentle slide of my body into hers, the way her back arches off the polished wood with each thrust. She runs her nails down my arms, gripping my wrists for leverage. Her touch fuels the need to come racing through my body.

My hips piston on their own, desire driving me past the point of control. Her eyes are wild as she moans with each thrust, each noise the sweetest melody I've ever heard. I grip her hips, thrusting inside the tightness of her body. She's so wet that I can feel her juices dripping off the underside of my balls.

"Payton," I whisper hoarsely, a plea for mercy.

"Feels so good. So, so good." Her words are broken, panting as she struggles to breathe.

"You feel so damn amazing," I tell her between thrusts. "Being inside you is fucking heaven."

She lifts her hips, changing up the angle ever so slightly. My eyes practically cross from the gratification of the moment. The familiar tingle starts in the base of my spine, and I know the end is near. As much as I try to hold off, I'm just not able to turn back now.

It's as if she senses my impending release. Payton lifts her hips as I slam into her, hitting that sweet spot deep inside her. She shivers as I pull out and crash into her once more, rolling my hips to maximize impact. On the third thrust, she detonates like a bomb beneath me. Goose bumps pepper her naked skin as her eyes close. My name seeps from her lips as a beautiful smile lights up her face.

The image of pure bliss sends me over the edge. My balls practically explode as I release myself into the confines of the rubber, repeating her name over and over. My body continues to draw out every ounce of pleasure it can, the internal muscles of her pussy milking my cock. Yet, I'm unable to stop moving.

Aftershocks sweep through my body moments before exhaustion. I practically collapse on top of her, her wet skin molding to mine. Her hands slide softly through my hair, her heart practically beating through her chest beneath my cheek. I can't help but close my eyes and savor the feel, the scent, and the taste of her against me. I'll hold her close until reality steps in, reminding us both of why we can't be together.

Running my hands up and down her arms, I savor the softness of her skin. I'm sure I'm crushing her, but neither of us makes an attempt to move. It's as if we're both ignoring the inevitable and just enjoying our time together, for however long we've got.

I can tell the moment reality sets in. Payton tenses beneath my touch. Exhaling deeply, I slowly stand up, pulling out of her body as I go. I grab the box of Kleenex behind my desk and hand her a few. Then I take some for myself, removing the condom and cleaning up the mess before disposing of it all in the trash.

By the time I'm finished cleaning up, she's halfway dressed. Neither of us speaks, nor makes eye contact as we dress. I wouldn't even know what to say anyway. Too quickly, I'm standing there in my pants, undershirt, and button-down hanging open. She's completely dressed and sliding on her flats. When she stands to her full height, it takes everything I have inside me to not close the distance between us and take her in my arms. My body burns for her, but the consequences of a relationship mixed with business keep me rooted in place.

Her eyes scan over me, stopping and staring at my open shirt. I wonder if she's going to ask me for this one too, like she did that first night together. Not that she really asked, but she was wearing that shirt–open of course–as we slept in her bed, our bodies touching and intertwined as much as humanly possible. If she asks, I'd gladly give this one to her too.

When her eyes finally land on my face, sorrow fills them. I can see her struggling with what we've done–again. It pains me even more that she's so torn. The last thing I'd want is for her to regret our time together; lord knows I haven't in the least. I want her to look back and smile and remember how dynamic and explosive we were in bed (and out of it).

Unable to resist the invisible pull I have towards her, I close the distance and stand before her. Softly, I run my thumb down her jaw before cupping her cheek in my hand.

"Why can't I stay away from you?" she whispers, her eyes shining with what could possibly be tears.

"I'm pretty irresistible," I reply, trying to keep it light.

She chuckles. "You are."

Together, we each take a deep breath as she turns and kisses my palm. "Nothing's changed." I say the words to myself as much as to her.

"I know." I can feel the regret pouring from her.

"I wish it were different," I say, pulling her into my arms and kissing her lips.

"Me too. I'd pick you if I could."

"I'd pick you too." And I would.

There's something astonishing and wonderful about Payton Summer, and it pains me that I'll never know the true extent of her amazingness. Someday soon, she'll meet someone and he'll never let her go. He'll realize the gift he has and cherish it for the rest of his life. He'll be the luckiest son of a bitch in the universe.

Damn, I wish I could be that man.

As she kisses me back, there's resolve in her touch. It's something I've become familiar with in the last few months. Every time we're together, we both vow that it'll be our last. Yet something jerks us together, like an invisible string pulling us back towards each other.

My heartbeat speeds up as she walks towards my office door. I had the forethought to lock it when we entered my space, not because I expected to screw her on my desk, but because I wanted to ensure no one interrupted our time together. Even if it would have remained completely professional, I treasure any solitary moments I can steal with her.

"Goodbye, Dean." Her words drip with melancholy, her eyes matching. It takes everything I have not to go to her and take her in my arms. I yearn to throw every rule in the rulebook out the fucking window.

But I can't.

Instead of speaking the words I long to say, I go with the right ones. "Goodbye, Payton."

7

Payton

My legs are shaky as I make my way from my car to my house. I feel like I just completed a marathon, all rubbery limbs and uneven breathing. I know walking away from Dean was the right thing to do, but why does it always feel like my dog died all over again every time I turn around and he's not there.

I can't justify a relationship with him, or anyone else, when it won't end the way I want it to. Because it *will* end. Why get involved with someone, potentially falling in love with him, only to have it end a short time later? Who would willingly subject themselves to that kinda torture? As soon as he finds out about my secret, he'll be gone.

They always are.

After unlocking my door, I let myself in, setting my computer bag and purse down on the table. The light is on above the sink, just the way I left it when I headed in to work this morning. It's a subtle reminder of my independent state. No one comes or goes but me, no one leaves their dirty clothes on the floor but me, and no one pays the bills but me. It's quiet, just the way I like it.

Until the silence takes over.

Turning around, I scream when a shadow falls on the kitchen floor.

"I'm sorry! I didn't mean to scare you," AJ says, her hands covering her heart.

"What are you doing here?" I ask, willing my heart rate to drop from stroke level.

"I stopped by to say hello, but you weren't home yet. I let myself in." Figures. "Where have you been? Working late?"

My cheeks blush involuntarily. "Yes." The one word comes out a croak. I'm sure she'll see right through my lie.

Her eyes turn all squinty as she stares, reading me like one of those romance novels she's always raving about. I keep my eyes trained on her, fighting the urge to shy away from the scrutiny. Finally, her eyebrows shoot into her bangs. Damn her and her Summer detective skills.

"Why do you smell like cologne?" She steps into my personal space and takes a giant, overly dramatic whiff around my neck.

"I…what are you…that's not…what?"

"You smell like a man." She steps back in and takes another whiff. "A very nice man."

I turn around and grab a glass from the cabinet and fill it with tap water, greedily chugging half the glass. "Must have been from one of my customers. I had a male customer in the store right when I closed," I answer, averting my gaze.

"And what about that whisker burn on your neck? Did that customer fall into you with his face before he left?" My hand instantly wraps around my neck, rubbing against the sensitive skin. I feel the flames burn beneath my hands, realizing that she's right.

Turning and straightening my resolve, I say, "Maybe he did. Maybe he tripped and rubbed his stubbled jaw against my neck.

You know, I could have caught him, saved him from falling completely down and injuring himself."

"You're a regular Florence Nightingale. I'm sure he's at home right now, handwriting his thank you card for saving him the insurance deductible."

I laugh at her sarcasm, which she responses with her own smile. "So?"

Exhaling, I grab my water and walk into the living room. I don't have to look around to know she's following me. Taking my seat on the couch, I fold my legs beneath me and get comfy. I let out a long, deep breath before I speak. "There's this guy," I start.

"Of course there is," she quips.

I offer her a quick smirk. "He's...well, he's kinda great. We have this killer chemistry, and frankly, the sex is amazing." We both laugh. "Like hitting a Grand Slam in game seven of the World Series amazing."

"God, when was the last time I had World Series sex?" she says absently, almost as if saying it to herself.

"I can't answer that, but I can tell you that if you have to ask that question, it's probably been a long time."

"If ever," she mumbles, taking a drink of her own glass she helped herself to. "So," she adds before clearing her throat, "if he's so great, why are you here and not with him getting whisker burn on other parts of your body?"

I clench my thighs together at the thought of Dean's stubble dragging along the sensitive skin between my legs. My sister stares at me, waiting for me to continue. I exhale deeply. "It's really complicated. I'm not really looking for a relationship, and he's kinda in the same boat. It could never go anywhere, so why try?"

AJ looks at me like she doesn't understand anything I just said. "Wait, what? First off, why wouldn't either of you be interested in a relationship, and second, why wouldn't it go anywhere? You're amazing and anyone would be lucky to have you."

My heart beats wildly and I smile automatically at her compliment. "Thank you. It's just...complicated, AJ."

"Yeah, you said that. So tell me something else."

"We kinda work together."

"Wait, you don't have a male employee so it has to be someone…" She leaves the sentence hanging wide open like a door for me to walk through.

Another deep breath. "Dean McIntire from Corbin and Denton." The words practically fly from my lips like a fighter jet taking off an aircraft carrier. My eyes widen at the confession, surprised that I've finally spoken his name aloud in a manner other than pertaining to my taxes.

"Why does that name sound familiar? Wait! Isn't he —"

"Yes!" I exclaim, cutting her off. "Now you see, right? You see why we can't have a relationship." And while I do feel that we should keep it professional, that's completely Dean's hang up, not mine. Mine is more personal. *Very* personal. Something else I've never spoken to another soul alive. Well, besides Cole.

"That's not working together; not really. You can totally diddle on the side with someone who does your taxes, Pay. I say if it's World Series sex, then diddle away!"

"Anyway, he has a rule, and he's right. It won't happen again. What's going on with you?" I ask, searching desperately for a redirect. Anything to turn the spotlight away from me and towards one of my sisters. It's actually one of my specialties as the oldest sibling. "How come you haven't been having World Series sex?"

She chugs a bit of water and shakes her head. "I went out with the drummer from Levi's band last weekend."

Levi is my littlest sister, Abby's, best friend. They have a *thing* for each other. We all see it and know it, while they, apparently, choose to ignore it. He's in a local band as a guitarist and backup vocalist, and therefore has no shortage of women eager to keep him company afterwards. It kills me to see the sadness in Abby's eyes when she sees him with other women, but she's too afraid to do something about her mega crush. I'm sure she's terrified of wrecking their friendship. So instead, she chooses to be miserable.

Go figure.

Pot, meet kettle.

"Why didn't we know you were going out with him?" I ask, interested in why she kept this from all of us.

"I didn't want it to be weird for Levi or Abby if things didn't go well," she states.

"And things didn't go well?"

"I fell asleep."

I give her a look, confused as to where she's going with this. "On the date?"

"Afterwards. In bed." I blink several times before she continues. "You'd think a drummer in a band would have excellent stamina in bed, right? I mean, it's so clichéd and practically a rule. Well, this wasn't even close to World Series sex, Pay. I. Fell. Asleep. It was elevator sex, but with a sprint for the finish line. I don't even know if he realized I was there or not. When I realized he was pounding the hell out of me in a frenzy to get himself off, I totally faked it."

"You faked an orgasm?"

"Hell yes I faked an orgasm! Then I grabbed my clothes, told him I was coming down with something contagious, and got the fuck out of there!"

I can't help it, I burst out laughing. "Laugh it up. It was horrible. He was a two-pump chump. I bet, start to finish, it was a total of four minutes. His idea of foreplay was to shake his ass at me when he stripped off his skinny jeans. It was like I was expected to stick a dollar bill down his tighty whities"

Laughter. Oh God, I can't breathe. I'm laughing so hard tears are rolling down my face. "That's horrible," I finally choke out through fits of giggles.

"It was. So my point is, not everyone gets to experience World Series sex. If you find a slugger who hits a grand slam, then you should definitely round the bases as much as humanly possible."

"What's with the baseball analogies?"

"You started it. I don't even like baseball."

We sit in comfortable silence for a while, watching whatever dramedy is playing on the Hallmark Channel. I don't even really notice she's still there until her stomach growls, drawing my attention from the television. The clock on the wall says nine-thirty, which completely surprised me, considering I'm usually in bed around now.

"Do you want to order food?"

"No, I better get home," she says, standing up and stretching. "I've still got papers to grade for tomorrow."

I follow as she walks the short distance to my front door and slips on her coat. "Thanks for stopping by," I tell her, reaching for the knob. "Oh, and what I told you about you know who? Can we keep that between us?"

AJ gives me a direct look, her matching green eyes full of compassion and understanding. "Of course. As long as you don't say anything about the drummer."

"Mum's the word," I say, opening the door. She steps out onto my little porch before I remember part of my conversation earlier with Grandma. "Oh, wait. I'm going away for a few days next week to some big florist convention. Rachel is going to work full-time, but my only other option for help is Grandma. I was going to ask Jaime because she used to work there, but she's so busy sucking face, and other things, with Ryan. Do you think you can pop in and just check on things for me?"

I know AJ understands what I'm asking. It's not that I don't trust my grandma, but I've spent my entire adult life building up this business and I want to make sure it goes smoothly in my absence.

"Of course. I'll stop in on my lunch break each day and after work. I don't think she'll be too suspicious if I bring her chocolate," she says with a wink and a smile. Grandma's sweet tooth is legendary, and using that to our advantage is something my sisters and I learned a long time ago.

"Thanks, A."

"You're welcome, Pay. Get inside and dream about baseball," she hollers before slipping into her car. Even in the darkness, I can see her smile reflecting in the moonlight.

Making my way back into the house, I lock up and head for the kitchen. Even though it's late, my eating schedule isn't exactly what you'd call normal. Not when you put in crazy hours to maintain a small business. I grab the bread and peanut butter out of the cabinet and the jelly from the fridge. This was my favorite sandwich growing up, and surprisingly, I've never gotten tired of it. Even in college, I could eat a PB&J every day and still want more.

I wouldn't mind taking a bath and relaxing a little, but it's already getting late for a weeknight. No, ten o'clock isn't exactly late, but for me, it is. I opt for a quick shower instead. As I strip in my room, I zero in on the red burn on my neck that AJ noticed. Memories of being laid out on his desk while he slid inside of me assault my mind, a tingle of something more than awareness slips down my spine.

The warm water does nothing to ebb the ache in my body, especially after I replay the entire scene over and over again in my head, and by the time I'm washed up, I find myself spending extra time washing a certain area. How can a woman go from completely sated to crawling out of her skin in need only a few hours later?

It's him.

Being single most of my adult life, I'm not ashamed to admit I have to take matters into my own hands every now and again. And by hands, I mean my fingers or my vibrator. Since I'm without Waterproof Waylon, that's my seven-inch vibrating, swirling, and pulsating vibrator that leaves me in a quivering pile of hormonal goo where I stand, I have to resort to the old fashioned way.

Closing my eyes, I picture a big hand skimming down my belly, angling towards the place I ache. I slide my fingers between my legs, letting the water cascade over my body. I recall the way his breath tickled my neck right before his mouth skimmed from my collarbone to my jaw. I slide two fingers inside my body, while my other hand concentrates on my clit. A groan slips from my lips and my body starts to shake as I remember his words. *"Being inside you is fucking heaven."*

I explode around my fingers, tightening and pulsing as the orgasm sweeps violently through me. Not worrying about anyone hearing me, I vocalize my release, Dean's name slipping from my lips. It's always his name, or at least it has been since I met him in his office last spring. It's his body I picture, his dick I pretend to ride, or his mouth I feel between my legs.

Washing up a second time, I shut off the water and wrap a big fluffy towel around my body. I'm still weak in the knees and my legs are shaky, but I manage to make my way into my bedroom. I don't even bother with pajamas; instead I go for the one shirt I sleep in more than I probably should. I fasten a few of the white buttons before bringing the material up to my nose and inhaling. It doesn't carry his scent anymore, but I can picture it in my mind so vividly, it's as if he wore the garment just yesterday. Of course, being in his arms a few short hours ago helps trigger that particular sense.

I set my alarm before climbing into bed. I'm a belly sleeper usually, but with him, I reveled in the feel of his body against mine as he spooned me from behind. Of course, it didn't hurt that it was the perfect position for a midnight romp when all he had to do was basically surge forward and into my wet, waiting body.

And there I go with the memories again.

Closing my eyes, I try to think about things *other* than Dean. Mrs. Simmons was so surprised when I delivered a beautiful bouquet from her husband in celebration of their twenty-ninth anniversary. The nursing home residents loved the winter holly and berry mix I arranged for their dining room tables. And I picture the delight written on the face of a high school senior whose boyfriend sent her three roses for her birthday. All smiles that are part of my day, but it's Dean's that I can't get out of my head right now.

And it's his that will likely fill my dreams again tonight.

Dean

"Remember to brush your teeth before bed, and make sure you listen and are a good girl for Mimi, okay?"

Bri rolls her eyes at me, something she's recently picked up from one of the older kids at the sitter's. I give her a stern look, letting her know I'm not a fan of her eye roll. "Sorry," she says sweetly with a shy smile. "I'm always a good girl for Mimi."

"I know," I say, kissing the top of her forehead. "I just have to remind you every once in a while."

"You're gonna be gone three whole nights?" she asks while pouring water into her Hello Kitty watering can.

"Three whole nights, sweetheart. I'll be here Friday when you get home from school. My sessions are supposed to end at noon, so I'll drive back as soon as I'm done and pick you up from Miss Nancy's, okay?"

"Otay! Mimi is gonna sleep in your bed, Daddy. She said I can have Frosted Flakes for breakfast, too. And pancakes! She'll make me pancakes or maybe waffles. Do you think she'll bring her waffle eye-ron?"

"It's an iron, and I'm sure she can grab it if you want." I pour clean water over the top of her head, rinsing the remainder of the suds clean.

"Can you text her tonight? This way she doesn't forget to bring it tomorrow?"

"I'll call her when I get you in bed, okay?"

"And tell her that I have Home Alone that we can watch on Blue Ray."

I can't help but chuckle at her ability to bounce from subject to subject so quickly. If only I were able to do the same; maybe I wouldn't have spent the last week thinking about the noises Payton made while she came on my cock.

"I'll tell her," I tell my daughter.

"Oh! And tell her that I'm going to have Edward sleep in bed with her so she doesn't get scared 'cause she's in a new place."

Laughing, I say, "I'm sure she'll be grateful to have your stuffed cat sleeping in bed with her."

Thirty minutes later, I'm tucking her into bed after drying her hair and reading her a bedtime story. If you would have asked me ten, twelve, hell, even six years ago, I would have thought you'd be full of shit at the idea of being a single dad, doing this twenty-four seven. Sure, I've always wanted kids, but I never thought this was how I'd do it.

I shake my head, gazing down at Brielle, and mentally chastise Brooke and curse her for what she's missing. She'll never know how amazing her daughter is. She'll never know that her favorite cereal is Frosted Flakes or that her favorite color is orange, and it's even better with pink polka dots. She missed her first words, the first time she rolled over, her first steps. Not to mention her first Christmas, first birthday, and every one in between.

Bri seems content, though. She rarely asks about her mom. I wouldn't say that I've lied to her, per se, but I don't tell her the complete truth. She knows Brooke wasn't part of her life, so God gave her a dad who would move mountains for her. All she needs to know is that I was there for her, always.

The truth is Brooke wasn't cut out to be a mother. I realized it about halfway through her pregnancy. The rounder she got with our daughter, the more miserable she was, and the more excited I became. We had dated for six months before the condom mishap that resulted in Brielle. I vowed the moment we saw the plus sign on the pregnancy test that I would do everything I could to protect her.

Unfortunately, Brooke didn't see the pregnancy as anything but a nuisance. I know she tried, she really did, in the beginning, but she just wasn't cut out for the road we were heading down. She was always larger than life, with big dreams and a big checking account. And being saddled to a baby and a boyfriend that she tolerated wasn't what she pictured for herself.

So she left.

I was understandably upset, but only for a minute. I had a three-month-old baby to raise, so there was no time for wallowing in self-pity. My days consisted of poopy diapers, dirty, spit-up clothes, and falling asleep sitting up. I worked full-time from home and the office, and had my mom to help me in between. We made it work because that was our only option.

I dial the familiar number after making sure Bri is settled into bed for the night. She'll be up once or twice to get a drink or use the bathroom, anything she can use as a stall tactic. I'm onto her game, but still let her get away with it for a bit before I pull the plug. A little girl can only go to the bathroom so many times in a thirty minute time period.

"Hello?"

"Good evening, I have an important message for you from your granddaughter."

She chuckles as she says, "Oh, I can't wait to hear this."

"First off, please bring your waffle iron."

"Already have it sitting on the table by my bag," she says, the sound of the television filtering through the phone.

"And you're sleeping with Edward."

"Of course I am. Every time she spends the night, Edward sleeps in my bed. She says he'll keep me company if I wake up in the night to use the bathroom."

"So what you're saying is Edward gets around."

"He does," she says with a laugh. "Speaking of getting around, are you going to tell me why you came home last week smelling like perfume?"

My heart stops beating; like literally stops beating in my chest. I know exactly what she's talking about. The last time I came home late from work was the night I christened my desk with Payton. It was hard to miss the knowing looks Mom gave me, but I didn't think she'd bring it up now, a week later.

"I don't know what you're talking about." It's a weak defense, but once you've committed to it, you have to stick with your story. And it's either that or deny, deny, deny.

"Listen, Dean, I'm not asking for details or anything. I just like listening to you squirm."

"That's not nice," I tell her as I start the dishwasher.

"Yeah, well, parents aren't supposed to be nice. Really, I don't care what you were doing or who you were doing it with, but I want you to know that you don't have to hide anything from me. If you have a date or something, that's okay. In fact, I'm pretty sure you've been on exactly three dates since Bri was born," she says, the remorse evident in her voice.

"I don't need to date, Mom. I have Bri and she takes up all of my time."

"Oh, honey, you don't have to try to convince me of anything. I was a single parent too, remember?"

"How could I forget?"

"My point is that Bri is getting older. It would be perfectly acceptable to go out every now and again with a woman. Who knows, you might actually meet someone that you want to spend the rest of your life with."

Is it bad that Payton flashes through my mind at her statement? It is when a relationship with her isn't an option. But for some reason, images of Payton sitting beside me on the couch with her feet in my lap parades through my mind. It's a cozy image until she moves and straddles me. Then the picture turns dirty. Very dirty.

"Thank you for the offer to watch my kid while I date, but I'm okay."

"That's subjective," she says with a laugh. "All I'm saying is that I'm available to help so you can go out and live your life every once in a while. Your life can have a personal side to it too, Dean. It doesn't have to be all about Brielle."

I know she's right, but for someone who's spent the last five years of his life with his daughter as his sole focus, it's hard to picture a point where I share myself with another woman. Even if that woman were Payton. As much as my body craves her, I just don't know if I'm capable of splitting myself between my daughter and a woman. It's a challenge I'm not really ready to undertake.

"Okay. How about this? I'll agree that if I find someone I'm interested in going out with, I'll get your help with Payton."

There's silence for a few seconds before she finally speaks again. "Payton? Who's Payton?" I can hear the smile in her voice.

Shit. Did I say Payton? How in the hell am I going to backtrack out of this one? This is one of those times I should deny, deny, deny. "I didn't say Payton."

"No? I must have made it up. I'm sure you don't even know anyone named Payton, do you?"

Shit. A. Brick. She's going to make me lie to her face, or at least over the phone. But I can't lie to her outright like that; I've never been able to do that. And let's not forget the fact that she'll know the instant I lie to begin with. She's baiting me like always. She's giving me just enough rope to hang myself with. So I'll give her just enough info to appease her.

"The only Payton I know is a client of the firm."

"Is she pretty?"

Damn her.

"She's not ugly," I say, mumbling the words. Jesus, what am I? Fourteen? Why can't I just tell my mom that I think she's hot?

"Hmmmm." That's all she says. Hmmmm. I'm pretty sure she has everything figured out just like she did when I was seventeen and I told her the pack of cigarettes in my room where my buddy Wes's.

"Anyway, I need to get another load of laundry done so I can finish packing. I'll meet you here after you get off work, right?"

"Mmmhmmm." It's more of a noise than a word. Shit, she doesn't believe a word I've said. Why the hell did I have to say Payton's name?

"Okay, see you tomorrow, Mom. Love you."

"Love you, too, Dean. See you tomorrow." There's wittiness in her words. She's definitely humoring me and knows that I'm completely full of shit. Great.

After finishing up the kitchen and the last load of laundry for the evening, I lock everything up and head to bed. Even though I'm exhausted, I'm just not sure I can sleep. Not with the knowledge of leaving Bri for three nights looming in the morning. It's going to be awkward, me being solo for multiple nights for the first time in over five years. I suppose this would be the perfect time to potentially meet someone. I mean, I'm going to be in a strange city at a hotel, right? It doesn't get more convenient than that.

Even though that's never been my forte, it wouldn't hurt me to keep my options open. Three whole nights without my daughter could prove to be beneficial in that respect. I mean, I am still a man. Even if this man has been more celibate than not in the last few years.

Except for my time with Payton. That's something I'm not likely to forget anytime soon.

The drive to Richmond is peaceful, something I'm not accustomed to. I bask in the solitude of listening to my own music, not whatever Bri wants to listen to or whatever movie she's watching. It's actually enjoyable to have a little *me* time, though I'd never admit that to my mom. I'll never hear the end of it if I do.

The convention is in one of Richmond's largest hotels, The Freemont. They've hosted the annual event for several years as accountants and CPAs from all over the country attend this informative and educational 3-day event. Even though it falls during the beginning of tax season (who's bright idea was that anyway?), they still sell out tickets every year.

When I pull into the parking garage, it isn't until the third level that I finally find a parking spot, and even then, it's way in back. The temperature is brisk with a chill in the air. It's not quite as salty as the Bay weather, but feels much of the same anyway.

After parking my car, I retrieve my briefcase, roller suitcase, and my garment bag. I'm not required to wear business suits to the event, but I brought one just in case. There's a dinner on Thursday night at the hotel where it's a little more of a dressed-up event. Otherwise, Dockers or dress slacks, dress shirt, and tie are the attire for men, and business dress for the women. Though, I'm sure I'll still see plenty of suits over the next three days. Some old school guys still wear them daily.

The check-in process is pretty painless. My reservation for a king-sized bed, non-smoking room is pretty standard. I have the company card that my reservation was made under, so after signing my name a few times, I'm handed the plastic key card and told which elevator will take me to my floor. Technically, they all will, but the one at the far end of the corridor will get me closest to my home away from home for the next three nights.

I make quick work of unpacking my suit, my suitcase and shaving kit, and computer. Even though I'm required to attend this thing doesn't mean work stops. Not at the end of January. I grab my phone to text Mom when my stomach growls, reminding me that I didn't eat dinner tonight before I left the house. It sounds childish, but I couldn't eat. My stomach was in knots as I watched my daughter smile and carry on without a care in the world. And for her, there isn't a care. She'll be perfectly fine and content with her grandma, and me, I'll be missing her every second of every day.

That's the first thing I learned about being a parent: unconditional, never-ending love.

I fire off a quick text to Mom. Even though it's after nine, I know she'll be waiting to hear from me. Her reply comes before I can even set the phone down.

> **Mom:** She was out before I finished the second story. We're fine. Have fun.
>
> **Me:** I'm glad. Don't let her sweet talk you in to ice cream for breakfast.
>
> **Mom:** Don't you worry about it. What happens when Dad is away stays between Bri and me.
>
> **Me:** That makes me question why I left her in your hands.
>
> **Mom:** You turned out just fine.
>
> **Me:** I also never had ice cream for breakfast.
>
> **Mom:** One of the joys of having grandkids. Go. Enjoy yourself. We're fine.

I put my phone in the back pocket of my jeans and grab my key card. I'm starved, and could honestly use a drink. Pushing aside all thoughts of what's waiting for me at home, I head out of my room and down to the restaurant. Maybe with a full belly and a glass of something strong, I'll be able to get a little sleep tonight.

Payton

"What do you mean you don't see my completed reservation?" I ask, my voice dangerously close to reaching a pitch that only dogs can hear.

"Well, it appears you made the reservation, but a room wasn't held for you," the young blond manager says sheepishly with a look of sympathy in her light blue eyes.

"So give me another room."

"I'm sorry, but we don't have any available. There's three conventions going on this week, and we're booked solid."

"Let me get this straight. You took my registration, charged my credit card for the room, but there's no room available?"

"I'm terribly sorry, ma'am. The hotel will gladly refund the charge to your card for the room."

"But, I'm attending the convention here. I'm supposed to be here through Friday."

"Again, I'm terribly sorry for the inconvenience. Country Gardens will happily provide you with a voucher for a free stay at any one of our Country Garden Inns in the United States."

"Really?" I ask, giving her a look of shock. "I don't want your voucher. I want the room that I reserved."

"I'm very sorry, ma'am."

"And stop calling me ma'am!" I exclaim as I grab my bag and turn towards the entrance.

"I could happily call around and see about finding another room for you at a nearby hotel. Unfortunately, with the conventions in town, finding a room in downtown will be rather difficult."

I almost turn around and give her a piece of my mind once more, but opt to just leave. Keeping my back ramrod straight, I pull my bag right out the front door. I don't care about the voucher. I don't really care about the hotel room. I don't even care about the stupid convention right now. I want to admit defeat and jump back in my car, heading home.

But I won't do that.

I won't put my tail between my legs and head home when everyone else helped make this trip possible. Between Rachel, Grandma, and Jaime, the shop is taken care of. AJ and Lexi both agreed to stop in and check on things, and Abby volunteered to stop by my house and water my plants. I didn't have the heart to tell her I don't have any plants.

Walking down the street, I step inside the first hotel I come across. Unfortunately, the manager at the first hotel is right: there's no availability. Not here, not anywhere. Just to be sure, I try four more before backtracking on the opposite side of the street. There's one more down the block. If that one doesn't have availability, then I'll admit defeat. I'll head home, wasting the money on my ticket and taking a huge hit to my pride. Sure I could stay at a smaller, cheaper hotel out of the downtown area, but then I'll have to pay double for parking and deal with traffic.

And I hate dealing with traffic.

I stroll into The Freemont hotel, tired and a little sweaty underneath my coat. I wasn't planning on taking a Sunday stroll when I wore my favorite pair of heeled black boots, resulting in achy feet. Pasting on my best smile, I walk up to the front desk. It's after ten so the lobby seems cleared out, but there's plenty of noise coming from the hallway. A bar, if I had to guess.

Damn, could I really use a drink.

"Checking in?" the pleasant man says with a smile.

"Actually, I'm looking for a room."

"I'm sorry, we're completely booked this evening."

Closing my eyes, I drop my head. "Of course you are. Everyone's full."

"There are three major events going on this week," he says sensitively.

"I know. I'm supposed to be at one at Country Garden but they didn't reserve my room."

"I'm terribly sorry to hear that. Unfortunately, we don't have any available until Friday night."

Friday night. The night *after* my flower show ends. "Thank you for your assistance. I guess I'll just head home."

"You might get lucky and find something on the edge of town, but honestly, most hotels are reporting maximum capacity for this week. Good luck." His eyes are kind as he reaches for the ringing telephone.

"Thank you," I mumble as I grab my suitcase and turn around.

I'm exhausted from the walk and the time of night, and not looking forward to driving home. It'll be well after midnight by the time I actually make it back to Jupiter Bay. Tears well up in my eyes uncontrollably as I check to make sure I have all of the stuff I've been lugging around for the last hour. Making sure I have my keys handy, I grab the handle on my suitcase (thank freaking all things holy that it's on wheels) and take a step towards the entrance.

"Payton?"

I turn sharply, surprised to hear my name being called in the unfamiliar hotel lobby, but even more shocked at the voice calling my name. Turning towards the long corridor, I see Dean walking towards me, a tall redhead hot on his heels.

The sight of him here, at a freaking hotel, has me stop in my tracks. All words evaporate from my brain as I see him standing close enough to touch. In a freaking hotel. A hotel three hours away. With a woman beside him.

Christ Almighty, I can't believe it. He's seeing someone? A week after screwing me into the polished wood of his desk top, and he's now seeing someone? Hell, maybe he's been with her all along and I've been the sidepiece. Wouldn't that just be the apple pie on the Fourth of July? Fucking great, now I'm a whore.

"What are you doing here?" he asks, concern evident in his sparkling brown eyes.

"I'm here for a trade show, or at least I was supposed to be," I answer, my eyes instantly zeroing back in on Barbie's best friend standing next to him.

"You're staying here? At The Freemont?" Is that excitement I see in his eyes? Can't be. Unless he's excited to have me close by so he can bed-hop like a freaking sixties hippy. You know, free love and all that shit.

"No. I was supposed to stay at the Country Garden but they didn't actually reserve my room. There's no availability anywhere tonight, so I'm going to head home."

He's about to reply, but a throat clears behind him. "Oh, I'm sorry. Payton, this is Althea. Althea, this is a friend from home, Payton Summer."

The Cosmo magazine model steps forward and shoves her perfectly manicured hand in my face. I give it an awkward shake as she says, "Pleasure to meet a friend of Dean's. I'm sorry you won't be joining us this evening. We were just heading upstairs." She then places those claws on Dean's forearm, essentially putting her body between him and I, as a shield.

"I better let you get up to your room. It's getting late," I mumble before grabbing my suitcase and turning towards the door. My feet can't get me out of this place fast enough.

Before I get to the entrance, though, I hear his voice once more behind me. "Payton, wait."

Turning around, I come face to face with the man who haunts my dreams pretty much nightly. Except now I see him in a whole new light. Dean always had this, how can I say this politely, *nerdy* aura about him. I never pictured him as the manwhore type, but hey, to each his own. Just goes to show you that you never really know someone. Even if that someone lays you across a piece of wood and does naughty things to your body.

And cue the blush. No, not from embarrassment, but desire. Apparently my body doesn't care that Dean diddles with more than one woman at a time because I'm suddenly tingly and hot in places that I'd rather not talk about right now. Especially with the redhead standing over his shoulder looking bored and annoyed.

"What show are you here for?"

Even though I'd prefer to run from the hotel screaming, maybe even kick him in the balls for not telling me he was seeing someone, I swallow hard and answer his question. "There's a flower show across the street at Country Garden. I'm supposed to be there till Friday, but since they don't have my room, I'll be heading back to Jupiter Bay." Glancing down at my watch, I add, "And it's getting late so I better get on the road."

"Wait," he says anxiously as I turn towards the door. "Don't go. Stay. You can share my room with me."

Wait, what?!

"Oh, thank you, but I couldn't possibly do that," I say in a rush, glancing over his shoulder and watching Althea give me a look of total displeasure.

"You're already here and you have a ticket. We could share a room." He says it so simply, like I wouldn't be the third wheel in his sexcapades. Or maybe that's what he wants? Maybe he's one of those guys that wants a threesome. He already has the room, and I'm already here, right?

Gross.

"I can't. I'm sure there's no room anyway," I say, glancing over his shoulder one more time after the redhead sighs loudly.

"No room?" he asks, looking over his shoulder. "Oh! No! Althea isn't staying in my room. We just met at the restaurant. We're both attending a convention in the hall this week, and were walking up to our rooms–our *separate* rooms–when I saw you." His eyes are big and round, wide open and there's no way to mask the sincerity and honesty in his words.

"You're not together?" I say aloud without realizing it.

"No."

Glancing over his shoulder, I add in a whisper, "Does she know that?"

"I'm not sure," he replies sheepishly with that cute boyish grin I've come to love in such a short amount of time. "She seems nice, but I'm not interested. I really was going to drop her off at her floor and head up to mine."

I consider his offer. It feels like I'm playing with matches while wearing pants doused in lighter fluid. Am I really considering sharing a room with this man? A man I've spent amazing nights with over the course of six months, but can't have a relationship with? I mean, even if we share a room, that doesn't mean we have to sleep together in it, right?

Oh, who the hell am I kidding?

There's no way in hell I'll be able to resist him once we're alone, sharing a small hotel room. He'll be sleeping mere feet away from me, showering in the same stall that I'll be in. It's pretty much a recipe for disaster, and the scary part is that I'm actually considering it. I want to share a room with him. I want to take the olive branch he's extending and attend the show I've been looking forward to since the day I signed up. I want to enjoy time with him, even if it remains platonic the entire time.

"You have to let me pay you for half of the room," I say cautiously.

"My company is footing the bill so it won't matter."

I give him a long look, weighing all of my options. It doesn't take me very long because I don't have any. It's either share a room with Dean or hop in my car and head back home. Simple as that.

Except I know this will be anything but simple.

But even knowing that, I still find myself saying, "Okay."

His brown eyes light up in a way I'm not expecting. He seems genuinely happy that I'm bunking in his room for the next few nights. I can't help but feel a little excited myself as I give him a small smile.

"Great!" he exclaims, reaching for my suitcase.

"I can get it," I say the moment his hand touches mine on the handle.

Surely the sparks that fly from the touch are visible to everyone in the lobby, including Barbie's beautiful friend, who still happens to be standing back, watching the entire scene, while tapping her foot in irritation. When her face registers that Dean's pulling my suitcase behind him and I'm walking beside him towards the elevators it takes on this twisted look that reminds me of someone who sucked on a lemon.

"Your friend is staying?" she asks, trying to sound casual but failing.

"She is. It was nice meeting you, Althea. I'm sure we'll see each other in passing over the next few days," he says as he calls the elevator.

"Oh, I'm sure we will. Let's have dinner tomorrow night," she says enthusiastically, tossing her long red hair over her shoulder and basically straight into my face.

"I have plans tomorrow night." His reply is polite, but seems to cut her deeply.

"Well, we'll for sure see each other at the big dinner Thursday night. It's for convention attendees *only*. I'll save you a seat at my table," she says, glancing over her shoulder at me once more.

"If I attend, I'm sure I'll see you there."

"You have to attend. Everyone is going to be there. Please," she coos, stepping closer and rubbing up and down his arm. I also can't miss the way she plasters her perfect boobs against his arm.

The elevator arrives, saving him from having to answer. He allows us both to enter the car before stepping in himself. Althea pushes the button for the fifth floor, while Dean steps forward and cues up the seventh.

Silence fills the car as it starts to ascend upward. The scent of his cologne permeates my entire being as he steps up behind me, the heat of his body felt through my clothes and coat. "I have to warn you, I only have one bed," he says softly, his breath fanning across my neck, causing me to shiver.

Air lodges in my throat and my eyes widen in a very un-lovely way. I'm sure I resemble a blow-up doll with her eyes wide and mouth gaping open. Not exactly the best look for someone who isn't staring in a smut film. "You only have one bed?" I whisper, turning slightly to face him.

"I'll sleep on the pullout couch."

"No," I beg. "I'm the one crashing your room. I'll take the couch."

"I could never let a lady sleep on the couch while I sleep in a bed, Payton."

"Or, Dean can join me in my room since I have two queen sized beds. This way, Payton can have her own room. You won't have to bother her with all of the coming and going we'll be doing for the convention. We'll be on the same schedule, so it seems like the most logical solution." Althea smiles sweetly at Dean, clearly offering more than just the extra bed in her hotel room.

"That's nice of you to offer, but I'm not leaving Payton. She's here and I can't think of anything better than sharing a room with her." His eyes never leave mine and the temperature rises a thousand degrees. The meaning is clear. Even Althea must understand that her efforts are fruitless because she finally zips her lips and turns to face forward.

From this point on, Dean and I will be sharing a room. A hotel room.

And from the look in his eyes, I don't think there'll be much sleeping going on.

10

Dean

My dick is already hard when I slip the key card into the door. Apparently the wayward appendage doesn't care that I shouldn't touch her. I'm helping out a friend, but the little guy trying to claw out of my trousers to get to Payton doesn't seem to care about that. He wants one thing, and one thing only.

Payton. Naked.

I push open the door and wait for her to enter. She glances around, her gaze landing firmly on the king-sized bed in the middle of the room. The awkward silence quickly becomes sexually charged as we both stare at the mass of pillows and blankets. I can picture her body splayed out, as if on display, while I feast on every curve she has. And, damn, does she have them in spades. Beautiful, delicate, sexy-as-sin curves.

My focus right now needs to be on getting my friend settled, not settling myself between her thighs. There's a reason a relationship with her isn't in the cards, and that won't change tonight, tomorrow, or even next week. The fact still remains that she's my client, and I won't risk damaging the work relationship we've built just because the sex is fantastic. My dick twitches in my pants at the memories.

"There's a few open drawers in the dresser. Feel free to put your stuff in there and in the closet," I say, scanning the room for anything left out of place. Of course, I wasn't in here long enough to do anything but put stuff away, so everything's where it's supposed to be; not one pair of dirty underwear in sight.

Payton stands in the middle of the room and gives a slow turn before her eyes come to rest on mine. "Are you sure about this?" Her voice is laced with apprehension and concern. I completely understand where she's coming from. It's not like we're buddies who are sharing a room. We know each other intimately, in a way that only lovers do.

"It'll be fine, Pay. I can be on my best behavior," I say with a chuckle. "I can be man enough not to maul you when we're staying in a hotel room together."

My plan was to sound relaxed and casual, but for some reason, my brain only focuses on two words in my statement: hotel and together. The air becomes stuffy, making it hard to breathe. I pull at my tie, loosening it, along with the top button. There's no missing that she watches my motions, swallowing hard when I pull at the collar.

"I'm sure this will be fine," she says, still staring at my throat.

"Easy."

"Piece of cake."

"No big deal."

But it is a big deal. She knows it and I know it. The greatest challenge of my life may not have been raising a daughter, practically from birth, completely on my own. My greatest challenge may be facing me in this moment: sharing a room with Payton and not touching her. Friends without the benefits.

And because I'm playing the martyr, there's only one thing to do.

Accept the challenge.

Payton puts away all of her stuff in the drawers beside mine. I'm sitting at the round table, sending off a few emails, but my mind isn't focused on work. I'm struck by how easy it is to share the space with her, and how right it feels to have her belongings in the same place as mine.

It's almost eleven when she lets me know that she's going to take a quick shower. Listening to the water, knowing that she's naked and wet just on the other side of that closed door is torturous. We're talking pulling off all of your fingernails just to get you to talk cruelty. And, honestly, as I listen to her move around as the water cascades over her lush body, I'd almost prefer the fingernail treatment right now. It's sure to be just as painful but without the raging boner in my pants.

I've been staring at the same email for ten minutes when I hear the water shut off. My mind instantly imagines what she'd look like fresh from the shower. Her hair slicked back and her face free of makeup, a towel knotted between her full breasts, that barely covers her ass.

Jesus, what is wrong with me? Why in the hell am I tormenting myself so damn much? There's no way I'll be able to sleep tonight with the Louisville Slugger in my pants wanting to come out for batting practice. The only relief I'm going to get tonight, the only way I'll be able to sleep a wink, is a shower of my own; one that has me taking my throbbing dick in my hand while I mentally picture her on her knees with my cock in her warm mouth. I audibly groan as that delicious little image starts to play out in my mind.

"Are you okay?" she asks, standing in front of me. I didn't even hear her come into the room.

"I'm fine," I reply quickly, clearing my throat as I glance back down at my laptop. Then something catches my attention and my eyes fly back up to Payton. She's walking towards the bed, her hair wetting the top of her pajamas. Only these aren't pajamas. She's wearing a shirt. A big, white, collared, button-down shirt. One that looks awfully fucking familiar.

"What are you wearing?" I ask, my voice sounding foreign and husky, even to my own ears.

She turns around and I swear to God I'm having a heart attack. My dress shirt hits mid-thigh and is buttoned up to the top of her breasts. It covers all of the pertinent areas, except those mile-long legs, but the fact that it's *my* shirt she's wearing is like an aphrodisiac in and of itself.

Payton glances down. Her face flushes as she gives me a slight, shy smile. "I, uh, wasn't expecting to be sharing a room with anyone."

"You sleep in my shirt?" I think about that morning so many months ago that I woke up to find her sleeping in it. I'd gladly leave my entire wardrobe if it meant seeing her in them every night.

No. Wait.

Not every night.

That can't happen.

Friends. We're friends.

"Not all the time, but, I guess, sometimes. It's super comfortable and it's long sleeved so it keeps me warm without getting hot." She says it so matter-of-factly, like it's completely logical for her to be sleeping in the shirt I left. But the fact still remains: she sleeps in my shirt.

"Sure, I can see that." I decide to let her off the hook with her sorry excuse, but I can't help but smile as I force my attention back to my computer. It's futile, though, trying to work. Instead, I'm picturing those smooth legs as they disappear beneath the starch-white material. My hard-on is steel and reaching epic levels.

Shutting down the laptop, I grab a pair of running shorts from the dresser. "I'm going to take a quick shower."

"Are you sure you don't want the bed?" she asks, drawing the covers back. "I'd happily take the pullout."

"No, it's fine. I like sleeping on carpet-thin mattresses with a bar running across my back." I throw her a big smile so that she knows I'm kidding.

"Just for that, I'm only giving you one pillow," she says as she tosses an extra pillow from the bed straight into my face. Her laughter follows me all the way into the bathroom.

The hot water beats down on my neck as I stand beneath the water. It ebbs away the tightness in my muscles, except the one between my legs. My cock still throbs with need, and seeing Payton in my shirt hasn't helped the situation in the slightest. Instead of taking my problem in hand, I turn the hot water almost completely off. The frigid temperature helps alleviate the ache, but doesn't remedy it completely. There's only one thing that'll fix that problem, and she's sleeping on the other side of the bathroom wall.

The lights are off when I step into the room. There's a glow from the television bouncing off the walls, and it helps illuminate the woman lying on her side, watching an episode of *Friends*. I throw my wet towel over the bar in the closet and make my way to the couch, which is already pulled out.

My shorts are comfortable, even though the pullout isn't. I was right that the mattress is paper-thin, and I'm rewarded with not just one, but two metals bars under my body. Looks like Payton's presence isn't going to be the only thing keeping me from getting any sleep tonight.

It's quiet for a while, but through the glow of the TV, I can see the contours of her face. She's propping her head up on her hand, her soft brown hair falling in waves around her face. She's, without a doubt, the most gorgeous woman I've ever seen. Brooke was beautiful, but has nothing on Payton.

I roll to my side and watch her for several minutes, inundated with a fierce longing that it almost causes physical pain. She smiles at the television, the episode where Monica wears the turkey on her head and dances for Chandler. He answers by telling her he loves her. I've been in love before, but not the way you'd expect. I love my mom and daughter fiercely, I loved Staci Jordan in high school the way you always treasure a first love, and I loved Brooke as much as I could. She was difficult, though, and loving her wasn't easy.

"Payton?" I ask when I notice her eyes starting to droop. She glances over at me, those gorgeous green eyes focusing on me. "I wasn't going to sleep with her."

She stares straight at me as if trying to get a read on the conversation. "It's not any of my business, really," she says as if trying to brush it all off.

"I know, but I want you to know."

"Okay," she whispers. One word but it's laced with understanding and longing.

"Good night," I tell her, desperation starting to take over. Not only does my body want to climb in bed with her, but so does my head. And don't get me started on my heart. That pesky organ is beating wildly, ready to jump off the cliff without even giving a glance to the dangers down below.

"Good night, Dean," she mumbles as her eyes close.

I watch for several more minutes, like the creepy stalker I apparently am. Her eyes flutter softly and her mouth opens faintly, the slightest little moan slipping from her lush lips. I realize I could watch her sleep every night if given the chance. In fact, I did watch her for a long time that night I stayed at her place. I watched until I couldn't keep my eyes open any longer and finally succumbed to sleep.

Which is what's happening now. My own eyelids start to droop and my body relaxes. Even Jennifer Aniston and Courteney Cox can't keep me awake any longer. As exhaustion sweeps through my body, my last conscious thought is of the breathtaking brunette sleeping across from me. We're not even in the same bed, but I feel joy and a calmness I haven't experienced in I don't even know how long. Just being in the same room with her brings me peace.

I should run from that.

But I can't.

I won't.

Coffee is great. Coffee is my best friend. I'm pretty sure I lived on coffee and toast when Brielle was an infant. And now it's just a regular part of my morning routine. When Payton was in the shower, I slipped from the room to retrieve us both a coffee. Sure, there's a tiny coffee pot in our room, but that little thing isn't enough to make one large cup of joe, let alone two. And listening to the sweet sounds of her working through her morning routine was doing a number on my mind and my groin. So here I am, carrying two large coffees back up to our room. I wasn't sure how she took hers so I snatched packets of cream and sugar from the restaurant, just in case.

When I enter the room, the bathroom door is wide open. She's standing before the mirror in a pair of black slacks and a purple top that flows beautifully around her curvy body, putting on makeup. Her hair is already dry. She brushes one color across her eyelids, followed quickly by a second. She has always worn natural colors. When our eyes connect, I realize I've been standing there watching her getting ready for her day as if I'm witnessing the behind the scenes secrets of NASA. I feel elated to be able to see this part of her, a concealed part of her day that no one gets to see.

Except me.

We've been staring for several moments when the warmth of the coffee cups starts to permeate the palm of my hand. "I grabbed you a coffee," I say casually, stepping inside the bathroom and setting it down on the counter.

Big mistake.

Her scent is everywhere. It's floral with a hint of fruitiness. I've dreamed about this particular smell for months, and now it's standing in my bathroom, putting on makeup. Her eyes are sparkling emeralds under the harsh florescent lighting of the small bathroom. She's so close, close enough to touch. I crave her and almost groan aloud in need.

"Thank you," she replies, husky and low.

"I didn't know how you took it so I grabbed sugar and cream." I notice a slight tremble to my hand as I set the small bag of coffee fixings on the counter beside the cup.

"Sweet and not at all tasting like coffee," she quips with the hint of a smile.

"What?"

"I have to add a bunch of crap to my coffee. I need it to get my day started, but I don't like the actual taste of black coffee."

"Good to know."

That invisible electrical current sparks to life in the confines of that small bathroom. We're lost in a mixture of newness and familiarity. Newness as we learn to navigate a shared space with someone we've spent mere hours with, and a familiarity because even though we don't really know each other, the other person is comfortable and right.

"I should get ready to head down. There's a breakfast meeting to kick things off at eight." As difficult as it is, I break eye contact and take a step backwards.

"Yeah, I need to register by nine A.M. and I want to spend as much times as I can browsing the booths."

Grabbing my tie from the hanger in the closet, I get to work on creating the little knot. My fingers fumble the silky material twice, though, proving just how out of sorts I am with Payton's presence.

"Let me," she says behind me, startling me. I could tie a necktie in my sleep, so when I look up in the mirror, I'm surprised to find her standing right behind me again, gazing at me in the reflection over my shoulder.

I drop the two ends of the tie and turn towards her. She's not that much shorter than I am, so it's comfortable to stand before her. I'm not short, but not tall either. I've always been average at five eleven. Payton's on the tall side for a female, standing only about 2 or three inches shorter than me.

She works quickly at creating the perfect knot. I'm able to watch her face as she concentrates on each flip, pull, and tug of the material. When she smiles that brilliant smile, pride swells up in my chest. Why? I have no clue, but for some reason, knowing that she can tie a tie and is smiling happily at the result makes me grin widely back.

I turn to the mirror and only need to push the knot up slightly to cover the top of the button. It's the perfect knot. "Where'd you learn to do that?" I ask, smiling at her through the mirror.

"My dad. He's a pilot, and when I was younger, I used to love watching him get ready for work. He taught me how when I was probably eight. I used to always tie his necktie before he left." She smiles fondly as if she's lost in the joy of the memory.

"Most men don't know how to tie a tie, so to see a woman do it is pretty cool."

"I haven't done it in a long time, but when I saw you, my fingers twitched to get a hold of that satiny material."

Speaking of twitches, my dick jumps in my pants. Just another reminder of the tremendous amount of sexual desire I feel for her. Payton Summer could easily become an addiction I can't quit.

"Well," I start, clearing my throat, "you did a great job."

I watch, mesmerized, as she reaches around my shoulders and runs warm hands over my shoulders and chest, as if brushing off wrinkles. My skin tingles under her touch, my eyes locked on those nimble fingers with the orange nails as they move in contrast to my white shirt. Suddenly, I picture those fingers sliding over *other* parts of my body, her nails raking over my sensitive skin.

"Have dinner with me tonight." The words are out of my mouth before I can consider the ramification. Her green eyes jump to mine, wide and full of wonder.

"What?" she whispers, the tip of her cherry red tongue slipping out and wetting her lips.

"I want to take you to dinner tonight."

Silence fills the void for several moments before she finally responds. "I'm not sure that's such a great idea."

"It's a wonderful idea."

"Like a date?" The words are almost inaudible.

"Yes." My words, however, are clear, calm, and direct. "I want to take you to dinner tonight. Not as a client or as a friend. I'm having a very hard time staying away from you and I think we both owe it to ourselves to see what could happen."

"I can already picture what will happen," she quips with another small smile.

"Me too. But if you didn't want that to happen or it didn't lead there, then fine. I want to take you to dinner because I enjoy spending time with you, and I think you enjoy it just as much."

"I do." She stares at me through the mirror for several heartbeats before finally saying, "Yes. I'll have dinner with you."

We smile at each other for several seconds like dopey kids before I glance down at my wristwatch. "I need to get downstairs. Are you going to be okay getting to your show?"

Payton takes a step back and grabs her stuff. "Yes, it's just across the street."

"I'd walk you if you wanted," I say as I grab my laptop bag and reading glasses off the table.

"I know you would, but it's not necessary."

"All right. I'll meet you back up here this evening. What time does your stuff end today?"

"Five."

"We'll get freshened up and head out around six or six-thirty then. I'll meet you back here," I say, heading towards the door.

"Wait," she hollers behind me. "I don't have a key."

Reaching into my pocket, I pull out the plastic key card and hand it her. "Take this one. I'll stop by the front desk and grab another." As she takes the card from my hand, I can't help but slide my thumb over the top of her hand. Electricity charges through my blood. She must feel it too because the sexiest little gasp slips from her plump lips and her eyes widen in shock.

I don't pull her into my arms the way I'd prefer, because if I did, we would never leave the room. Instead, I turn and walk towards the door, smiling a real smile for what feels like forever. I'm having dinner with Payton tonight, and if things go right, she'll be in my bed. Not because I'm cocky about my moves, but because it's inevitable. Like an alcoholic to the bottle, I'm drawn to her. She's the fix I need.

Tonight, she'll be mine.

Payton

11

It's hard to concentrate on gladiolus and gerbera daisies when your mind keeps replaying the way Dean's Adam's apple bobbed when I tied his necktie. Or the look of pure lust reverberating from his very soul as he watched me through the mirror. I'm sure I wasn't able to hide the raw need that tore through my own body.

The first day of the show has been enlightening, to say the least. The booths from big named florists and designers from all over the United States and other countries were almost overwhelming. There were so many talented people in the building that I didn't know where to look first. I took dozens of photos of displays and arrangements in hope of implementing some of those ideas into my own shop.

A late morning session on thinking outside of the box was my favorite of the day. The designer, Carlos Santiago from New York, explained that everything doesn't have to be traditional and symmetrical. The same roses and carnations bouquets that are perfectly round aren't what are in style at the moment. Sure, those have a time and a place, but most customers will see the beauty in rarity and different. He encouraged us to go with our hearts and come up with unique bouquets that would dazzle the clients.

Needless to say, I left the first day eager and excited to get back to Jupiter Bay.

However, something else stepped in as I walked through the entrance of The Freemont. Nervousness.

Do you know how long it's been since I had a date? I mean a real date, like with dinner and conversation? The possibilities of handholding and a goodnight kiss? Okay, fine. There will definitely be a goodnight kiss, but all of the other stuff?

Dates over the last few years have become few and far between as I've worked to build my business. Long hours and very late nights have been my norm for as long as I can remember. Those dates were always casual, someone I may have met at the bank or at my shop, but never anyone I pictured myself being with for longer than the right now. A few turned into a handful of dates, which translates into some romps in the hay, as Grandma would so bluntly state. But there was never that spark, that desire to really just *be* with a person because being without them wasn't an option.

Not like it is with Dean.

Not like it is for Jaime and Ryan and Meghan and Josh.

Notice how I didn't say Lexi and Chris? That's because I don't feel like they have that spark anymore. Did they ever really have it? I'm not sure. They met in high school where hormones rule and everything was just comfortable for them. But now? I see less comfort and more tension. Even when he's around, he's not mentally present. I would never encourage her to leave him, but I no longer feel like he's the right choice for her. She'll discover this on her own, I know, so for now, mum's the word.

I use the key card to enter our room. *Our* room. The one I share with Dean. Just thinking that makes me shiver with anticipation.

There's no point in denying it any longer: I want him. He's probably bad for me, like smoking or drinking, but I can't stop myself. He'll probably be an even worse habit to kick.

But as long as I keep my eyes open, I shouldn't have any issues when this ends on Friday. When we go back home, he'll go his way and I'll go mine. He'll serve as my accountant and handle my taxes. He'll no longer handle *other* things. Things that I really want him to handle–and rub and kiss and fondle and lick–tonight.

When I walk in, Dean's already there. He's fresh from the shower, his towel hung low on his hips. I stare openly at his body like I'm a wolf about to devour a baby deer. He's lean, but defined with a six-pack and that delicious little V that travels from his hips to the place I suddenly want to explore. With my tongue.

"Hey, sorry. I forgot to take my clothes into the bathroom with me. I'm kinda new at this roommate thing," he says with a sheepish grin.

Oh, no. No need to apologize. Please, go ahead. Drop the towel. Please, for the love of God, drop it.

"It's okay," I reply with what I'm sure is my version of a predatory smile.

Dean grabs a pair of jeans and a pair of boxers from the dresser. "I'll throw on some clothes and then you can have the bathroom to get ready."

"That's fine," I reply, dropping my stuff on one of the chairs beside the small table.

Dean's computer is sitting on top with a small stack of folders. The reusable tote bag I've been carrying was a freebie from one of the many vendors. It's loaded up with brochures, pictures, and free samples that I picked up from the numerous businesses at the show. Before I head over tomorrow, I'll be sure to empty it out so that I'm ready for tomorrow's offerings.

My roommate reemerges a few minutes later, fresh in a pair of jeans and a tight t-shirt. I watch as he walks over to the closet, barefoot, and grabs a blue button down from the hanger. There's something incredibly sexy about a man walking around barefoot in a pair of great-fitting jeans. It's like an aphrodisiac. Throw in a nice button-down with the sleeves rolled up a bit on the forearms? I'm practically a puddle of hormones.

Slipping into the bathroom, I take a quick shower, careful not to get my hair wet. I spend extra time shaving my legs, underarms, and the bikini area. As soon as I'm scrubbed clean, I apply lotion to every square inch of my body. There's no reason not to be smooth and smell great, right?

After freshening up my makeup and hair, I slide on my favorite pair of skinny jeans and a black three-quarter-sleeve sweater. Silver bangle bracelets, a long silver necklace with matching earrings, and a sexy pair of black pumps complete my outfit. With a spritz of perfume, I consider myself ready for the date and move to join Dean in the living space.

I wish I could have recorded his reaction when I walked into the room. As it is, it's something I'll never forget. When he turns around, his eyes burn with desire, as he looks me over from head to toe and back up again. In a moment, he's moving towards me. Pride swells inside of me, mixing with my own lust. It's a heady feeling, knowing that this man wants me the way he does. I see it blazing in his eyes, feel it in the way he touches me.

When he stands directly in front of me, my breath lodges in my throat. His big hand grazes against my cheek as he stares deeply into my eyes. "You're gorgeous," he says. His touch completely undoes me.

"Thank you. You look pretty fabulous yourself."

Dean takes a hold of my left hand and brings it to his lips. The touch is felt clear down to my toes, vibrating the junction of my legs. I'm wet, and the date has barely just begun.

"Ready?" he asks, keeping my hand in his as he leads me towards the doorway. We both grab our coats since the January air can be a bit brisk this time of year.

It's a short walk to the restaurant where he made reservations, so we opt to walk the block and a half instead of using a car. The cool air helps clear my mind. Well, until Dean places his hand on my lower back about halfway down the block. I can feel his warmth through the layers of clothing. There's something possessive, primitive about the gesture. It's as if he's making some sort of statement. It's not like he needs to guide me through throngs of people since the sidewalks are mostly empty.

We're seated at a great table beside the window. You can see the traffic lights in downtown Richmond, cars passing as they head home or wherever they're going for the night. The restaurant is casual with low lighting and dark wood. Most of the tables are full, even for a Wednesday night.

Our waitress arrives a few moments later and takes our drink order; a strawberry daiquiri for me and a Jack and Coke for him. As we browse the menu, he asks, "What looks good?"

"All of it," I reply with a laugh. "They had some sort of chicken salad on top of lettuce, with grapes for lunch. I was craving a big, juicy cheeseburger."

"Mmmmmm, I say we go for the grease," he says, closing his menu with a smile.

"I can get on board with that." Following suit, I close my menu.

After the waitress brings us our drinks and takes our order of cheeseburgers and fries, we jump into small talk. It's comfortable and easy, as if we've shared a table for days, weeks, hell, months before. I've never experienced this effortlessness with another person before outside of my family. It's strange and wonderful all at the same time.

"Tell me about growing up with five sisters."

The prospect makes me laugh. "One time when my dad was off, and before my mom died, she took us all to church. There were usually eight of us, when Dad was home, so we generally took up our own pew. We could be a bit unruly so Mom always picked one of the back pews and sat close to the middle so she could reach all of us easier."

I glance over his shoulder, smiling, as I get lost in the memory. "Well, the pastor had just started his sermon and was encouraging all of the adults to take these portable prayer books that were by the back door. As soon as he dove into his sermon, Abby glanced over at me and whispered, 'Grandpa keeps his portable prayer book on the back of the toilet.' I started to giggle, and the next thing I knew, all five of my sisters were giggling as well. Mom looked horrified as the pastor stopped his sermon and the entire congregation turned to look at us."

He laughs a hearty laugh. "I take it by keeping it on the back of the toilet, she meant..."

"Oh, yeah. Grandpa used to read his prayers when he was *using* the facility. Abby must have been four at the time, and she had no clue what she was saying. To her, it was just an observation, but to me, it was talking about poop in church."

We both laugh as a parade of memories flash through my mind. Most of them star my mom. Those are the memories that hurt. For years, I pushed aside all of those reminiscences because it was too painful. I was seventeen when it happened, so close to officially becoming a woman. When she passed, I felt like I lost a huge piece of myself.

"I remember when I was thirteen, I learned from some boys on the school bus to take those little poppers that you throw on the ground, you know the ones that come out for the fourth of July, and carefully tape one to the bottom of one of the little supports of the toilet seat. Then when someone sits down, it applies pressure, makes a loud pop, and scares them to death."

"You did this?"

"Of course I did! I talked Jaime into helping. We got our sister AJ first, and then our dad. Let's just say that when that happened, we quickly decided *not* to do that again."

"You got in trouble?"

"Oh yeah. I'm sure the fact that AJ cried for two days and didn't want to use the toilet was a big part of the punishment we received."

"Sounds like you guys were trouble when all together," Dean says in observance before taking a drink.

"Definitely. We gave our parents plenty of sleepless nights, I'm sure. Lexi was the worst though. She was trouble with a capital T. Though, she sort of mellowed out when she married Chris right out of high school. Our grandparents instigated a lot, the older we got."

"And Grandma would be the one who added a few zeros to your financial statement a couple of weeks back, right?"

"Yeah, that's her. She has this uncanny ability to embarrass all of us, especially my sister Jaime. Grandma and Grandpa always busted Jaime and Ryan when they were in a *compromising* position."

"Were they dating in high school or something?" he asks when our loaded burgers and fries are delivered to the table.

Plucking a fry from my plate, I reply, "Oh no. Jaime and Ryan are together now. This happened last year. The first time Jaime stayed at Ryan's house, Grandma called us all in, telling us Jaime had gone missing. Then she called the National Guard. She was in bed with Ryan when we found her, which didn't surprise any of us. Grandma just wanted to make a big deal out of nothing and embarrass her. It worked too. Jaime's face was scarlet for three days."

"Sounds like you have your hands full with them." I watch, mesmerized, as he takes a big bite of his cheeseburger.

"Definitely."

"Did you ever ask her about the extra zeros?"

"Not yet. I will, but I was busy the last week before I left for this show. Plus, I'm pretty sure she was avoiding me, which pretty much admits guilt." I load up my fries with ketchup before diving in again. "What about you? You're not from here, right? I'm pretty sure I would have remembered you."

"No, I'm originally from Ridgewood. I lived there until about a year ago when I relocated to Jupiter Bay to work at Corbin and Denton. I was raised by a single mom who did the best she could, while working multiple jobs and barely making pennies. It was hard, but she did everything she could for me. When I was in high school, I knew I wanted to help and make something of myself, so I focused on my studies. Put in a lot of time and was able to get scholarships for college, graduating with a degree in accounting and mathematics."

"I can picture you, with your little glasses, studying all night for a test. It's actually kinda hot," I tell him with a coy smile.

"Really? Well, if you find nerds attractive, then I have plenty of late night historical cost and matching principle study groups where we all discussed the Algebraic K-theory stories to make your panties wet," he whispers conspiratorially with darkening eyes.

"I think they already are." My words are dripping with heat and desire. "The problem is I've been in this perpetual state of arousal since I met you." My confession is rushed, but not any less true.

His eyes are rich and full of need. The way he's looking at me, like he wants to gobble me up instead of his burger, leaves me aching and ready to throw down right here on top of this table; fellow diners be damned.

"I have something else I want to tell you," he says. It's as if we're the only two people in the room. I'm transfixed with the way those plush lips move, remembering exactly what they felt like against my heated skin. My body heats up to a thousand degrees.

"What's that?" I whisper.

"I'm still really close to my mom. Actually, she's back at my place, helping me with —" he says, but is interrupted when Althea makes her presence known by hollering Dean's name in the restaurant.

"I can't believe it! What a coincidence you're here having dinner tonight, too." Completely ignoring my presence at the table, the redhead walks up and stands directly beside Dean and bends down, dangling her boobs in his face.

"Mind if I join you?" Before we can even reply, she's grabbing an unused chair from a nearby table and plops it right next to

Dean. We're talking side-by-side, can't even slide a piece of paper between them kinda close. Thank God it's only their arms. Otherwise, I might turn green with jealousy, and besides my eyes, I've never been a fan of the color green.

"Actually, we were just finishing up," Dean says, dropping his napkin on the table next to him. "Maybe next time."

"Oh, too bad. I was hoping to hang out with some familiar faces this evening." Even though she says faces as in multiples, she has yet to even acknowledge my presence at the table.

Hell, for all I know, she has some other dude picked out and plans to have a threesome later this evening. And that image isn't all that bad, except I've discovered I'm sort of territorial where he's concerned, and not only do I *not* want to picture him and some other guy having their way with Althea, but I don't really want to think about some other dude joining him and I in bed either. I'm perfectly content with it being just the two of us.

"Maybe another time," she says politely while he throws a few bills down on the table. We hadn't finished our meal so our check hasn't been brought to the table yet, but I don't think either of us minds. Right now, getting as far away from Althea, the redheaded supermodel with her eagle talons set on my guy, is my primary concern.

Completely ignoring her reply, Dean reaches over and takes my hand in one hand and both of our coats in the other. We're practically sprinting towards the door, both anxious to be alone.

When we step outside, he helps me into my coat before putting his on. It's a completely gentlemanly gesture, one that makes me swoon just a little bit more. If that were possible.

"Come on," he says with a smile, pulling me in the opposite direction of the hotel. I think my body silently weeps for a moment.

"Where are we going?"

"Over there," he says, pointing to a park entrance.

He wraps his arm around my shoulder as we walk towards the park entrance. Rod iron fencing as a large gateway greets us as we step into the wide space. Even though the sun has long ago set, the moon illuminates a large playground area with everything from jungle gyms for all ages, basketball courts, and even a skate park. A walking path winds through the park, which we stick to for quite a ways. We come across park benches and picnic areas, trees and flowers. It's a beautiful area, one I wouldn't mind enjoying during the daytime.

"It's a beautiful night," I say, my arm wrapped around his waist as we leisurely stroll by a large fishing pond.

"It is," he confirms, looking up at the night sky. Even with all of the lights and sounds of the city around us, you can still see the stars shining brightly in the clear sky.

We stroll along, making our way around the outskirts of the park. We run into the occasional joggers, a few power-walkers, and even a couple holding hands and enjoying a walk in the park, but for the most part, it's a quiet, serene moment. A perfect moment.

Eventually, towards the back of the park, we come upon a grouping of trees. It's dark but not in a scary way; it just speaks of seclusion. Apparently, he feels the same way, because the next thing I know, we're not on the walking path any longer. I'm startled when I feel the coarse bark of a tree at my back.

But there's no time to think.

I feel the warmth of his body pressed against me moments before I feel his hands on my cheeks. My skin tingles as he slides his big hands down, grazing over the long column of my throat. A hearty moan rips from my throat, but it's swallowed by his mouth. The kiss is primal, urgent, and not anything less than perfect. My tongue slides along his, tangled in a sexual dance that makes my blood boil and my panties soaking wet. I pulse with want, my flesh on fire with need.

"You taste so fucking good," he whispers harshly without removing his lips from my own. "I can't wait to taste every inch of your body later."

I shiver in anticipation at his words. "Yes. I want that. All of that."

"It's a long walk back to the hotel," he says his hands sliding down my chest. "Unless…"

"Unless?" I ask, that one word throaty and high-pitched.

"Unless you can keep quiet for a minute."

Before I can register the meaning of his words, he's unbuttoning my jeans. Another shiver rakes through my body, but not because of the cool air. This one's of eagerness. I feel his touch as he places his hand on my lower stomach and gently slides it down into my panties. I'm on fire, my legs quivering and barely keeping me upright.

"I love touching you," he says as he moves his fingers between the lips of my drenched pussy.

"I love it when you touch me." I moan when two of his fingers press into my wetness. My legs long to spread, to wrap around his waist and ride the waves of pleasure he's about to inflict.

His fingers are more insistent as he thrusts them in and out of my body. My lips latch on to his hungrily and frenzied, the only way I can keep from screaming out in ecstasy. He works me over thoroughly and completely, like a maestro orchestrating a symphony, and before long, I'm climbing towards an epic orgasm.

"I can feel your body clenching around my fingers. You're so close, beautiful."

"So, so close," I whisper in a rush of broken words.

"Come for me. I want to feel it on my fingers and see it on your face."

As if on cue, I detonate like a bomb, bliss gushing from my body in waves. He prolongs my release by rubbing over my clit. I practically melt into a pile of mush, and if he weren't holding me up, I'm sure I'd be lying on the ground by now. My legs shake and my core trembles as his dark brown eyes pierce through my post-orgasmic haze. They're rich and alive with yearning, a desire so profound I feel it deep in my soul.

"That was the hottest thing ever." He kisses me square on the lips, his fingers still buried inside me. "I want to do it again, but this time, I'm going to taste it on my tongue." He nips at my swollen bottom lip. "And then I'm going to feel how fucking amazing it is on my cock."

He goes in for another bruising kiss that leaves me breathless. Blood starts to pump recklessly in my body again, and my slick pussy clenches around his fingers again. I've never had this sort of sexual drive before; not before Dean.

Quickly, he pulls his hand from my pants and secures the button. I'm left panting and brainless as I lean against the tree, thankful for its presence to help hold me upright. He pulls my shirt down, followed by my coat, and gazes into my eyes.

"I'm about to Hulk out of my pants. I need to get you to a bed. Now."

Unable to form words, I nod my head in response. There's no other place I want to be than below him, above him, around him. As long as he's inside me, that's the only thing that matters, the only thing I crave.

Standing up and taking his hand in mine, I try my best to convey just how much I want him. "Let's go."

12

Dean

I move as fast as I can without dragging her behind me, but my legs are being driven by pure lust. I'm dying to have her, to feel her body wrap around my cock like a glove. Last night was the worst night of sleep I've had in I don't even know how long. The glow from the television illuminated her flawless skin and her rich brown hair. Her mouth was slightly agape as she slept, the occasional soft snore slipping from her sweet lips. I was pretty much hard as a rock the entire night, unable to close my eyes for fear that I'd miss out on one moment of watching her. Yeah, it might sound a little creepy, but whatever. I was completely enamored and transfixed and wasn't even touching her.

While she showered tonight, I had to get my mind off her nakedness, so I called home. Bri told me all about her day, from the time she woke up through the very phone call we were having. Mom said she was good and that everything was fine. I knew it would be, but when your entire life is wrapped up in one little girl, you still can't help but worry a little bit. Since I got the phone call out of the way, I'm free and clear to consume myself on everything Payton for the rest of the night.

And, fuck, am I ready to devour.

Our hands are still tangled as we step inside the hotel. Heat pelts us in the face causing my cheeks to sting a little. It didn't feel that cool outside when we were in the park, but that could very well have been because my blood was boiling and my hand was down her pants, coated in her juices.

There's no one else waiting for the elevators as I push the call button. It arrives just a few moments later, and as soon as we step inside, I'm engaging the close door button. The moment we're ascending, I pounce. She's expecting my assault, her mouth open and tongue greedy. The kiss is searing, the kinda kiss that brands you for life. She tastes like heaven as my hands slide up her sweater, eager to touch more of that warm, soft flesh.

Her moan fills my mouth and the empty elevator. It's fuel to my already burning desire for her. I almost fall to my knees and rejoice when her hand grasps my cock through my jeans. Suddenly, it's my own groan of ecstasy that fills the small car. Everything inside of me begs to hit the stop button so we can finish right here, right now.

"God, I want to fuck you so bad. I want to take you hard and then slow and then fast again. I want to make you come so many times you can't remember your name. I want to make you scream my name until your throat is raw and your voice a whisper. And then I'm going to go agonizingly slow and worship your entire body with my mouth. I'll do it over and over, until we're both so exhausted that sleep is the only option left. And when we wake, I'll start all. Over. Again."

My own words surprise me. I'm not usually this vocal about my wants and needs. Heaven knows I would have never said any of that stuff to Brooke. But Payton? She brings out this primal, edgy, raw hunger that's buried deep inside me.

Her hand flexes around my engorged cock as the sexiest gasp slides from her lips. Mentally, I strip us both naked, lift her in my arms, and bury my cock in her wetness. But the ding of the elevator reminds me that we're still in a public setting. Even though we're alone in the car, there's a good chance we're giving some security officer in a little room somewhere enough spank bank material to keep him busy for a while.

A group of men that I recognize from the convention are laughing, waiting for us to disembark the elevator car. I keep my head down as I grab her hand, rushing her behind me. I don't even try to mask the erection in my pants. They must notice her swollen lips and my raging boner because their laughter stops instantly as we walk past. They step in the car and immediately start laughing again. I should be embarrassed about being busted in my current state of horniness, but I'm not. I couldn't care less.

Keeping one hand still locked on hers, I slide the key card into the slot, noticing a slight tremor to my hand. Payton steps up behind me and plasters her curves against my back. With our fingers still locked, she slides her hands around me, gripping at my chest and sliding down my abdomen. I close my eyes, rejoicing in the way her breasts smash against my back and her hands roam over my torso.

Finally, the little light turns green. I drag her inside the room as if the hallway were on fire. The loud click of the door shutting is the last thought I have before I'm lost in her. Her touch, her taste, her scent. It's everywhere, wrapping around me like a vice and refusing to let up its grip. Not that I want it to.

With a little more force than I intend, I push her against the wall. "I'm sorry. I didn't mean to be rough," I pant, searching her emerald green eyes.

"Please be rough. I like it when you take what you want, because you make it feel so good when you do."

Flame, meet gasoline.

My hands are a frenzy of gripping fingers and grabby palms. There's no couth to my movements as I remove her coat and sweater. She's panting with need as I watch, hypnotized, by the way her chest quickly rises and falls. Those glorious breasts are being contained by a thin, black lace bra, her nipples straining against the coarse material.

Removing my own coat, I never take my eyes off her. My need to be inside her is overwhelming, my control completely gone. Hell, did I ever really have it when it came to her? Even in the beginning, the first time she walked into my office, I've been hanging on by a tiny thread. One look from those spellbinding eyes was enough to send me spiraling out of control.

I unbutton my shirt, leaving it hanging wide open. She has a thing for my shirts; this proven by the fact that she wears one to bed at night. Her pupils dilate further until you can barely tell what color her eyes are. Reaching down, I unsnap her jeans. My hands are itching to touch her, so as I slide down the material, I do it with both palms firmly against her skin.

When I reach her ankles, I regrettably remove her heels. I'd leave them on if I could get her jeans off without having to eliminate them. The way her body looks in a pair of black heels and lace is sexier than any Victoria's Secret model I've seen. Payton has curves, the body of a real woman. And I'm about to worship at her altar.

"I want these back on," I instruct as I decide to slip the heels back on her bare feet.

The moment becomes surreal, like an out of body experience. As I regain my full height, I openly stare, transfixed by her radiance. In nothing but the lace bra and matching panties and fuck-me heels, I'm forever gone, lost in an image I will never forget. Her hair cascading down her shoulders, lips plump from my kisses, and the scent of her arousal; it's all part of my greatest fantasy come to life.

I kick off my shoes, pull off my socks, and drop my jeans. My hard-on has practically taken on a life of its own, jetting painfully out of my body, standing at complete attention. Regrettably, I slide my shirt off so that I can get to the undershirt beneath. While pulling it over my head, Payton bends down and grabs the button-down.

"I want this back on," she says with a teasing smile, dangling the material from her pointer finger.

Hell, I guess we all have our own vices. Unable to hide my own smile, I slip the shirt back on and lose my boxers. I step forward, caging her against the wall with my body. Placing my forearms against the hard surface brings me close to her, but not close enough. My lips devour hers slowly, a sensual kiss that will surely build into something more, something epic. They always do with her.

Payton pants against my lips when I finally break the kiss. Her eyes are molten and her body sways, as if pulled towards my touch. A need for pleasure has completely taken over my body. I know I should slow things down, should taste her with my mouth, but I can't fight it any longer. I need to be inside her.

Quickly, I unclasp her bra and grab the thin straps of her panties. "I'll buy you new ones," I say as I rip them from her body.

She gasps and moans at the same time. "Oh, God."

Lifting her in my arms, Payton wraps her legs around my waist and her arms around my neck. I've never done this against a wall, and it's already proving to be a little more difficult than I anticipated. But my cock lines up perfectly with her pussy, so I've got that going for me.

"Shit, I need to grab a condom." Regret filters through me. Moving away from her is the last thing I want to do right now.

"I'm clean. I haven't been with anyone but you in a while."

"Me too. It's only been you since you walked into my office." Not that they were lined up before then either. There was only one woman between Brooke and Payton and that was the result of a drunken night at a bachelor party more than two years ago. "You're protected?"

Something flashes in her eyes. I'm not sure what it means. It speaks of hurt and sadness, but she quickly pushes it away and answers. "Yeah."

That one word is music to my ears. Pulling back slightly, I thrust forward, engulfing my cock in her tight, wet heat. Neither of us filters our moans. It's fucking perfection. Giving her a second to adjust to my size, I slowly begin to move my body in and out. My legs and arms are burning and her heels are biting into my lower back, but I don't care. This? This is pure magic.

"So good." I'm surprised the words are coherent considering my eyes are practically crossed in pleasure.

My hips start to buck wildly as I begin to chase the release I know is inevitable. I've teased myself too long without any relief, and this is the ultimate respite. I find her lips with my own once more as her pussy starts to tighten around me. Her hands dive into my hair, gripping and pulling as she rides me. It's a sweet pain that coincides with the indulgence.

Pushing her into the wall, I use it as leverage. My thighs are on fire, but I don't pay any attention to it. I focus solely on giving this gorgeous woman another mind-blowing orgasm. Keeping both hands on her hips, I pull back, looking down and watching my cock disappear into her pussy. The base of my spine starts to tingle, and I know I won't be able to hold off much longer.

Payton arches her back into the wall, pushing her breasts upward, as if offering them to me on a buffet. I'm able to bend down slightly and still pump my hips, so I lick from the top of one breast down to her erect nipple. Another moan fills the room, driving me further into insanity. Using my teeth, I latch on to her, sending her soaring over the edge. She comes violently in my arms and on my dick, practically screaming her release.

Mine follows.

Removing my mouth with a pop, I thrust and succumb to the magnitude of my orgasm. Blinding white light infiltrates my mind and I swear I lose consciousness. I've never come so hard in my life.

When I open my eyes, Payton's eyes are closed, but she's smiling. We're also a knot of legs and arms. I'm not exactly sure how we ended up on the floor, but I'm guessing somewhere between the most powerful orgasm of my life and my legs giving out.

"You're not hurt, are you?" I ask, looking her over as much as I can.

"Are you kidding? I've never been better." She never opens her eyes, but her smile widens.

She's straddling my lap, legs still wrapped around me. I'm still buried inside her. I can feel my dick twitching, probably seizing from exertion. Payton leans forward, wrapping her arms around my neck. I can feel her breathing starting to even out as little puffs of hot air hits my neck.

"Come on, sweetheart," I say, gently moving her. "Let's get into bed."

She murmurs something incoherent as I attempt to stand on shaky legs. My arms are Jell-O, but I somehow manage to pick her up and carry her to the bed. It's still made from the maid service earlier in the day, so I one-handedly pull the thin white blanket and sheet back before lying her down. Chuckling, I grab those black heels and toss them on the floor before pulling the sheet up.

In the bathroom, I lose my dress shirt and grab a washcloth. Honestly, I could use a quick shower, but opt for just a wash-down with the cloth so I can get in bed with Payton quicker. There'll be time in the morning for a shower. Hopefully together.

Rewetting and wringing out the washcloth, I head back into the main room. She's sleeping peacefully, her soft brown hair splayed out on the pillow. Holding that cloth, I gingerly pull the sheet back. I'm not sure if this is chivalrous or creepy, but I move her legs and wipe up the mess I made. It actually gives me some weird sense of pride when I see my mark running down her leg.

I know. I'm not right.

Tossing the wet cloth on the floor, I slide into bed beside her, scooping her into my arms. My entire body screams with exertion, my lids drooping the moment my head hits the soft pillow. Payton snuggles in close, resting her head on my shoulder and wrapping her arm around my chest. When she throws her leg up onto mine, my wayward dick starts to stir again. See what happens when you actually use it for its intended purpose?

My last conscious thought is how good it feels to have her in my arms. When I stayed that first time, I was gone before the sun. Tomorrow, however, I get to wake with her in my arms, and hopefully, make slow, sweet love to her. I'm not making any pretenses that this is just a one-time thing. It can't be. It feels too right for it not to be.

Convincing my head and her that we should continue is going to be the challenge. Is it wrong to sleep with a client? Sure. But it's not forbidden. I'm just afraid of getting myself into a situation similar to the one I found with Brooke six years ago.

And Payton? She has a serious hang-up about the possibility of a relationship. In just a short period of time, I can tell she has some sort of past hurt. Something keeps her from going all-in with a guy, and I'm sure it's going to be my greatest test to build up her trust to take down her walls. And her walls are thick, this I can already see. That'll take some serious effort on my part, but my mind is made up. She's the one that I want. And I'm up to the challenge.

I can already tell she's worth it.

Payton

13

Warmth. I'm wrapped in it to the point of sweating. My skin feels damp, my limbs heavy as I try to pull myself from whatever deep slumber I was in last night. But, oh, what a glorious night it must have been. I awake feeling completely refreshed and ready to tackle day two of the show.

But then I move and encounter the reason for the heat.

Opening my eyes, I find Dean sleeping on his side, his arm wrapped around my abdomen. A flush creeps up my face as I remember everything about our *date* last night. The park, the elevator ride, the wall by the entrance. My skin starts to tingle again, but for another entirely different reason. Heat floods between my legs, reviving that dull ache I've had since I agreed to share a room with him.

Ah, who am I kidding? I've had this need since the first moment I saw him.

Glancing up at his face, I take in the peacefulness of his features while he sleeps. His angled jaw is more relaxed and his full lips slightly agape. His hair is tussled from sleeping, or maybe from me gripping it in my fists last night right before I came so hard I was temporarily blind.

The sheet is pulled up to his waist, but there's no camouflaging the erection just beneath the surface. He's pitching a tent that would have made my old Girl Scouts troop leader proud. My mouth salivates at the sight of his dick. Could I really be ready to go another round? The way my breasts feel tingly and heavy and the apex of my legs wet, I'd say the answer is an undeniable yes.

As I stare lustfully, a little drop of liquid appears on the sheet right where the tip of his dick is. My fingers itch to touch and my tongue tingles to lick that little droplet. Before I can stop myself, a little moan slips from my lips.

When I finally pull my eyes away from his erection, I glance back up to find Dean awake, eyes ablaze and filled with desire. The breath in my throat lodges as our eyes connect. And if I were being honest with myself, something more than just our eyes is making a connection. I feel something different, something crazy, something scary when we're together. But there's no way I'm ready or willing to think too much about those pesky feelings right now.

Right now? I want to devour the man beside me.

I'm moving before I have the chance to chicken out. Tossing the sheet back, I reveal the most mouthwatering specimen of man-meat I've ever seen. *Damn, I've been hanging around Grandma too much.*

Crouching between his legs, I take his cock in my hand. I'm licking my lips in anticipation of finally getting to taste him. Even after half a dozen of sexual encounters, I realize that I have yet to return the oral sex favor. And we can't have that, now can we?

Bending down, I lick the moisture on the tip of his dick. "What are you doing?" his question is harsh, breathy.

"Doing something I've wanted to do for a while now." I swipe my tongue over the tip again and swirl it around the wide crown.

"Don't let me stop you. Please, continue."

He inhales sharply as I take him inside my mouth. His skin is velvety and pulled taut, the scent of him infiltrating my senses. Slowly, I move down his shaft, licking and wetting his skin as I go. Keeping my hand firmly wrapped around the root, I lower myself as far down onto him as I can go. I have to mentally turn off my gag reflex the closer I get to my throat. A deep garbled groan rips from his throat.

Slowly, I begin to pump my other hand with long, fluid strokes. Glancing up, his eyes are locked onto the action, his breathing labored and choppy. Using my other hand, I reach down and grab his balls. When I glance up again to see his reaction, I watch his eyes roll back in his head.

Dean reaches down and gently grabs a hold of my head, guiding me down onto his shaft. I begin to bob in earnest now, taking him into my throat as far as I can.

"Fuck, Payton." It's a mix between a choke and a moan.

I feel his balls draw up and take that as my cue that the end is drawing near. His hips start to buck, his grip in my hair tightening almost to the point of pain. But I ignore it. Instead, I focus on the way he moves, the way he tastes, and the way he sounds. He's so sexy when he's on the verge of coming.

"You need to stop. I'm going to come," he grits through his teeth.

There's no way I'm stopping now. I want to taste him–all of him. Tightening my hold on his shaft, I hollow out my cheeks, sucking him with everything I have. He curses like a sailor moments before stilling momentarily and thrusting upward into my mouth one last time. His release is warm and tangy and slides down my throat easily. His dick twitches in my hand as he falls back onto the pillow utterly spent.

"Jesus."

I smile. That one word was the greatest compliment I could have possibly received. That, and the fact that he can't even move right now. His breathing is reflective of someone who just ran a full marathon in record time.

With a quick pat on his thigh, I turn and smile. "Time to go!"

"Wait, go? Where?"

"You have a very compelling accounting conference to get to, while I go play with flowers all day," I say as I start to slide off the bed.

He reaches for me, halting my progress. "I say we just stay here and do more of *that* all day."

"Can't. Very important things to do today," I say as he lines up our lips, mere inches apart.

"I can't think of anything more important than burying myself between your thighs."

"Hmmmm," I respond, contemplating. "How about you go do your thing and I'll go do my thing and we'll meet back here tonight and do more of that thing you suggested."

He grazes his soft lips over the top of mine. "I'm going to hold you to that."

"You're promising me an orgasm. I'm not going to flake out on you," I quip with a smile.

Our kiss is interrupted by the ringing of his cell phone. While he goes to answer it, I slip into the bathroom to shower. While a part of me wants to know who's calling at seven in the morning, it's not really any of my business. So I shut the door and crank on the water under the pretense of giving him privacy. But really it's because I don't want to be tempted to press one of those glasses against the door to hear his conversation.

After my shower, Dean jumps in, taking a quick one while I get ready. He dresses in another button-down shirt, this one in a light green color, with tan slacks. His tie is green and brown plaid, and I don't even have to offer to tie it. He turns towards me with a smile on his face and hands me the material.

When the knot is perfect, we both head towards the door. Before I can open it, though, he pulls me into his arms. My legs turn to noodles as his lips take mine in a bruising, perfect kiss that leaves me breathless. Dean's hands wrap around my back and pull me flush against his body. He's hard already. Wrapping my arms around his neck, I give myself into the kiss.

It ends before we have the chance to rip each other's clothes off, and frankly, I was ready. With a sly smile, he takes my hand and pulls me out of the room. We walk together to the elevator and wait for it to arrive. While inside the car, memories of last night filter through my mind, causing more warmth to flood my already soaked panties.

"Tonight," he whispers into my ear as our car fills up with other hotel guests.

Dean continues to hold my hand as we make our way into the lobby of The Freemont. He offers to escort me across the street, but again, I tell him it's not necessary. Honestly, I could use the little bit of alone time in the cool air to calm my racing heart and raging hormones. If he walks over with me, I'm liable to find the closest supply closet as soon as we set foot through the door.

"I have to attend the convention dinner tonight, but I'll be upstairs as soon as I can break free."

"Don't rush on my behalf. I can order room service and watch a movie. You certainly aren't required to entertain me."

He steps closer, invading my personal space. "I'd much rather spend tonight entertaining you. And I will. Unfortunately, I have to make an appearance at the dinner, but know that I'd much rather be spending every second of my time with you, naked, in bed. Or in the shower. I'm not picky."

I smile at the thought. "I'll see you tonight," I confirm before stepping out into the sunny January morning.

After detouring to the gourmet coffee shop down the block, I head inside The Country Garden, wide-awake and full of energy. I'm ready for day two of the floral show. I didn't have an opportunity to chat with some of the vendors and businesses in the massive convention hall, so that's on my agenda today. As well as attending two of the featured programs; one on bringing out the natural fragrances of the flowers, and the other on working with exotics and hard to care for buds.

Stepping in through the front door, I feel my phone vibrate in my pocket. Upon digging it out, I find a text from Grandma. Considering the shop has only been open for an hour, I hope nothing is wrong. I received message from AJ and Rachel yesterday stating that everything was going well.

Grandma: Code Blue, Payters. Code Blue!

Me: OMG! What does Code Blue mean?

Grandma: Nothing. I just wanted to get your attention.

Me: What?!?!?!? *insert growling emoji*

Grandma: Did you know there's a flower named Clitoris?

Me: Are you kidding me right now? I thought the place was burning down!

Grandma: The only thing burning is my loins, Payters. The flower. Clitoris. Should I order some?

Me: NOOOOO! They're called Clitoria, Grandma. I don't want to sell flowers named Clitoria. That's gross.

Grandma: I admit, they're a little odd. Plus they're native to Asia so the shipping will probably cost you a fortune.

Rubbing my head, I gaze down, dumbfounded, at my phone.

Me: Do not order those. And do not order anything, please. I already ordered before I left.

Grandma: Yes, I know. I sent back the poppies.

Me: Why?

Grandma: They looked like hairy vaginas. *insert photo* Even grandpa said they look like they need a good wax job. I can't, in good conscience, sell hairy vaginas to your customers, Payters. That's just wrong. Even I think so.

Me: They're not hairy! And when they open, they're beautiful!

Grandma:	Oh, well, no one told me that.
Me:	*insert eye roll gif* Never mind. I'll order more next week.
Grandma:	Grandpa says hello. Oh! Have you found a strapping young stud to do a little service work underneath the hood?
Me:	Am I a car now?
Grandma:	Never underestimate the power of a good mechanic, Payters. If you find one with a good dipstick, you might not mind a good servicin' every now and again.
Me:	How are we related? Seriously.
Grandma:	I'm your favorite relative, and you know it. Anyway, I have go. Gpa has a handful of my poppies right now.
Me:	GRANDMA! You're at my shop!
Grandma:	I know where I am, Payton. No one is here so it's ok.
Me:	No. No, it is most definitely NOT ok! *insert angry face emoji*
Grandma:	Don't act all high and mighty. I already found ass prints on the stainless steel table. I'm not pointing any fingers, but it's not my ass print and it's not Rachel's – I asked her. That only leaves one ass, Payton.

I stare wide-eyed and shocked at my phone. That romp on my workbench was weeks ago. There's no way there's butt prints, but how else could she know about them? Unless she's making it up in hopes that I'll give myself away, and that'll open a whole new can of worms I'd rather not open with Grandma.

Grandma:	Got a customer! Gotta go! Toodles! *insert kissy face emoji*

See, this is why I can't have nice things. My family is whack, and it started two generations before me.

Dean

The dinner drones on and on as the president of AICPA, or the America Institute of CPA's, talks about proposed IRS changes in the upcoming year. Usually, discussing and debating the pros and cons of tax law changes with fellow numbers nerds would be the highlight of my night, but not tonight. Not with Payton in my room.

I'm stuck at a table with nine other professionals, one of which is Althea. She keeps smiling at me, giving me that flirty little smirk that basically says she's game for anything sexual I'd suggest. But the thing is, even before I found Payton standing in the lobby of my hotel, I just wasn't feeling it with her. Althea is gorgeous, sure, but not in that simple, natural way. She's pretty with three hundred dollar shoes and pristine and professionally applied makeup. Her hair is perfect and her business suit spotless.

But she's not Payton.

Payton wearing a pair of jeans and a simple tee. Payton with her hair pulled high in a ponytail. Payton with smudges of dirt on her cheek from replanting a potted plant. Payton in nothing but my dress shirt, unbuttoned and gaping open to reveal soft curves and luscious breasts.

There's only one woman who piques my interest and makes my cock throb, and it's not the beautiful woman sitting across from me.

Payton. That's where my focus seems to be, no matter how much I try to listen to the speakers or to my tablemates sharing client horror stories. There's plenty of stories of my own I could contribute. My personal favorite was the time a male client tried to write off hookers as a business expense. He called it stress management. Or what about the woman who wanted to start a business with her late husband's insurance money. Did I mention he wasn't actually dead yet when she submitted to cash in the insurance policy?

My point is that I have something to contribute to the conversation around me, but my mind is stuck in the gutter. Specifically, how quickly I could get Payton naked and moaning beneath me.

"What about you, Dean? How do you think this new legislation will affect the economy? Rumor has it that it'll be harder on the middle class, therefore changing the way they spend and save money." This question comes from Raymond, a tax advisor from Detroit.

I blink rapidly, trying to catch my bearings. No way can I confess that I've basically completely ignored all discussion around me for the last hour and a half. No way can I admit to be so distracted by a woman that I can't even carry on a casual dinner conversation without all thoughts drifting. Because then I'd be *that* guy. You know the one; the guy who basically follows his woman around like a puppy dog, sending cute little text messages throughout the day like *Miss you* and *Thinking of you*.

Fine. I'm soooooooo that guy. I'm man enough to admit that I'm completely smitten with Payton Summer. Even if it's one hundred percent the worst decision in the history of mankind, I'm still willing to take the chance. Just like that, my mind did a complete one-eighty, and I find myself racing towards Payton, not in the opposite direction I've been going for the last several months. Even though I'm certain I'll come out mangled and destroyed when it ends, and heaven knows, it will end.

Life is anything but predictable. I've learned that lesson the hard way. The only thing right–perfect, even–in my life is Bri. My daughter's the one thing I did right. Even if the way I got her wasn't so right. She's my light in total darkness, my sun breaking through the clouds.

"I'm sure Dean would agree that the economy will forever fluctuate, but people will always still spend. Whether it's a want or a need, society will still spend more, and if we're lucky, saving a little bit along the way," Tim adds to the conversation. Relief courses through me, and I'm grateful for the help.

Before I can add anything to the discussion, my cell phone vibrates in my pocket. Normally, I'd let my voicemail catch the call, but with Bri and Mom out of the area, I jump at the distraction of a phone call.

"Excuse me," I state as I stand up. "I need to take this," I add, indicating my phone.

"Hello?" I ask quietly as I slip out the big double doors and into the expansive hallway.

"Hi, Daddy!"

"Hi, pumpkin. Are you having fun with Mimi?"

"Yep! We're drawing horses and monkeys."

"Horses and monkeys? That's a great combination."

"I miss you." My gut clenches tightly.

"I miss you, too. But I'm going to be home by the time you get out of school tomorrow. I'll pick you up from Miss Nancy's house after school, okay?"

"Okay! I can't wait to see you! I made you lots of new pictures for your office." I smile at the thought of adding one more drawing to the side of my filing cabinet.

"Sounds good, sweetheart. I can't wait to give you tickles."

"No tickles, Daddy. You'll make me pee!" she exclaims through fits of giggles. And that's why I say it. Just to hear that sweet sound from her little lips.

"Okay, no tickles. I'd hate to get peed on," I reply through my laugh.

"It's time for my bath. We had grilled cheese for dinner and Mimi says I have butter everywhere."

"Sounds good, angel. Tell Mimi I'll call her tomorrow when I'm on my way home. I'll see you tomorrow, all right? I love you."

"Love you too, Daddy."

My. Heart.

Doesn't matter how many times I hear those words, they still render me speechless every time.

"'Night, pumpkin."

I hang up just as fellow conference-goers start to file out of the banquet hall. Raymond, Tim, and Althea, amongst a few others, come out, laughing and talking.

"Hey, Dean! We're heading into the bar for a drink. Care to join us?"

Are you kidding me? I have a gorgeous, probably naked woman upstairs in my hotel room right now. Hanging out with you guys, talking taxes doesn't even come close as reason as to why I'd delay heading up to the room a second longer than necessary.

"Thanks for the offer, Tim. I'm actually heading out pretty early in the morning. I'm going to head up and pack before hitting the hay." Althea's eyebrows shoot skyward, but she doesn't call me out on my obvious lie. Especially in light of the fact there's one final meeting in the morning before being dismissed from the conference at noon.

"Too bad, man. If you change your mind, we'll be in there," he says, indicating the doorway to the hotel bar.

We say our goodbyes before I'm able to escape to the elevator. I'm smiling broadly as I push the button for my floor, anxious to get to the woman waiting in my room. My pants start to tighten just thinking about her luscious curves. Bouncing on my toes, it doesn't take long before I'm deposited on my floor and heading towards my room.

Towards Payton.

The door isn't even closed, and my cock is thickening in my trousers. Her voice is seeping through the crack in the bathroom door. It's a Carrie Underwood song, and it's definitely off-key. A huge grin sweeps across my face as she sings about a cheating man and tearing apart his pickup. If it wasn't so comical, I'd be slightly terrified of the underlying message.

Instead, I take the opportunity to strip out of my clothes until I'm naked. On any other day, I'd go ahead and hang my dress shirt in the closet and fold my pants in my suitcase, but that was before a very naked, very wet Payton Summer was singing horribly in my shower about maiming a man.

I'm so fucking turned on.

I slowly open the door, thankful that it doesn't squeak, and slip inside. The air is thick and humid, the mirror completely fogged up. That only makes me that much more anxious to join her beneath the hot water spray.

Payton's attempting to hit high notes that would make dogs bark. I have to bite the inside of my lip to keep from laughing and giving away my position. And my position is a breath away from the singing beauty. My hard-on could practically reach out and knock on the shower curtain.

Unable to stay away any longer, I grab the curtain and gently pull it back. Glancing inside, I'm treated to the sight of Payton's gyrating hips as she sings along to the music in her head. As I step inside, I try to avoid scaring her, but she doesn't hear me, so when I reach out and touch her back, the room is filled with a scream.

"It's me," I say as I try to peal her body off the side of the shower.

"Jesus, you scared me," she gasps, trying to get her breathing under control. "You're all finished with your dinner?"

"Yep. Lots of boring speakers and conversations with my peers. The dinner was good, though. Did you eat?" I ask, running a finger from her shoulder down her arm and watching the way my fingers glide over her wet skin.

"Not yet." She's breathless. I can feel her eyes burning into me as she watches me touch her.

"You should have eaten." I run my finger back up her arm and down the center of her chest. When they reach her belly button, I return my eyes to hers. "You're going to need your energy."

She shivers.

Stepping forward, my arms wrap around her waist, drawing her into my embrace. Before she can even wrap her own arms around me, my lips taste skin. I start at the hollow of her neck and slowly drag them upward. My tongue slips out, drawing a long, wet trail up her chin. When my lips reach hers, I hit pay dirt. Her lips taste like heaven. Sweet, succulent, and addicting.

Her groan fills the bathroom, the sound going straight to my groin. She immediately opens her mouth to me, and I gladly take it. My tongue has an urgency I've never experienced. It's more than just a quick 'hey, we gotta hurry up before someone catches us' need. This is something that consumes me, ravishes me. My need for her is infinite, and frankly, that scares the crap out of me.

So I won't think about that now.

Now, I'll concentrate on pleasure. On the way she makes me feel. On Payton.

Without breaking the connection of our mouths, I move her backwards half a step until she's leaning against the shower wall. Payton arches into me, her glorious tits rubbing against my body.

If I wasn't hard before, I'm painfully stiff now. Knife-like throbbing in my balls kinda pain.

But I welcome it, because any amount of time with this woman is worth it.

"Stay right here," I instruct after breaking the kiss. She whimpers, but stays put.

Grabbing the fragrant bar of soap, I squat in front of her and, frankly, am treated to the best view in the house. Carefully, I lift her left leg and set it on the side of the tub. Then, I lather up my hands and grab the foot resting on the ledge.

Starting at her instep, I apply pressure to her foot, rubbing and washing her body. Her moan is deep and goes straight to my dick. As much as I'd like to say forget this round of foreplay and bury myself balls deep, I have this overwhelming desire to touch every inch of her skin. So that's what I do.

I work my way up from her foot to her calf. When I reach behind her knee, she giggles and squirms. Glancing up, she looks breathless and gorgeous, with water streaming down her body. The water cascades over her breasts and winds down her stomach to her pussy. It's like an aquatic path leading me to the Promised Land.

Her thighs are beckoning me. Leaning forward, I run my tongue from her kneecap straight up to where her legs meet. She's sweeter than any sugar concoction available, and her scent is heavenly. I can hear her heavy breathing over the water, and the sound does things to me. It drives me, fuels me. My sole need right now is to taste her.

When I swipe my tongue between the folds of her pussy, her moan echoes off the walls. I can feel her legs shaking as I place the one I was just washing back up on the ledge, opening her up for what's coming. As soon as she's stable, I slide nearer, getting up close and personal with my favorite part of her body. Well, besides her gorgeous smile. And her green eyes. And her perfect ass.

Fine. Every part of Payton's body is my favorite.

I start with slow, long strokes of my tongue against her swollen clit. She's moving against my mouth, seeking out my touch. The noises she makes, her uproars of pleasure, is like throwing gas onto an already blazing inferno. It ignites my blood and sends lust racing recklessly through my taut body.

Grabbing the backs of her thighs, I pull her forward, tilting her pelvis forward and upward, aligning her perfectly with my mouth. My tongue starts to move with a fierceness I didn't know it possessed. And possessed is another adjective, because it's taken a mind of its own, licking and stroking against her core with a ferocity that surprised even me.

She's close. I can tell by her noises and the way her body is gyrating against my face. She's taking everything she wants and needs, and hell, if that isn't a turn-on all on its own. I move slowly and slide my tongue into her wet, hot pussy. Muscles tighten around me as she moans once more.

"More," she begs.

And who am I to deny her anything she wants?

So I slide my tongue into her body, savoring every ounce of her taste, drawing out every bit of pleasure I can. I use one hand on the back of her thigh for leverage, and bring the other up front to join the party. With two fingers, I gently caress her swollen nub, and her legs instantly start to shake. She's so close, I can feel it.

I let her body lead me as I continue to pierce her wetness with my tongue and rub circles over her clit. Her body grinds against my face as I breathe in every part of her. She comes apart against me, in my mouth, with loud moans of pure, raw release. Her taste floods me, and not just my mouth. It invades my sanity, my soul. I need her, and I need her now.

Payton starts to weaken immediately. I can feel her body starting to sag against me, so I quickly stand up and grab a hold of her. She's pliant in my arms, wrecked by her orgasm. And that's my cue to get her into bed and do it all over again.

Shutting off the water, I grab a towel and wrap it around her body. Grabbing the second one, I wrap it loosely around my waist before turning my full attention back to her. She's heavy lidded and smiling lazily as she watches me watch her. My mouth desperately seeks hers. The kiss is bruising and fierce and full of promise. It's the kinda kiss I could drown in.

Without breaking the connection of our lips, I move and lead her towards the bedroom. The air is cooler in the main part of the hotel room and goose bumps cover Payton's arms. I lead her towards the bed and grab the blankets, pulling them back and lowering her. When I glance down, her hair is soaking wet with big clumps of drenched brown tendrils leaving marks all over the sheets.

It's sexy as hell.

And that's before I remove the towel. That's like Christmas morning and my birthday all wrapped up in one succulent gift as I expose her body. Even though I just had my hands and mouth all over her, I realize I'll never get enough. I crave her with a fierceness I had never expected, and certainly never experienced.

Dropping my towel, I cover her body with my own and resume the kiss. Her lips are eager, and she opens immediately for me. My tongue slides inside, caressing and stroking hers as my hands cover every inch of her chest. Her nipples are hard and press against me, making my mouth water even more than it already is.

"I want to continue my exploration of your body, but I don't think I can wait any longer," I say, kissing her neck.

"I need you." Her words are breathless and, like an arrow, strike me straight in the heart.

Gazing up, my eyes lock on hers. They're full of lust and need, but something else too. She wants me, wants this, but she's afraid. She has no idea how terrified I am by the rapidly developing feelings I have for her. Every moment I'm with her, I feel myself being pulled further under the water, until I'll be completely drowning in her. But while the fear is still very much present, my need to be with her takes over. The self-created rules have been thrown out the window. The proverbial line has been drawn in the sand and crossed. There's no going back to any sort of client/accountant relationship after I've tasted and felt her naked body.

So the only thing to do now is go with the current. I won't fight it. I can't.

I just need to convince her to take the plunge with me.

"Are you going to kiss me again?" she asks, drawing my attention back to the task at hand.

"Would you like me to kiss you again?" I ask, moving my mouth back to her neck. She purrs like a cat, craning her neck to give me better access.

Nipping at her ear, I ask, "Is this what you want?"

"Almost."

"What else do you want?" I ask, moving her legs up and over my hips.

"You're getting there," she quips with a smile on her face.

I rub my erection against her wetness. "Is this it?"

"Getting there."

Reaching over her shoulder, I grab a condom from the nightstand. She doesn't make it easy to sheath my erection when she won't let me up off her and keeps grinding against the very cock I'm trying to cover.

Returning to my position between her thighs, I slide against her clit, causing the sexiest gasp to slip from her lips. "How about now?" I ask.

"So close."

"But not quite there?"

"Not quite."

"Hmmmm," I reply before bending down and taking her lips with mine. This time, I keep a slow paced kiss, savoring and cherishing her mouth with my own.

With one slow thrust, I slide inside her wet pussy. Her muscles tighten around me and almost cause temporary blindness. "What about now?" I ask against her lips.

"That's it," she moans.

Slowly, I move in and out of her body. My hands are everywhere: in her hair, caressing her neck, stroking her breasts. It's brutal keeping my pace slow and steady. My own body is craving an epic release, but I keep it held off as long as I can. Instead, I revel in the feel of her body wrapped around mine.

"God, you're so fucking beautiful." The words are out there before I can stop them. But I'm not sorry I said them because she is. More than beautiful actually, but she's like a timid deer when it comes to relationships.

But she doesn't seem to mind the crudeness that comes with my compliment. A stunning smile crosses her flushed face as she gazes up at me with lust-filled, hungry eyes. Running her hand through my hair, she doesn't convey her thanks with words, but with her eyes. They're deep green and full of happiness, and it's a view of her I'll never forget. So venerable, so open, so real.

My lips claim hers once more as my body starts to move on its own. I'm actually surprised I've held out this long, my need for her completely consuming me. She runs her hands up my back, gripping and digging her nails into my shoulder blades. I can feel her starting to tighten around me, pulling me into the depths of her body as far as I'll possibly go.

I pump hard into her, giving in fully to the desire. My pelvis slams into her thighs hard enough she'll surely have bruises. I'd never intentionally–or unintentionally–mark a woman, but the thought of her having indications of our night on the delicate skin of her thighs makes me wild.

Her orgasm slams into her moments before my own. I'm swept away in the euphoria as her loud moans bounce off the hotel room walls. Her pussy pulses as I empty myself into the condom, my body shaking and convulsing with aftershocks of another epic orgasm.

My arms give out and I drop on top of her like my body weighs a thousand pounds. We mold together, a combination of water from the shower and sweat, and our labored breathing mixes. I could stay right here forever, and die a happy man. Being with this woman gets better every time, and considering the first few times were hot as hell, that's saying something.

"I'm squishing you," I mumble against her head.

"I like it."

"You're weird," I say with a laugh.

"True, but you like me, so what does that make you?"

"Weirder?" I quip.

Slowly, I roll to my back, taking her with me until she's tucked perfectly against my side. I need to get rid of the condom, but I'm enjoying the way she feels too much to care about getting rid of the rubber.

After a few minutes, I gently slide out from under her and head into the bathroom. I throw the rubber in the trash and take a leak before grabbing a warm washcloth to take to Payton. When I catch a glimpse at my reflection, I'm not startled to see what's staring back at me. The man in the mirror is flushed. He looks excited and eager to get back to the woman waiting in his bed.

But there's also weariness there. Tonight could be the start of something I wasn't looking for. It could lead to a relationship that I find myself, surprisingly, wanting. But it could also go the other way just as quickly. Payton could easily decide that tonight's the last time she'll be warming my bed. We've both proclaimed that a relationship isn't in the cards, but maybe that's all changed.

Maybe I've changed my mind.

Now I just need to change hers.

15

Payton

My stomach growls angrily beneath the covers, but I'm not in any condition to move. Dean has his arms wrapped around me, our naked and sated bodies entwined beneath starch white sheets. It's the most comfortable–and lest I forget, the most natural–feeling in the world. I'm content. Happy, even, and that can't happen.

It's not that I don't believe in happiness, because I do. I see it every time Jaime and Ryan or Meghan and Josh are in the room. It's just that it's not for me. Sometimes, life deals you a hand that leaves a void that you're unable to fill with laughter, kisses, and great sex. And I'll be the first to admit, I've never really had all three of those simultaneously before. With Cole, I thought I had it all, until I didn't. Even though we were young, the kisses were nice and the sex satisfying, but the communication was definitely left lacking. The laughter turned to tears, and there wasn't anything he could do to change it.

Now after experiencing sex with Dean? I realize that what Cole and I had was subpar, at best. And it wasn't just him; it was me too. I'm adult enough to admit that our relationship wasn't easy or perfect. At the end, I forced the issue that we weren't meant to be, and I still stand by that decision. Not that I'm writing Dean's name on the line beside the words *The One*, but things are definitely a little different this time around. It's complex and easy at the same time, and that's what concerns me the most.

I can actually picture a relationship with Dean McIntire. I can't and *won't* go as far as to see white picket fences and two point five kids, but that doesn't mean I don't picture him and I snuggled up on the couch late at night on a Friday watching *CSI* reruns. And that's why I need to stop this charade before it gets carried away and ends in hurt.

"I can feel your brain working overtime. What are you thinking about?" he asks, his hand drifting down my side and resting on my hip.

"Nothing much."

"Something tells me that it's a lot more than nothing much." Dean turns us both until we're facing each other. The concern is written all over his handsome face, in his rich, caramel brown eyes. "What's the matter?"

I guess this conversation is going to happen sooner, rather than later. I just hope he still lets me share his hotel room on our last night in Richmond. If finding an available room was impossible two nights ago, there's no way I'll find one now at almost midnight.

"I was just thinking about this *thing* between us," I state.

"I don't think you're referring to the impressive bulge that's getting unbearably hard between us right now, are you?" His smirk makes me laugh. It also draws my attention to the fact that his very hard erection is front and center and pressed against my stomach.

"No, I'm not. This thing between us, I mean, even though we've spent the last couple of nights together, it's still not...well, it can't go any further than just friends." My heart is hammering in my chest, my brain screaming at me to quit lying, because this could easily turn into something more than *just friends*.

"Really? Because I was just thinking the complete opposite of that."

My breathing stalls in my throat, and I start to shake my head. Damn it! I was afraid of this. Up until we shared a hotel room, we were like-minded in the whole 'a relationship is bad' scenario. I have to blink rapidly to keep a sudden bout of tears at bay. And I'm not a crier, so why in the hell am I so emotional right now?

"No, hear me out," he says, putting just a little space between us as he backs up, but doesn't remove his arm from beneath my head. "I have rules about dating clients. There's not something in the agency by-laws or employee handbook, but something I determined for myself a few years back. I want to tell you all about that, but not right now."

He looks thoughtful at me, and I can tell there's a story behind his self-imposed no dating clients rule.

"When we're together, you make me smile. You make me laugh. And you damn sure turn me on so much I can't think straight in your presence. I'm not proposing marriage or a new living arrangement, or anything of that caliber, but I'd love to spend more time getting to know you. I already know you're incredible, passionate, beautiful, and loyal. There are probably a million more qualities that make you *you*, and I want to find out what those are."

"Dean, I just don't think it's a good idea. I really like you, but this can't go further than what it is now."

"I'm not asking for a big leap, Payton. I'm asking for a chance. I'm asking you to have dinner with me publicly, and maybe if someone asks, you can say we're seeing each other. Nothing more. I want to be able to call you and talk about your day, and maybe even kiss you whenever I want without feeling like it's against the rules. I just want to spend more time with you. That's all."

God, does that sound nice. I mean, to have someone besides one of my sisters to call when I need to talk or to have dinner with an actual person instead of the hero starring in whatever movie I'm watching.

But could it really be that simple?

He makes it sound so easy, and maybe it is. I've known all along that I made my relationship with Cole harder than it needed to be because it was the only way I could think of to protect myself, my heart. And even then, in the end, I felt every broken shard. Of course, that ache in my chest was so much bigger than mourning the ending of a relationship, it was saying goodbye to a dream.

And that still fucking hurt.

But having dinner and talking to Dean doesn't mean I'm destined to dig up ghosts best left buried. It means I need to be on guard and take this nice and easy. Baby steps, if you would.

Wow, Payton. Bad choice of wording.

Pulling my attention back to Dean, he's anxiously awaiting a response to his declaration. The way it rolled off his tongue let me know that he'd probably been thinking about it, possibly planning his words for some time now. Me, on the other hand, felt off kilter and caught off guard. Maybe that's the reason I found myself saying something I never expected to come from my mouth.

"Okay." I take a shaky breath and blink off the onslaught of tears I feel prickling the back of my eyes again. Dammit, with the stupid tears!

Another deep breath, I get lost in the black speckles in his dark brown eyes. "I really do enjoy spending time with you, Dean, so please know that has never been the issue. I have things, things in my life that have kept me from jumping into an actual relationship. Someday, maybe I'll tell you about them, but not now."

"I'm not pushing you. I just want to go home tomorrow and know that calling you before bed is an option."

"I'd like that." And I would. Talking to him is so easy, easier than anyone ever before. It makes me optimistic about having someone like Dean in my life.

"Good," he says before pulling me back against his chest. My stomach chooses that moment to remind me that I haven't eaten since the light lunch at the convention. The laughter in his chest rumbles against my cheek. "I can't believe I haven't fed you tonight before ravishing your body."

"I'm a big girl. I don't need you to feed me."

"I know, honey, but I should have thought of that before I jumped in the shower with you, and definitely before I took you to bed."

"Did you hear me complaining?" I ask with a smile.

"No complaining, no. I heard a lot of moaning, a little groaning, and my name repeated over and over while you came so hard you almost passed out."

I slap his shoulder. "Whatever, Mr. Grunter. I did *not* almost pass out."

"Maybe not, but I don't think you could have gotten up off the bed if we had a fire alarm at that moment."

"No, probably not," I concede.

Dean reaches over and grabs the phone on the nightstand. "Cheeseburger and fries?"

"I never turn down a cheeseburger and greasy fries. That's why my butt is so big."

He sets the receiver back on the cradle and turns stern eyes back on me. "This butt?" he asks, grabbing a handful of my rear. "This butt is the finest ass I've ever seen in the flesh. I've jacked off more in the last six months to images of this ass than I care to admit, so I don't ever want to hear you say anything negative about it or the rest of your spectacular body."

Oh.

I've never been ashamed of my body. I was always fine with being a little curvier than my sisters. Not that a size ten is big, but when your other sisters are sixes and able to share clothes, you just get used to being different. I've always enjoyed food too much to care about the size of my jeans or the letter on the tag of my shirt.

"Thank you. I'm fine with my size, really."

"Good, because your size is hot." To prove his point, he grinds his hard cock against my thigh, making me giggle. "Now, how about some dinner?"

"Yes, please. I'm starving."

I smile the entire time he phones in an order of cheeseburger, fries, and fried mushrooms. Life doesn't get much better than a sexy naked man ordering room service at midnight. Except when we realize we have about thirty minutes before our food is delivered.

What's a girl to do with herself and a gorgeously nude man for thirty minutes?

We're about to find out.

There weren't any awkward goodbyes when we left Richmond, mainly because, as we speak, his car is following behind mine. I mean, we are heading back to the same town.

When he was getting ready this morning to go down for the final seminar of his convention, I finally mentioned that my show finished up yesterday. There was no reason for me to stay last night, except that I wanted to spend more time with him. That was hard for me to acknowledge to myself, let alone him, but it was something I needed to say. Dean seemed pretty happy about my confession if the way he kissed me breathless was any indication.

I felt lighter when he left to go downstairs. With three hours to myself in the hotel room, I called the shop and checked in. Grandma and Rachel both adamantly claim they took good care of my baby in my absence, but it was the way Rachel said she would be happy to have me back that left me curious. I know how my Grandma is, but she can sometimes leave a funny taste in your mouth if you're not used to her brashness.

I've decided there's a few things I need to catch up on at the shop, but I won't let myself stay past six o'clock. No, Dean and I didn't make plans for tonight, but I'm going to have dinner with Abby. She called me out of the blue earlier, and while that isn't completely odd, it made me realize that outside of sisters' Saturday nights I haven't spent much time with her lately.

As we start to approach the edge of town, I pull into the gas station to fill up my tank. Not surprising, the car behind me pulls into the station and parks at the pump beside me.

"Funny meeting you here," he smirks as he walks over and grabs the pump nozzle. While I swipe my card, he gets the pump all ready and then stands beside me and pumps my gas while I'm left standing there gawking. No one has ever pumped my gas. Well, with the exception of my dad when I was sixteen, but no one else has ever made the chivalrous gesture.

I can't help but smile broadly at him. It feels kinda good to have someone there to help, even though it's just pumping gas. Not exactly rocket science.

"What?" he asks, pushing his glasses up higher on his nose.

"You wear your glasses when you drive?"

"Yeah, reading and driving, mostly. Sometimes I just get so used to wearing them I don't realize I hadn't taken them off."

The pump shuts off, and he makes quick work of turning it off and closing my cap. After grabbing the receipt from the pump, I step up until we're practically chest to chest. "Thank you," I state before brushing my lips across his.

"I didn't do anything," he says.

"You pumped my gas. No one has ever done that for me before. Thank you."

"No one's pumped your gas? Honey, I'm not exactly worldly in my dating history, but even I can see you've dated the wrong guys," he quips with a sexy smile.

"You're telling me," I reply, unable to wipe the smile off my face.

"It's getting chilly. Get inside your car and head home. I'm gonna fill up and then get home. Can I call you later?" he asks while grabbing his nozzle and starting to fill up his own car.

"Yeah. I'm having dinner with Abby tonight, but we both have to work tomorrow so it won't be a late night."

He walks over to me once more and kisses me. His lips are warm compared to the cold air, but I'm pretty sure it's the man that causes my blood to heat up and a dampness to flood my panties.

"Talk to you later."

"Bye."

Getting in the driver's seat, I glance over at the man just outside the window. He grins and waves again before turning his attention back to the pump. I'm left with my thoughts as I continue my drive into Jupiter Bay. The air is crisp off the Bay, and for some reason, it feels like I've been gone weeks instead of a couple of days. Maybe that's because I don't get out of town much.

When you're running your own small business, you give it everything you have, including all of your free time and energy. But even as exhausting as it has been, the rewards outweigh the stresses. I couldn't imagine doing anything else with my life, and hope to still be doing this for the next thirty or forty years. I pray I'm just as active as my grandparents are now. You'd never know they were in their early eighties by the way they act and get around.

Pulling into the rear parking lot, I hop out, excited to get inside the shop and see how they did in my absence. When I reach the back door, I can hear voices coming from the work area. I let myself inside the business I grew from an empty building and find my grandparents in a compromising position.

"Jesus, Mary, and Joseph!" I yell, desperately shielding my eyes. If I weren't already inside the back door I would have turned and ran. Instead, I take a step to the right and walk right into a metal shelving unit that houses Styrofoam pieces, excess ribbon, and peat moss. When things start to hit the floor, I don't even glance up.

"What are you two doing?" I ask, not only shielding my eyes but squeezing them shut in a double attempt to spare myself nightmares.

"Well, we were about to play hide the salami before you interrupted," Grandpa chastises.

"Payters, you have horrible timing," Grandma adds, making me gasp. "We're decent. You can open your eyes."

Of course, I don't right away–just in case they're joking. Things like this you can't unsee. I learned that the hard way when I was fifteen and forgot to knock. One time. One friggin' time I forgot to knock.

Well, I never forgot again.

"Why are you two getting frisky in my storage room? Who's up front taking care of customers?" I blink several times as my eyes adjust to the florescent lighting. When they settle on my grandparents, I notice her face is flushed, her neck is whisker burnt, and his belt is undone. This whole scenario is just wrong on so many different levels.

"Abby's here. I was taking a break, and Orvie took one of his little blue pills," she states sweetly. "We just couldn't waste it."

"It?" I ask before realizing my question. Then it hits me. "No! Oh God, no! Don't you dare say anymore!"

"Payton," Grandpa starts.

Rubbing the side of my head where a massive headache is budding, I say, "It's almost closing time. Why don't you two head home, and I'll help Abby close up?"

"Then we won't waste a perfectly good hard-on, Orvie."

Again, I groan. "Please stop saying hard-on and go before I end up in therapy."

"I'm not sure I should drive in my condition," Grandpa adds, pointing down at his tented trousers. And I look.

My eyes!

"Thank you for all your help! I appreciate everything you guys did while I was gone. Gotta go check on things," I holler over my shoulder, it coming out all in one long breathy run-on sentence.

"Are they still at it back there?" Abby asks from her perch atop the barstool behind the counter, her face full of mortification.

"For the love of all things holy, what is wrong with them?" I ask before hugging my youngest sister.

"Nothing, I suppose. I guess if I were in their shoes, I'd pray my husband looked at me and wanted me the way they still do after almost sixty years."

I concede her point, though that kind of fairytale happily ever after isn't in my deck of cards. Believe it or not, I'm not a hearts and flowers kinda girl, even though that's the nature of my business. I enjoy watching a woman's face light up when she receives a big bouquet from someone special. I relish turning a pile of blooms and greenery into something respectable to honor the memory of someone past. I love the feeling I get when a man comes in and personally picks out something magnificent and then handwrites the card.

But is that for me? No. I learned that life is messy and unfair, and there's no point in glossing over that fact with beautiful flowers. The problems will still be there long after the flowers die, patiently waiting for the next opportunity to rear its ugly head.

I never used to be this cynical. Back when I was in my early twenties, I believed in the fairytale, the happy ending, the forever love. But life doesn't work that way. Sometimes, things happen. Things that are out of your control but dictate the rest of your life the same.

"How was today?" I ask, steering the conversation away from the cause of my anxiety.

"You had a great afternoon. I came in after lunch and helped man the front while Rachel made bouquets."

"Thank you. I really appreciate you all stepping in and helping while I was gone."

"It's no problem. I had flextime I needed to use so I took the afternoon off."

"Well, I still appreciate it. Let me run to the office and do a few things and then we can go. Do you have ideas for dinner?" I ask, grabbing the receipts below the counter.

"Actually, Lexi wants to go too. Chris has a *thing* again tonight."

My eyebrows shoot straight skyward and her pretty face shows her concern. "A thing?"

"Something with work. Again. She wants to go eat Chicago dogs down at the Bay. Since she seemed a little gloomy, I told her that was fine. I hope you don't mind," she says.

"Of course not. That sounds great, actually. Let me finish a few things up and we'll head out."

But when I get to my office, my head is elsewhere. It's on Abby and the kindness I see pouring from her soul, and the fact that *someone* uses that kindness without really seeing her. It's on Lexi and the sadness she tries to hide from everyone. It's on Dean and the fact that he wants more when I originally said no. And more so, the fact that I changed my mind and told him yes. Why? I know this can't go any further than the occasional dates, but I can't deny that I'm drawn to him. He's like a magnetic charge, slowly drawing me towards him. I just pray I don't get smacked when we're slammed together and try to pull apart.

It takes me twice as long as it should have to finish my work, and when I finally glance at the clock, it's almost six. Shutting down my computer, I throw the rest of the papers on my desk in a bin to file tomorrow. I never got to the order forms, but that's something I can do tomorrow after I close and take a quick inventory. Rachel's on point when it comes to numbers, but I always like to look everything over with my own eyes before I order supplies.

My sisters call it a trait of being the oldest. I'm bossy–rightfully so. I'm always right–I am older and wiser. I'm probably a pain in the ass–hey, aren't we all? Even though I trust my employees with my business, I still have to appease my own stupid curiosity and just verify everything. It's vital to my mental health. Otherwise, I'd be wondering and stewing all night, and the next thing you'd know I'd be coming in at nearly midnight just to verify that everything is, in fact, fine.

Been there, done that. Have the t-shirt.

Heading out of my office, I hear the harmonic sounds of my sisters giggling, and it brings a smile to my face. "What are you two hens snickering about out here?" I ask, stepping around the corner and finding Abby and Lexi with their heads in one of their phones.

"Grandma's Twitter page," Lexi says with a big grin and tears brimming in her green eyes.

"Grandma has a Twitter page?"

"Yep. Of course, no one knew until she mentioned yesterday that she was off to Twit."

"Twit?"

"Tweet. I didn't realize she had one until she started following me yesterday."

"Why on earth does she have a Twitter page? Who does she follow?" I ask, shutting off the front lights.

"Who doesn't she follow?" Lexi replies with another giggle. "She follows all of us now and a few locals in town. But mostly she follows male movie stars, models, and porn stars. And there's this guy who takes dick pics and dresses it up and draws faces on them. She actually tweets him directly, complimenting him on his mad hard-on skills."

"My God! The woman has no shame," I groan.

"True, but we've always known that. You ready? I'm starving for hotdogs." Lexi grabs her jacket and follows us towards the back door.

We pile into Abby's little hybrid car and make our way to the vendor along the Bay who sells the best hotdogs and cheese fries. Lexi talks about everyone *other* than Chris, and Abby talks about everything *other* than Levi. And I'm not ready to talk about Dean, so what does that make us?

"Did I tell you guys about what happened right before I left for that trade show in Richmond earlier in the week?" I ask after we order our food and wait for it by the window.

"No. I didn't get to speak to you before you left," Abby says, sipping her Coke.

"Well, Grandma volunteered to run my monthly financials to Dean. He called me a little later to see what the hell was going on. Apparently, Grandma thought it'd be a brilliant idea to add a few zeros to my income line."

"Holy shit," Lexi says.

"Why would she do that?" This from Abby.

"No clue, but Dean called me before I could be arrested for tax fraud."

"Seriously?"

"I mean, I don't know if it would be that bad, but if he wasn't paying attention and he filed those numbers, I could have gotten into big trouble, I'm sure."

When neither of them respond, I glance over. They look from each other back to me, each with their own conspirator smirk on their faces. "What?"

"You called him Dean."

"Yeah, you always talk about your accountant, but never by name."

Dumbfounded, I scramble for an explanation. "He is my accountant. That's his name."

"Yes, but you never use it."

"Whatever," I grumble, reaching for my food as Hank, the food vendor, shoves it through the window.

"Good response," Lexi says before shoveling half of her hotdog into her mouth. "I'll let it slide right now, because this? Seriously, so fucking goooooooooood."

And just like that, we're stuffing our faces with Chicago-style hotdogs and soda. It's the perfect way to end a pretty spectacular week. And maybe, if I'm lucky, I'll get a text message from a certain sexy accountant.

One can only hope.

16

Dean

It feels great to walk back into my own domain, but the longing to have Payton in my arms again doesn't go unnoticed. The house is empty, but not for long. Bri will be home soon, which leaves me just enough time to unpack my bag and start a load of laundry. Yet, when I take my dirty clothes from my trip into the utility room, the room is empty, not a dirty sock in sight.

Mom.

I smile as I separate my darks from my whites, and get my suit and pants ready to go to the dry cleaners tomorrow. I shouldn't be surprised, but the house is practically spotless. Mom always cleans the kitchen and gets dinner going for me when she stays with Bri on my late work nights, and today isn't any different, even though it's a Friday. There are chicken breasts marinating in the fridge, with sweet potatoes and green beans on the counter.

There are a handful of things I could do before my daughter comes home, but there's only one thing holding my attention and it isn't prepping the grill for supper. The only thing I can think about is Payton Summer. Her scent, her smile and laugh, the way her brown hair fluttered in the breeze while we walked through the park, the look on her face when pleasure steamrolled her body and she came on my cock. It's all there in spades, replaying in bright porno Technicolor.

Of course, the only thing that seems to do is cause my pants to tighten and my cock to throb. But, hell, that has been a natural response since the first moment I laid eyes on her. She was wearing her hair in a high ponytail and her cheeks were flushed from being in and out of the summer heat. I remember the succulent curve of her hips and how those tight khakis she wore for work molded to her ass like a second skin. Her name was written across the file set on the conference room table, but when I saw her rush into the room, she stole my breath and my sanity, and I couldn't have repeated the name typed across the folder if my life depended on it.

She was that amazing.

And that was before I knew her.

Before I realize it, I've lost track of time and it's well after four. Time to grab Bri from the sitter's house. I walk down the block and didn't even get my hand raised to knock on the hard wooden door when it flies open and my gorgeous five-year-old little girl smiles a wide toothless grin at me.

"Daddy!" There's no greater sound.

I barely have time to step inside before she launches herself into my arms. I inhale the scent of the shampoo I've bought for her since she moved on from the baby kind. I realize I'm being a total sappy schmuck right now, especially since it's only been three nights since I last saw my daughter, but I don't care. I missed the hell out of her.

"Hi, pumpkin! Did you have a good day at school?"

"Yep! I missed you!"

"Well, I missed you so much," I add with a chuckle.

"Can we go home? I have to show you the new pictures I made you while you were gone for work. And Mimi is coming over to cook and eat with us." After setting her down, she runs over and grabs her jacket and book bag from the hook by the front door.

"She's been talking nonstop since she got off the bus about your return home tonight," Nancy says from the doorway to the living room.

"I've been pretty excited to see her too," I reply with a smile as I dig money out of my wallet to pay her for her time this week.

Nancy takes the bills and helps Bri slip her book bag on her back. As soon as she's set, my daughter is out the door and standing on the porch. "I guess that's my cue," I say, shaking my head.

"See you next week, Dean."

With a quick wave, I head out, closing the door behind me, to meet my girl. We walk down the block hand-in-hand, her talking a mile a minute about everything I missed over the last few days. And in the eyes of a kindergartener, everything from gluing, coloring, painting, drawing, writing, and playing is a very important part of the day. So I hear about every detail, and smile the entire time. Even when we get back home, the stories continue while I clean and snip the green beans and peel and slice the sweet potatoes to go on the grill with the chicken.

At five thirty, Mom arrives with a wide smile. She's carrying a container with something that smells sweet. Cupcakes, if I had to wager a guess because if there's anything my mom can't resist, it's cupcakes with buttercream frosting.

"Welcome home," she says as she sets her container down on the counter.

"What's that?" Bri asks from the barstool she's perched on, coloring.

"Dessert, if you eat all your dinner," Mom says before placing a kiss on Bri's forehead.

"Thanks for getting all of this stuff ready for tonight," I tell her, wrapping the sweet potatoes in an aluminum foil packet with tons of butter and brown sugar.

"I figured you'd be tired from the drive, so I planned on doing it for you."

"Ehh, I got it. Besides, I enjoy cooking while my assistant makes me pretty new pictures for the fridge," I add with a wink at my smiling daughter.

Dinner revolves around my daughter's stories, her drawings, and her stuffed animals. She keeps us entertained and unable to carry much of an adult conversation. We're used to it, though. Mom and I get to have pieces of talks whenever we can. Like now. There's something I'd like to discuss, but can't until after little ears are occupied.

After putting Bri in the bathtub, I finally have my chance.

"So," I start, trying to retrieve the words I've been practicing in my head all night.

"So?" Mom asks, drying the last plate and sliding it in the cabinet.

"Remember the woman I mentioned? Payton?"

"I do remember. I also remember you adamantly denying speaking the name out loud."

"Well, the thing is," I stammer like a teenager, "I kinda like her."

"I figured as much." Her smile is bright when she tosses the towel on the counter and turns her full attention to me.

"Getting to this point where she's agreed to go have dinner with me has been…difficult."

"Difficult how?" she asks, sitting down on the barstool beside me.

"Well, besides the fact that I don't date clients, which she is, she's been very unyielding to the idea of dating."

"But that's changed?"

"Yeah," I tell her. "We've been… friendly." I swear to God, my face blushes four shades of fuchsia in a three second time span.

Mom's quiet for a few minutes, which only makes my level of anxiety kick up a few hundred notches. She was the master of the Mom look when I was younger and could make me crack in less time than a CIA interrogator. I start to feel a little hot under the collar, yet the woman across from me is calm, cool, and completely collected.

Shit.

"You know, Dean, if you want to date, I'm more than happy to help with Bri. You just have to ask. And another option would be to find a high school girl that you trust to watch her for a few hours. Single parents have been doing it for quite some time. Just because you're a single parent doesn't mean you can't have a life outside of your child."

"You didn't," I find myself saying before I can reel the words back in.

"*Au, contraire*, my son. I actually dated quite a bit."

"You did?"

Mom laughs. Laughs. Right. In. My. Face.

"Not a lot, but enough. When you spent the night at David's house or when you had scholastic bowl practice after school, I had coffee or dinner with men."

I swear she grew three heads in that moment. My mom dated? How in the hell did I not know that?

"I just never found anyone worthy of introducing you to. So, go out with Payton, and I'll help when I can. When you're ready to introduce her to your daughter, I'll know that she's someone special." Mom reaches over and grabs my hand. "And I really hope you find that someone. You're a wonderful man with a huge heart."

"You have to say that. You're my mom."

"No, I have to say eat your vegetables because I'm your mom. Everything else I say is the truth."

Lying in bed, my phone in my hand, I think about texting her. She mentioned having dinner with one of her sisters tonight, but I can't imagine her staying out too late. But I also don't want to suffocate her with my neediness to talk. And I do. I feel the need, the desire, to talk to her. Sure, I wouldn't mind a little more right now, but we've always been good at the normal conversation stuff.

Touching the screen until it's lit up, I type a few words.

> **Me:** Hope you had a good night with your sister.

A few moments later, I see the bubbles appear on the screen, letting me know she's writing back. I smile instantly.

> **Payton:** Two sisters, actually. It was Chicago dogs by the Bay. A good night.
>
> **Me:** Glad to hear it.
>
> **Payton:** How about you?
>
> **Me:** Good. Trying to catch up on my files though. Hard to do when I'm thinking of you.

Those little bubbles don't appear. Why don't they appear? I wait, holding my breath, for the longest minute of my life until I finally see her replying. Exhaling deeply and willing my heartbeat to slow down, her message pops up on my screen.

> **Payton:** I've been thinking of you too. I kinda liked curling up against you the last couple of night.

That's what I'm talking about! I pump my fists in the air like I just scored the winning basket.

> **Me:** I miss you and your cold toes too.
>
> **Payton:** My toes aren't cold.
>
> **Me:** They are. And the only reason they weren't cold last night was because you had those little ice cubes plastered against my outer thigh.

Payton:	You have hot thighs.
Me:	*smirking emoji* You have hot thighs too.
Payton:	That's not what I meant.
Me:	I know, but that's where my mind went. And now I can't stop thinking about them.
Payton:	*flaming emoji* Stop thinking about my thighs. I'm never gonna get to sleep tonight now. Thanks.
Me:	Yeah, it'll be a little **hard** for me to sleep now too.

Who is this guy? I've never used emojis. I've never been so blunt and dirty in a text. Hell, I barely like to send texts. But throw in a little insinuating back and forth banter with Payton, and I'm completely outside of my comfortable little bubble. The fact that I'm smiling instead of worrying should be enough to make me panic, but it doesn't. Instead, I fire off another text.

Me:	Be thinking of me later when you're all alone in bed with your sleeping problem.
Payton:	Funny, I was gonna say the same to you.

Before I can send a reply, another text pops up.

Payton:	I should get to bed. I have so much work to catch up with at the shop tomorrow.
Me:	Good night, Payton.
Payton:	G'night. Oh, and Dean? I'm already thinking about you as I start to take care of my little problem. *smirky devil face emoji*

Well, fuck a duck. Beneath my sleep pants, my hard-on is slamming against my stomach, begging to be played with. Mental images of Payton lying in her bed, touching herself as she takes care of her problem are enough for me to get up, lock my door, and do the same.

And my mind never strays from my brown-haired goddess.

17

Payton

Yesterday was chaotic at work, but nothing compared to a family dinner. The Summer sisters have descended upon our childhood home for an afternoon of bickering over the pros and cons between Batman vs. Superman, and eating too much of Grandma's chili. I'm in favor of Batman. There's something about that hard plastic suit and pocketful of gadgets. And come on: Batmobile. That alone puts him over the top in the coolness factor.

"Superman can fly, Payton. Batman can't, even though he's a bat," Josh argues with me from across the table.

"Plus, he has heat-ray vision, Pay," Meghan adds, smiling adoringly at her fiancé.

Their over-the-top cutesiness is nauseating at times, but today, I find myself dealing with their cheesy pet names and constant heavy petting. Though, I will say that their groping isn't nearly as bad as Jaime and Ryan who are practically dry humping under the table.

"You're so right, babe," he coos, reaching over and touching the tip of her nose.

Okay, that's a little nauseating.

"Heat-ray vision doesn't even factor on the coolness chart compared to Batman's…well, all the cool things Batman can do!" I defend lamely.

"See! You can't even think of anything! Superman wins!" Meghan exclaims.

Talking to them is easy today. I'd rather deal with their eternal relationship bliss than whatever is going on down at the other end of the table. Jaime and Ryan are oblivious to it as they all but make little Ryans beneath the plastic floral tablecloth. Something is going on with Lexi and Abby. They both seemed all right Friday night when we had dinner, but they're both off today.

Lexi and Chris have barely spoken since they arrived, and she refuses to make eye contact. Probably to hide her red-rimmed eyes so that we wouldn't jump all over her for details on why she's been crying. And Levi arrived a few minutes before dinner was served, but Abby won't even look his way. In fact, she looks almost pained to be sitting beside him.

It makes me wonder what's going on there. Well, both relationships, actually. If you can actually call what Levi and Abby have a relationship. They're friends, first and foremost, and I'd bet the ownership papers on my shop, they both feel something deeper than friendship.

And Lexi and Chris? I just don't know. She wants a baby, this is a fact that she doesn't attempt to hide. When he's around, he acts as if they're the perfect couple, but refuses to acknowledge that something could be wrong with their baby-making abilities. I wonder if she's talked further to her OB or to her husband. She didn't bring it up Friday, and knowing that it's a sensitive subject, I stayed as far away from that topic as humanly possible.

"Ladies! Great news," Grandma says as she comes into the dining room with a pineapple upside down cake. "I signed up for a home party, and you are all required to be there." Grandma sets down the dessert and starts dishing up the sweet, gooey cake.

"Oh, is it a kitchen gadgets party? I really need to get a few things for the house," Jaime says, pulling her attention away from playing tonsil hockey with her boyfriend.

"No, not kitchen gadgets," Grandma says, passing around little plates.

"How about makeup? I've been thinking of doing a makeover," Abby says softly, almost too quietly to hear. Everyone glances over at her and there's no way to miss the look Levi gives her.

"A makeover? You don't need to change anything," he protests loudly. And while I agree with him, the look on my baby sister's face says she strongly disagrees.

"No, not makeup, Abs. This is something different. Something fun."

"Then what?" AJ asks between bites.

"A sex toy party."

Fortunately for me, I wasn't shoveling a heap of fluffy cake in my face when those words spilled from my grandmother's mouth. Unfortunately for AJ, she was, and she instantly begins choking. No, not really choking, but more of an it-went-down-the-wrong-pipe moment. Abby's lucky she didn't get sprayed with spitty cake particles from across the table.

"Dear God, did she just say sex toy party?" Jaime half-whispers, half-yells at Ryan.

"Oh, don't be a stick in the mud, Jaimers. We all have the sex. It's a natural part of life. I want to explore and revel in it."

"Yeah, but I don't think you're supposed to explore with your grandkids in the room," my dad says with a look that shows he's as unsettled by this as we all are.

"Why not? We're all adults here. We can talk about vibrators and butt plugs together."

"Jesus, she said butt plugs," Meghan groans.

"I expect you all to be there. I get a free Pocket Rocket for being the hostess," she adds, clapping her hands triumphantly. "Now, dig in. It's super moist."

"Is she talking about the cake?" Ryan asks, earning a slap across the shoulder from Jaime. "What? We were just discussing a sex party and Pocket Rocket at a family dinner, and I can't say moist? Excuse me for being confused, because it could have gone either way."

And then, because men will be men, Levi leans towards Ryan and adds, "I prefer my women like my cake."

The table erupts in groans.

"Me too, boy. Me too," Grandpa adds with a mouthful of cake.

"That's such a gross word," Abby gags, throwing a glare in Levi's direction.

"Agreed." This from Lexi. She throws her own glare at Chris, who's barely pulled his nose out of his cell phone.

I can't help but look around and wonder where Dean would fit in this picture. He's not exactly the numbers nerd I originally thought, but still likes organization and rules. I see him talking about his day with Josh and about building projects with Ryan. He'll discuss sports with my dad, and maybe even help man the grill. I can picture him laughing at everyone's jokes, even the dirty ones, and pray that he doesn't think my family's as crazy as they really are.

When I look around, I see Dean fitting in anywhere.

And maybe that's okay.

Maybe that's not as scary as I thought it would be.

Then reality creeps in and slaps me across the face like a cold wind off Lake Michigan. I still have my reasons for avoiding relationships, and those reasons are solid. But maybe I need to give Dean the chance and the choice. No, I'm not ready to tell him everything, but maybe, over time, I'll learn to trust him enough to share my secrets. I just pray he doesn't run for the hills, leaving me in a heap of mangled heart pieces and salty tears, when it's all said and done. But perhaps he won't. What if Dean actually isn't bothered by my shocking news, and wants to stick it out with me? No, I know it's too early in our budding relationship to think long-term, but I'm a girl. Even a pessimist like me thinks about this stuff every once in a while. I just won't let myself get too caught up in the fairytale, not for too long anyway.

Because…what if?

Maybe he'll be the one to actually stay.

Wednesday night. Dean's late night. I close up shop, send Rachel home early, and drive towards his work with a smile on my face and a condom in my pocket. Not exactly the most romantic locale for sexy times, but hey, when one of us is an accountant during tax season, you don't always get to be choosey.

And sex atop a desk is kinda hot.

When I enter the firm, I find the secretary sitting at her desk. She's filing a stack of papers with the phone perched on her shoulder. The lines under her eyes tell me she's as exhausted as she sounds, but she still greets me with a warm smile.

"Can I help you?" she asks as soon as she puts the phone down.

"I was hoping to speak with Dean McIntire for a moment." No, I probably don't need to use his last name since there are only three accountants here and only one with the first name of Dean, but I'm working on keeping this as professional as possible here.

"Do you have an appointment?"

"No, I don't. I'm a client of his and I was hoping to drop these off for him," I say, tapping the manila file folder in my hand.

"He's with a client, but I could leave them for him." She stands up, reaching for the folder.

"Well, I would just leave it, but there's a few things I was hoping to discuss with him. Professionally." Why did I say that? Might as well tattoo the word guilty across my forehead. Maybe add I'm planning to have sex with Dean on his desk down my arm.

"Of course. Well, he's with his final client of the evening. If you'd like to wait, it shouldn't be too much longer."

I thank her and take a seat on one of the vinyl chairs in the waiting area. The building is silent except for a few clicks on a keyboard, and the occasional sigh. Starting to seriously reconsider my plan, I think about getting up. There's still time to slip out without Dean knowing I was here. But I won't do that. *I can't.* He's like a magnet, pulling me towards him. There's no point in fighting it; it's futile.

When I glance down at my phone to check the time, I hear a door open. Dean follows a young couple out of his office. They're chatting politely, and he has yet to see me. I feel the pull clear down to my toes when our eyes meet across the waiting room. Everything and everyone around us fades away until we're the only two left in the entire world. Just us.

"I'll have your paperwork finalized tomorrow. Cora will give you a call when it's ready to be picked up," he says, giving the couple before him his full attention. They shake hands before Dean holds open the front door and bids them a good night.

His eyes are dark and full of something needy when they turn back to me. Before either of us can speak, Cora pipes up from behind her reception desk.

"Miss Summer doesn't have an appointment, Mr. McIntire, but was hoping to steal a moment of your time to drop something off."

"Of course. Come on back, Miss Summer," he says, a subtle smirk playing on the corner of his mouth.

His mouth. His lips are full and remind me of all the wicked things they did to me just a week ago. That mouth is part of the reason I'm here, while he's supposed to be working. Even talking to him every day has done nothing to squash the looming desire that's ready to flame to life with mere thoughts of him and his talented mouth.

And those glasses. He's in full business mode, and there's something sexy about the way they perch on the bridge of his nose. They give him a studious look. The perfect blend of smarts and erotic. Fortunately, I dig the hot nerdy accountant look because my body is flush and my panties soaked.

"Thank you for giving me a few moments, Mr. McIntire."

Again, I'm rewarded with the slightest curl of his lip. Silently, we walk past Cora's desk and down the short hall to Dean's space. As soon as I step inside, I feel his presence behind me. I'm being stalked. Glancing over my shoulder, his face is the picture of lust. Molten lava races through my bloodstream.

"This is a pleasant surprise," he says. I feel the heat of his body as he steps behind me and presses his body against my backside.

"I was in the neighborhood." My words are breathy and rushed.

"Really?" Dean runs his hands up my outer arms to my shoulders. "I'm glad you stopped by." He places a kiss on the back of my neck. "What's in the folder?"

"I couldn't exactly show up empty handed, could I?" Grabbing the folder, I flip the cover and reveal the paper inside.

He glances over my shoulder and laughs. "You drew me a cat?"

"Not just any cat. This cat is sunning itself in the window."

"Why does the cat only have three legs?"

"That's Sparky. He was our cat growing up. He got under the hood of my dad's work car one day when I was little and got his leg caught. My mom rushed it to a vet, who amputated the mangled leg. We loved that damn cat. He lived until he was almost eighteen as our three-legged baby."

"That's oddly sad and delightful at the same time." His lips return to my neck, making me shudder.

Tossing my hair over my right shoulder to give him complete, unobstructed access to my neck, I ask, "Do you have any more appointments tonight?"

"Not tonight," he says, nipping at my spine. "Cora will be leaving shortly. If I'm still back here, she'll lock me in."

"So we have a bit of alone time?" I ask, exhaling deeply as he runs his tongue towards my collarbone.

"Very much alone," he mumbles, his hands sliding around to my stomach. He pushes up my shirt, his large hands skimming effortlessly up to cup my breasts. "I've been thinking about you."

"Me too."

"What have you been thinking about?" Dean lightly pinches my nipples, causing me to squirm and push back against him. My ass connects with his very hard cock. I gasp.

"About how much I want to feel you inside me again."

"Is that what you want now?"

"Yes," I whisper as he keeps one hand on my breast and slides the other down and into my pants.

"I was thinking about this weekend," he says, moving his hand into my wet, useless panties.

"Yeah?"

"I'd love to take you to dinner Saturday night."

I pant; not from his words, but from the way his hands play me like a musical instrument. His fingers graze against my clit, causing a flood of sensations to bubble inside me.

"I can't Saturday night." Honestly, I'm not sure how I'm able to form coherent sentences at this point. Not with his fingers playing with my clit and his other hand massaging my nipple.

"No?"

"It's sisters' night. Oh God," I groan. "I have a standing date with my sisters. So good."

"Sisters' night is so good? Or this?" Dean slides two fingers into my pussy.

"This. So much this."

"You came to my office for this, did you not?" he asks, pumping his fingers into my body. I feel myself climbing higher and higher, inching towards the glorious cliff that'll send me flying.

"Yes," I gasp. "I needed to be with you. I couldn't wait any longer."

"Then, who am I to keep you from what you want?" he asks, pinching my nipple and rubbing his palm against my clit. The friction sends me soaring high above the clouds. The orgasm slams into me with force. My legs get weak as my body gyrates against him, silently begging for more.

I don't have to ask. He knows.

Leaning forward, I take a moment to catch my breath as he removes his hands from my body. The sound of his zipper, the removal of his pants, and the ripping of the condom wrapper are as loud as my breathing, and my body responds instantly.

"This is what you wanted?" I feel him step up behind me, his cock rubbing against my butt cheeks.

"Yes," I pant.

"I would never deny you this," he says as he pushes forward and into my still-pulsing pussy. From behind, I feel every inch of him as he slides inside, all the way to the root.

A hearty groan is the only response I give as I push back against him, taking him as deep as possible. My brain is officially no longer connected to my mouth, and I realize it the moment I start spouting off things I normally wouldn't say if it weren't for the blissful state of euphoria spreading through my body.

"You can come Saturday night," I whisper as he gently slides almost the entire length of him out and then slams back inside.

"Yeah?" he asks, grinding against me when he's fully seated once more.

"Yeah. All of the guys usually show up by the end of sisters' night, even though they're not supposed to."

Again, he pulls out, but this time slides in slowly, deliberately, and almost painfully. "You want me there with your sisters' guys?"

I should shut up, but I can't. "Yes."

"Where?" Dean grips my hips tightly but pauses his movements. My body craves him, needs him to move, to give me the release that's imminent.

"Please move," I beg, trying to push back against him.

"Where?" he commands, holding me still and not letting either of us move.

"The Beaver. We're doing some sort of pottery class in the back room."

"And you want me to be there when you're done with your class?"

"God yes," I groan, my inner muscles tightening around his cock, as if begging for more.

"Don't do that," he groans, still holding me completely hostage.

"What? This?" I flex my muscles around him, resulting in another moan.

"Yes, that. Stop it or Cora is going to hear us when I slam into you and make you come so hard you see stars."

"Yes. That. Do that."

"Make you come hard and see stars?"

A foreign noise slips from my lips, and I'm not sure it's an actual word.

"You have to be super quiet, honey, or she'll come in and check on us."

Again, I make a noise, but it's a noise of relief as Dean slides out and back in to the hilt. My body starts to shake and I feel myself bearing down on him. His grip is tight, and I'm sure I'll have marks on my hips for days. That's okay. The idea of being marked by Dean doesn't bother me in the least.

"Jesus," he grumbles, quickening his pace as the finish line stands before us.

With one deep thrust, I shatter into a million pieces around him, soaring high above the clouds, never wanting to come down. He follows, driving into me from behind with force before stilling and shaking. Dean bends over and places open-mouthed kisses along my shoulders before resting his head against my back. My legs are worthless, refusing to hold me up. His weight is heavy as he relaxes, pinning me between the desk and his body.

It's comfortable.

"I meant what I said. I'm going to come Saturday," he says as he tries to regain his breath. "There's something I need to discuss with you."

I gasp as he slowly starts to slide out of me. On shaky legs, I turn and face him. "I meant what I said too. I want you there."

It's not so scary to admit that I want him to attend, because I do. I guess I just always expected to see something burst into flames or for something equally as dramatic if I actually wanted a man to attend a family function or someplace where my family will be. But not just any man, I want Dean.

We've been talking a lot lately and I've enjoyed our banter and getting to know each other. Twice now, he mentioned he had something to tell me, but wanted to wait to do it in person. I'm not sure what it is, but maybe we can discuss it tonight, since I'm already here.

Silently, we both straighten up our clothes. Dean disposes of the condom in the wastepaper basket, while I right my top. "Do you have a few minutes to talk before you go?" he asks, fastening his work trousers.

"Yeah, a few minutes," I reply, buttoning my top.

Just as he goes to say something else, the door to his office bursts open. A little girl with the brownest eyes comes barreling through the door, a wide smile on her face. I gasp, anxiously working my fingers to fasten my own pants. I have no time to process the interruption or try to determine what in the world is going on because the child speaks two words that shock me to my core.

Two words.

And they change everything.

"Hi, Daddy!"

18

Dean

My daughter comes bouncing in, wide toothless grin plastered across her face, and all I can think is *shit!* Mostly because I've barely gotten my pants secure before she came busting in here. Also not exactly how I wanted to break it to Payton that I have a child. And if by the look on her face is any indication, I'd say she definitely wasn't prepared for that little nugget of information.

I glance quickly over at Payton who looks like she's seen a ghost. Her face is pale and her eyes wide. Her fingers, which moments ago were gripping a hold of my thighs, are stalled on her own pants. No one says anything, no one really moves as we all gape at each other, waiting on someone to speak.

I don't have the opportunity to, however, because my mom walks in. "Sweetie, you have to wait to make sure Daddy isn't in a meet—" The words die a cold death on her lips as she takes in our mostly put-together appearance. Mom's not dumb. I'm sure the guilty *I just had sex* look on my face is the same one I wore the day my freshman year I skipped school to watch a *Rocky* marathon with my buddy, Justin. Mom arrived home from work, and without saying a word, went about her day as if nothing happened. But I knew. She knew. I could feel it in my bones.

Here we are, seventeen years later, and I believe my face to show my guilt as easily as it did that day.

And to make it worse, Cora follows my mom into my office. "I'm so sorry, Mr. McIntire. I was in the restroom when…"

Our office secretary's round eyes bounce back and forth between Payton and myself, making me well aware that my hands are still firmly holding the two ends of my belt buckle.

"Oh, dear," Mom says at the same time Payton whispers, "Fricking hell."

Words seem to be stuck in my throat, however, and I'm unable to respond to anyone or anything. So we basically just stare at each other, all of us as uncomfortable as a prostitute in church on a Sunday morning.

"Daddy, Mimi has to go!" Brielle exclaims. Leave it to a child to break the tension with a sledgehammer.

"Go?" I ask when my belt buckle is finally secured and I'm able to face my family, albeit red-faced. "Where does Mimi have to go?" I ask my daughter as I pick her up and place a kiss on her forehead.

Mom steps forward, still slightly averting her eyes. "Aunt Kate called. She fell at home and believes she broke her hip. The ambulance was taking her to the hospital, and since I'm her power of attorney, I need to meet her there. I'm sure I'm going to be at the hospital for a while, so I didn't want to take Bri, and then have her stuck in a waiting room."

My aunt Kate is Mom's oldest sister. She became a widow about five years ago, and has been on her own since Uncle Frank died. With no kids of their own, my mom has stepped up and helped care for her sister when her health hasn't been the best. She has periods of weakness and shortness of breath, and I'm sure it's weighing heavily on Mom's mind that she fell when she wasn't around to help.

"I tried to call your phone, but it went to voicemail, so I thought we'd stop by and see if you were busy. When we came in, Cora wasn't at the desk. Before I could stop little miss anxious, she ran back here and just threw open the door." Mom gestures with her hand between Payton and me, as if we need a not-so-subtle reminder of the elephant in the room.

"It's fine. You should go be with Aunt Kate. Are you okay to drive? Do you want me to take you?"

"No, no," she says, turning and smiling at Payton. "I'll be fine. I'm sure Kate's going to be just fine, but I do need to be there."

"Go, Mom. We'll be fine."

"I didn't get dinner started," she hedges.

"We'll grab something on the ride home." Bri cheers in my arms.

Cora excuses herself back to the front as Mom heads towards the door. Before she vacates my office, she turns back towards Payton, who has yet to say anything. "I take it you must be Payton, dear. It's a pleasure to finally meet you," she says as she retracts her steps and walks over to the woman I've only begun to see.

"You too, Mrs. McIntire."

"Gretchen, please. I was never a McIntire. That was Dean's father's name. Anyway, I hope to have the chance to see you again soon."

"Likewise," Payton replies with a tentative smile.

"Be sure to let me know how Aunt Kate is doing," I add before Mom leaves.

It's just us in the room. Payton, me, and the daughter I have yet to tell her about. I've been trying to figure out the right way to tell her, but nothing has magically popped in my head. Not to mention the fact that every time I've attempted to tell her, we've been interrupted. Throw in the fact that when we're together, we're more interested in ripping each other's clothes off, and you have a recipe for lack-of-info disaster.

"So, this is Brielle, my daughter. Bri, this is my friend Payton. Can you say hi?"

"Hi," Bri replies, shying away from the other adult in the room, yet curiously keeping her eyes on her.

"H-hi, Brielle. It's nice to meet you."

"I like to draw cats. Do you like cats?"

"My sister Jaime has a cat. He's kinda evil, but looks cute when he's sleeping," Payton says, her words laced with nervousness and uncertainty.

"I like real cats. I want my dad to get me one, but he won't. He don't like 'em cause they tear up his trash and poop in the flowers."

"One time. I complained about the neighbor's cat one time and she hasn't forgotten." The smile I offer Payton seems to help alleviate some of her anxiety. "Honey, why don't you go draw me a picture at my desk while I talk to Payton. Then we'll head home and get something to eat."

"I want French fries! No, peanut butter and banana sandwiches. Oh, what about pizza?"

Payton laughs at Bri's menu choices for this evening, but I'm used to her hodgepodge of entrees. "We'll figure it out on the way home. Give me a minute, okay?"

Bri acknowledges me, but she's more interested in digging out the paper and crayons that I keep in my desk drawer for times like this. It definitely wouldn't be the first time I've had a surprise visitor at the office in the form of my daughter.

Walking over to the corner of my office, away from my daughter's all-hearing ears, I turn to find Payton following me. "Listen, I'm sorry you found out this way. It was always my intention to tell you, but lately, every time I started, something got in the way."

"You have a daughter," she mumbles, as if trying it on for size.

"Yeah. She's five."

"And her mother..." she starts, leaving it an open-ended question.

"Not in the picture. Hasn't been since Bri was a few months old."

"I'm sorry," she whispers, her eyes conveying sadness on our behalf. Her sympathy reaches into my chest and squeezes my heart.

That's one of the things I love about Payton. Her ability to adapt and roll with whatever situation she's presented with. Her emotions reflect in the depths of those hypnotic green eyes. She has a hard time masking her feelings, and has a heart that makes it easy to fall for her.

Wait. What?

Slow the horses, bucko.

Love? Did you just say love?

Like. One of the things I *like* about Payton.

No love. No. Love.

Just like.

"Thank you, but I came to terms with it years ago. It kills me that Brooke will never know how amazing her daughter is, but I can't dwell on it. I won't. She made her choice."

"Daddy, can we go for pizza? She can go too." Payton and I both glance over at my daughter and she's smiling up at the woman across from me. Again, with that damn heart squeeze.

"I shouldn't," she whispers.

"Come with us." That statement–three little words–is out of my mouth before I can worry about the implication. I don't concern myself with how this might confuse my daughter. I realize in the moment that I really want her to go.

"But…"

"I know we have a lot to talk about," I interrupt. "And we will. I want to tell you everything about her, but not here. And I really want to have dinner with you, even if it's just pizza and we have an audience. So, come with us. Please."

Her walls crumble right before my eyes. She wants to fight it, decline the offer, but she can't. She won't. Payton and I are in the same boat. No matter how stupid it may be, this *thing* developing between us is greater than both of us are prepared for. I've made my peace and am ready to roll with it. I can tell by the hint of trepidation in her eyes, she's not quite there. Baby steps, though. Baby steps and patience will get us to where we need to be. I can feel it

And I know she can too.

I can tell by the way she closes her eyes and smiles, and answers, "Okay. I'll go."

I'll admit the walk out of the office and past Cora was a bit embarrassing. We waited while she shut down her computer and gathered her things to leave, all while refusing to make eye contact. Thankfully, Bri is chatting a mile a minute, filling Payton in on everything about her day. It keeps my mind from wandering back to the scene they walked in on in my office.

Mental note to lock the door.

I lock up and head towards the parking lot, my daughter's hand firmly in mine. "Meet us at Checker's?" I ask as we approach my car. Payton's is parked a few slots over.

"Are you sure? I'm fine to go home. I don't want to intrude on your family time."

"No way!" Bri exclaims. "Checker's has the bestest pizza ever! You gotta go!"

"Bestest isn't a word; it's just best. And she's right. It is the best pizza. You really should join us." I watch as she seems to mentally weight her odds, and I pray they remain in our favor.

"Okay." *Mental fist pump!* "I'll meet you there."

When we get situated in my car, Payton follows us to the pizzeria in the heart of Jupiter Bay. You can smell the salty air mixed with the scent of tomato, basil, and garlic. The early night is breezy and the waves can be heard off in the distance crashing on the shore. It's the perfect winter night as the stars shine brightly above our heads. Together, we all make our way into the restaurant.

Once seated at a booth, Bri already begins begging to play some of the arcade games they have set up in a small room off to the side. The dining room has a few other adults seated at tables while their kids are off playing in the game room. It can get loud in here at times, but the atmosphere is fun and relaxed, not to mention delicious pizza that's not overpriced, which is exactly why so many families come to Checker's for dinner.

"Can I go play?"

"Wait until after we order. You can play for a few minutes until the pizza is ready, but then you have to come back to the table. No arguing. Got it?" I ask, helping take her jacket off.

"Got it!"

After we order a large thick crust pizza with extra cheese and sausage, garlic breadsticks, and a couple of drinks, Bri takes off into the game room with a handful of quarters.

"She's a huge fan of the pinball game, even though she can barely reach both sides of the flippers at the same time." I can't help but picturing how frustrated she gets when she can't flip both sides, but refuses to let anyone help her by manning one side of the game.

"She's adorable." Payton takes a sip of her diet pop and glances over at the little brunette in the other room.

"She's ornery. But, she's also sweet and caring and has me completely enamored with her." I'm rewarded with a small smile that makes her green eyes shine like brilliant emeralds.

"Tell me about her." Those words are an invitation to let her in, and I completely relent to the idea.

"Well, I was working at an accounting firm in Ridgewood when I met Brooke. She was a client. We dated for a while, about six months, and everything was fine. Brooke found out she was pregnant, and everything changed. I could feel her slipping away and didn't have the slightest clue what to do to fix it. She became emotional and completely withdrawn. I was working crazy hours as the newest accountant. They gave me all the late shifts and the most difficult clients. Things weren't good at home, but I didn't know what to do.

"When Brielle was just a couple of months old, Brooke left. I saw the writing on the wall when she barely wanted to hold her, refused to breastfeed, and hated to change her diaper. It was so stressful that when she walked out, I felt like I was finally able to breathe."

"She just left? What kind of woman does that?" Payton's eyes are wide with shock.

"A woman who isn't fit to be a mother. And that's okay. At least I was there to pick up where she left off. Bri will always be loved by me, even if I'm the only parent in the picture."

"That's very admirable of you. I'm sure it was difficult."

"It was downright excruciating at times. Lack of sleep and food will do crazy things to a person. But that stage doesn't last long. A few months more and she was starting to sleep longer through the night. My mom helped a lot with Bri and making sure I ate and didn't keel over dead from exhaustion."

She smiles at me again. God, that smile slays me. "That must be where you get your rule from."

Nodding my head, I grab my drink and take a sip.

"But, you're breaking it now," she hedges.

"I am." No hesitation.

"Why?" Her eyes are filled with question, and I'm pretty sure she's holding her breath.

"Because I finally found someone worth breaking the rule for," I say with the slightest shrug of my shoulder, as if it's no big deal to throw away every statute I set into place after my failed relationship with Brooke.

After a few moments, she finally says, "I've never dated anyone with a kid before." It's as if she doesn't know what to do about this development.

"Does that bother you? That I have a kid?"

She contemplates her answer for a few moments before she replies. "No, not really. It's just different. A little scary considering I've never really been around kids. None of my sisters have babies yet so my experience with them is limited."

"She's five which is much easier than if she were an infant or toddler. Do you want kids someday?" I ask innocently.

That's when I see the storm cloud sweep into her eyes. Those bright green orbs turn dark and somewhat dangerous. She sucks in a big breath of air and blinks rapidly. Her reaction to a seemingly innocent question catches my attention and makes me wonder. It happens quickly, the play of emotions across her face, but just as rapidly, Payton pushes it away and offers me a small smile.

Before I can ask her more, my daughter comes running up to the booth. "I almost beated the game, Daddy!"

"Beat the game, and I'm glad, pumpkin. The breadsticks should be here soon. Why don't you sit down and have a drink of milk while we wait."

She climbs up onto my bench of the booth and instantly starts grabbing her fork and plate and pushing them across the table. When she picks up her paper placemat and jumps down off the bench, I make a grab for her before she can take off across the restaurant. But she doesn't run away. She walks over to the bench across from me–the one where Payton sits–and climbs up.

"Do you want me to draw you a picture of a cat? I'm really good. You can take it home and hang it on your fridge. Do you have a fridge?"

"I do have one," Payton replies with a smile. "I would love to take it home and hang it there."

"My cat is a good cat, though. Not a crazy one like your sister's." She doesn't even look up, just gets to work outlining her cat with one of the black crayons in the bin on our table. Her tongue sticks out just the slightest bit as she concentrates on coloring in her masterpiece.

Payton and I both watch, me for the hundredth time and her for the first. Bri could sit around and color or draw for hours upon hours a day if you'd let her. During the weekends, we come up with lots of little craft and coloring projects to do. It sure beats the hell out of video games.

"I'm dunna take swimming lessons this summer," Bri adds while drawing whiskers onto the feline.

"You are? Are you going to the public pool?" Payton asks, watching every stroke Bri makes on the paper.

"Yep! I'm dunna swim like a fishy!"

My heart starts to race as Payton smiles affectionately down at my daughter. I never thought I'd be introducing my child to a woman I'm seeing, at least not until after a very significant amount of time dating, but here we are, right smack dab in the middle of another situation where I had to make a choice. But this one felt right. If it were any other woman, she wouldn't be sitting at the table with us. I wouldn't have introduced them to each other yet, if ever. Not until it got serious.

But this feels serious to me.

"They offer swim lessons at the public pool during the summer, and I want to sign her up. She's too young for the public lessons, but the head lifeguard was a classmate of mine and she's agreed to do some private lessons."

"That's good. You're never too young to learn. Especially since we live along the water."

"My thoughts exactly," I say, relieved that she gets it. I want to give my child every opportunity I can to protect and better herself, and if signing her up for swimming lessons so that she's comfortable in the water and I'm comfortable for her to be around it will help that, then I'm all for it.

Our breadsticks arrive a few minutes later. Breaking one in half, I set it on Bri's plate with a glob of warm marinara. She digs in, shoveling it into her mouth, which has me telling her to slow down and take smaller bites. I'm pretty sure she mumbles an apology, but I can't hear it because her mouth is full.

When the pizza arrives, steam rolls off the top and the cheese strings from the pan to our plates as I dish it up. I don't even have a chance to cut Bri's pizza into small bites. While I'm dishing out a slice on everyone's place, Payton instantly starts to cut up her piece into manageable chunks and blows on it to help it cool. I'm struck by the sheer ease and how natural it is for her to do that.

Dinner is enjoyable. Bri keeps us entertained with stories from school and some from our time at home. She's so comfortable with Payton that it makes my heart lurch in my chest and slam against my ribs. This crazy reaction to exchanges between my daughter and the woman I'm seeing is odd, but not scary. It just feels right.

I clean up the plates and stack them in the middle of the empty pizza pan. Bri is anxious to get back over and spend her last two quarters on a game of Pinball. "Payton, will you come play with me?" Bri asks, making my air lodge in my throat and my heart stop beating.

Payton glances up at me before answering, "I'd love to."

Before they can slip out of the booth, a shadow falls over our table. "Payters, I thought that was you."

"Grandma," Payton stutters, clearly surprised to see the older woman at our table.

"I ran inside to grab a pizza for supper when I glance over and saw you at the table. Who are your dinner companions?" the old woman asks, almost mischievously.

"This is my friend, Dean, and his daughter, Brielle." I'm pretty sure she choked on air when she stammered out that sentence.

"Brielle. What a beautiful name for such a gorgeous little girl."

"Tank you. I'm five."

"What a fun age. Are you going over to play some games?" the woman asks, nodding towards the remaining quarters on the table.

"Yep! Payton is gonna come help me win! Come on, Payton!" she exclaims as she jumps out of the booth and heads towards the game room.

"I'll be right behind you," she hollers before turning back to her grandmother. "Where's Grandpa?" she asks, looking over the visitor's shoulder.

"Oh, he stayed in the car. He figured out how to search for inspirational photographs on the Tumblr so he's busy saving things to his phone thingy."

"Inspirational photographs?" she asks, glancing my way with a look of question in her eyes.

"You know, porn. I don't like to use the dirty words before I've had my dinner." I almost spit out my mouthful of Coke.

"What? You use dirty words all the time!" The cutest blush creeps up her neck and spreads across her cheeks.

"That's neither here nor there, Payters."

Leaning forward, Payton whispers harshly, "And why is Grandpa looking at porn. That can't be good for his heart."

"Oh, fooey. His heart is just peachy. He's looking up new scenes for us to reenact later tonight after we've had our pizza and Fish Oil."

A loud smack echoes through the restaurant as Payton's head lands on the tabletop. "Why must you be so embarrassing?" she groans into the wood.

"Sex is not embarrassing, dear. And if it is, you're not doing it right. Maybe this young man can show you how it's supposed to be done," Grandma suggests, throwing me a wink.

I'm riveted in my seat, unable to look away even if I wanted. This tiny spitfire of a woman has me wanting to shy away and hide under the table one minute and laugh until my side hurts the next. I can't imagine what it was like growing up with her, assuming she has always been this brash and forward. And if the gleam in her eyes is telling, I'd say she has been.

"Come on, Payton! You gotta play with me!" Bri hollers from the doorway to the game room.

"I need to go in there. You go home," she says as she slides out of the booth, giving her grandma a very pointed look. "I don't trust you not to corrupt Dean."

The older woman tsks her disappointment. "I would do no such thing. Dean and I would be capable of having an adult conversation unsupervised."

"It's not Dean I'm worried about," Payton mumbles.

"Go play with that darling little girl, Payters. I'm going to take this pizza home before it gets cold. Dean, it was nice meeting you," she says seconds before I'm pulled into a big hug. The petite little thing is freakishly strong. Just as I go to pull back, I'm startled by a hand grabbing my ass firmly. "Oh, yes. It was very nice to meet you," Grandma adds with a wink before walking away.

I stare, wide-eyed and shell-shocked as she walks away.

"Did she grab your ass?" Payton asks, a mixture of mortification and exasperation.

"Yeah."

"Jeez. I'm so sorry. She has this thing with grabbing butts. She does it all the time to Ryan and has since the first time she met him. She rarely does it to Josh and never to Chris. I think it's some weird initiation."

"I don't know who all of those guys are, but it's okay. I can handle an eighty-year-old woman copping a feel on my rear," I reply with a chuckle.

"Just wait until she cops a feel on the *other* side." Payton's eyebrow rises. I can tell she's serious.

"Really?"

"Well, she's never actually grabbed it that I know of, but for a while there she was very friendly with Ryan, Jaime's boyfriend. She'd pull him in close and I swear you could see the moment he realized his junk was practically plastered to her stomach. Grandma just smiled and held on a little longer, though." I can't help but laugh. "My family's weird, Dean. I mean like really, really weird. Are you sure you want to continue this *thing*?" she asks, motioning between us.

Stepping forward, I invade her personal space until I can feel the heat of her body and smell the floral scent clinging to her hair. "I'm sure. In fact, I wouldn't mind continuing a little something else later." Running my hand down her arm, I feel her shiver in response.

"Payton!" my daughter yells from the entrance, breaking the spell I find myself in every time Payton is near.

"Come on. Let's go play some Pinball before they kick us out for yelling."

We barely make it into the game room when Payton's phone starts to go off. She ignores it at first, joining my daughter at the Pinball machine and manning the left side button to control the bumper. But after the fourth or fifth chime, I can tell she's worried about something. She grabs her phone from her pocket and swipes the screen.

I try to focus on my daughter's game, but I can't help but watch Payton. Her fingers are moving rapidly and her sweet little mouth is wide open. When she glances up at me, fire dances in her eyes, and I can tell whatever is on her phone doesn't make her happy.

"Everything okay?"

"No. I might kill my grandma."

19

Payton

Five texts.

Five messages, and all of them are pretty much the same.

Jaime:	You're having sex!?! Lots of sex???
Meghan:	Who's the guy?! Heard he's sexy!
AJ:	You are holding out! I need deets!
Lexi:	Hooker. ;)
Abby:	Yay! Can't wait to meet him!

There's only one explanation for this onslaught of annoying text assault: Grandma. Five bucks says she didn't even make it out to her car before she sent messages to my sisters. Hell, she probably had Grandpa drive home so she could enact the phone tree. I'm sure by the time our harmless little dinner got around to the last sister, I'm probably married with a baby on the way.

I blink rapidly, swallowing emotions I can't even deal with right now. The point is that as the conversation went down the line, I'm sure it was exaggerated immensely. Grandma won't even care either. She'll just stand there with her big spoon, stirring and stirring that pot, with a sweet little smile on her face.

Ornery ol' woman.

"Everything okay?" Dean asks beside me, glancing down at my phone.

"Well, Grandma wasted no time in calling all of my sisters and letting them know she saw us together. So now my sisters are texting, wanting all the dirty details of our sordid love affair."

"Are we having one of those? A sordid love affair?"

Beneath his glasses, his eyes are the brownest I've ever seen. They're dark and stormy and convey something I never expected to want again. But here I am. Staring at the first man I've considered something *more* with. Meeting his daughter today was a shocker. Part of me was ready to throw on my running shoes and take off like the devil was nipping at my heels.

Instead, I felt drawn to her, to him.

My life was stalled, but now? Everything is brighter, louder. I'm sure that has something to do with the little girl going to town on the button that controls half of the bumpers on the Pinball game. I'm struck by the look of excitement and fierceness in her matching brown eyes and something in my chest starts to flutter.

That lump in my throat returns as my heart rate picks up. This *thing* between us, between Dean and me, can easily turn into something more. I feel it. It causes exhilaration to bubble in my chest, making my heart beat even faster. But just as quickly, fear sets in, wrapping around my entire body like an old worn blanket.

How long am I going to let that fear control me?

"Everything okay? You slipped away for a few moments," Dean says, pulling me out of the trance I was lost in.

"Yes," I reply automatically. "I was just thinking about what I'm going to say to my sisters."

Dean studies me, and I can see it in his eyes. There's a look that tells me he doesn't believe me. He doesn't call me out on my lie though, instead gives me a quick smile before turning his attention to Brielle. Yeah, I know I should confess what I was thinking about, but I haven't even come close to coming to terms with the revelation myself, let alone tell Dean that I'm starting to fall for him.

And I am.

Falling.

It's a startling admission. I may not be able to say everything that's brewing in my head and in my heart, but I can admit one thing to him. "Yes."

"Yes?" he asks, glancing up from the game to give me his full attention.

"Yes." I swallow hard. "This might be the start of a sordid love affair." My words are hushed because of little ears, yet they sound like they're blasting through a megaphone all the same.

He smiles at me, one of his full-watt grins that starts slow and ends up lighting up his entire face. The results are the same every time: my panties are wet. "Yeah?" he asks, as if seeking confirmation. Of course I know why. I've been back and forth since the moment we met. Push him away, only to grab a hold of him and hold on tight. I've turned into one of those women who uses men as toy things.

Only this isn't a game to me. I'm legitimately torn between holding him close and running away. I think Dean gets that, gets me, and that's why he's not pushing me further than he already has. Convincing me to date him is already something of gargantuan magnitude, so maybe he recognizes my fear and is picking his battles.

Smart man.

We help Brielle play and win points on the Pinball machine, but before long, she's yawning. Dean must notice at the same time and glances down at his watch.

"Wow, I can't believe it's already seven thirty. Someone's already late for her bath."

"Daddy, I want to stay and play with Payton som'ore!"

He gives her a pointed, very stern look. "Not tonight. It's getting late and you have school in the morning."

"But Daddy…" Brielle whines, her gorgeous brown eyes filling with tears.

Dean's about to open his mouth, most likely to reprimand her for her fit, when my own mouth opens involuntarily. "Sorry, sweet girl, but it's getting close to my bedtime too. Us girls have to have our beauty sleep, you know?"

She gazes up at me with big, wide eyes. "Okay," she whispers, sniffling before any tears can fall.

I turn to head back to our table to grab my things when I feel her small hand slip into mine. Looking down, I'm in awe at the sight. Her little hand fits perfectly inside of mine and suddenly, I'm fighting off my own tears. She stares up at me with so much trust and innocence that it makes my heart lurch and slam into my rib cage somewhat painfully.

Slowly, I glance over my shoulder and come face to face with Dean's equally surprised face. He glances down and stares softly at our entwined hands, the faintest of smiles creeping across his lips. Me, on the other hand, suddenly feel like I'm about to have a heart attack.

"Come on, Payton," Brielle says, taking a step forward and pulling me towards our table. I follow willingly because I'm pretty sure, in this moment and every one that would follow, I'd do whatever this little girl wanted.

We're all quiet as we grab jackets and get ready to head out into the night. Dean settles the bill and refuses to let me pay for half of dinner. I argue my point that this wasn't a date, but it falls on deaf ears. Dean is adamantly shaking his head, refusing to listen, and Brielle is watching our exchange with a smile. Realizing I'm not getting anywhere, I settle for leaving the tip.

Outside, there's a slight breeze blowing off the Bay. Together, we all make our way towards the small lot beside the pizzeria where I parked my car beside Dean's. When we get there, I'm not sure what to do. He seems to be hesitant to say goodbye, and Brielle's grip on my hand tightens when we reach the vehicles.

"It was very nice meeting you, Brielle. I hope to see you again soon," I say, giving her a smile.

"Tomorrow? Can you come to my house and play with my stuffed animals?"

"Not tomorrow, sweetheart. It's a school night. I'm sure we'll see Payton soon," her father chimes in while opening up the door to the back where her booster seat is located.

Bri stomps her foot on the concrete and crosses her arms. "When?"

Dean mimics the move and stands his ground. "I don't know. This is not how a polite little lady behaves, missy."

Defeat pours from her little body like a faucet as her shoulders droop. Bri turns to look at me, wrapping her arms firmly around my waist. "Bye, Payton."

"Goodbye, Bri. I had lots of fun with you tonight," I say, hugging the little girl.

"When it's not a school night, you should come over and play with my animals with me. We can color and draw too. I love to draw kittens. And my daddy can make grilled cheese sammiches 'cause those are my favorite."

Giving her another warm smile, I respond, "Those are my favorite too."

As if my simple statement satisfies her, she climbs inside the car and sits in her seat. Dean helps secure her in the seatbelt before turning back towards me. "I'll walk you around to your car."

"You don't have to do that. She's ready to go," I say, nodding towards the little girl already playing with some stuffed animals in the back of the car.

"Bri, I'll be right back. I'm going to walk Payton around to her car. I'll be there," he says, pointing to my car parked right next to his.

"Okay."

Without saying a word, he places his hand at the base of my spine and leads me towards my driver's door one car over. Warmth spreads up my back and makes all my limbs tingle. My reaction to him is weird. I've never felt this instant connection with someone before, this all-consuming desire that steamrolls my entire being when he's around. And I'm not talking about sex, even though that's pretty freaking spectacular. I'm talking about him. Just his presence.

"Thank you for coming to dinner with us."

"Thank you for inviting me. Well, for agreeing after your daughter invited me," I add with a laugh.

"She has great taste, what can I say," he says with a smile. When it falls from his lips, he steps forward, completely invading my personal space. "I wasn't planning on introducing you to my daughter like this, but I'm glad it happened."

Air lodges in my throat. "Me too." It comes out a croak and a bit scratchy.

Dean leans forward, taking both of my upper arms in his hands and placing a kiss on my forehead. My entire face flushes under his warm lips and breath. "I wish I could kiss you properly."

"I wouldn't mind that."

"But we have an audience."

"I know."

"Drive safe, Payton."

"I will. You too." I notice he hasn't let go of my arms.

"Can I text you after she goes to bed?"

"I would like that."

Even though his eyes are burning into me, he quickly glances over my shoulder once before he's moving and his lips are on mine. The kiss is simple and quick, yet still ignites my blood all the way to my core. I almost whimper when he pulls back and drops his hands. "Good night," he whispers.

I try to reply, but the words just won't come. A simple good night is just gone from my vocabulary. Stupid hormones.

He holds open my door as I slide in and slip my key into the ignition. As soon as I'm belted in, I glance back in his direction. He gives me a knowing grin before shutting the door and heading towards his own vehicle.

My pulse is hammering in my neck and I'm breathing harder than I should be. Why do I always feel this way around him? The kiss was the simplest of kisses, one that you'd give a friend. Yet it sent desire and lust racing through my body as if it were qualifying for the pole position.

A racing metaphor? Really?

Sighing, I slip my car into reverse and pull from my parking spot. Dean's still there in his car, waiting for me to exit first. When I'm on the road, I continually glance back and watch his headlights in my rearview mirror until he reaches his turn, and suddenly, his lights are no longer behind me.

I can already tell I have company before I even reach my driveway. Lexi's car is on the street, but I don't see her inside, which tells me she's already made use of the spare key hidden on the porch. Gathering my belongings and my wits, I head inside to face one of my baby sisters.

Reaching the front door, I throw it open, knowing it's already unlocked. "Honey, I'm home," I holler. The light above the sink is still on, as well as one of the lamps in the living room.

I see her as soon as I step into the living room. She's sitting on the couch after helping herself to a glass of wine. "Mind if I get one of those before the inquisition begins?" I ask, dropping my purse and bag on the table.

"It's not my wine. Though, I'm already on my third glass so there's probably not too much left. Oh, by the way, you're almost out of wine."

"Noted. I only keep that stuff here for you guys anyway," I state and head into the kitchen to grab myself a glass. My plan was to use the time to collect my thoughts before having to go back inside the living room and explain Dean, but I quickly realize that no amount of time in my kitchen will give me the answers I need.

Grabbing a glass and the rest of the bottle, I join my sister in the living room.

Pouring myself a small amount, I ask, "Chris working late?"

"Of course."

"How's the baby making going?"

"Not. Rumor has it you have to have sex to make a baby. My husband would rather work himself into an early grave so that we can buy the perfect piece of land and build the perfect freaking house and have our finances in perfect fucking order before we try the fucking part."

"Ouch."

"Yeah, well, I have a plan," she says before taking a big gulp of wine. "I'm going to get him drunk, tie him to the bed, and screw him until he puts a baby in me. People have been making drunk-sex babies for decades. That's the only way I'm going to get knocked up, Pay. He thinks the mood has to be just right, but I'm here to tell you it doesn't. You just have to have a stiffy with plenty of swimmers to make it work.

"Remember that girl in high school who got pregnant our senior year? She doesn't even remember it. Too much to drink at a party and bam. Knocked up. That's what I'm going to do. Saturday night at sisters' night, I'm getting sloshed. I've already told Chris he's meeting me there this Saturday, no excuses. If I was as limber as I was in high school, I'd make him get naked in the car in the parking lot, but we'd probably never fit in the backseat anymore."

"And don't forget what happened to Ryan and Jaime when they went parking in old man Gerard's bean field."

"True. My luck someone would see the car rocking and call Barney."

"So, make sure you get home before you strip his clothes off and make him blow."

"See, that's the thing, Pay. I shouldn't have to *make* him do anything. He should *want* to get naked with me. I mean, isn't the best part about having a baby all of the practicing? Why doesn't he want to do that anymore?"

"I don't know, Lex," I reply softly. It's the honest to God's truth.

"I miss the practicing. We used to practice a lot. Now he gets home from work after I've gone to bed. I try to snuggle up against him, but he's virtually asleep the moment his head hits the pillow. And when we do have sex, he's not as thorough as he used to be. I mean, we both still get off, but, I don't know. It's just missing something."

"I'm sorry, Lex. I wish I knew what to say. It's not like I have a lot of experience in life lessons on love."

"Speaking of, let's not talk about my crappy sex life. Let's talk about yours. Apparently, you have one and didn't share."

I sigh loudly. *Dammit, Grandma.*

"Oh, don't act so surprised. You should have known she would call us before the cheese started to cool on her pizza. This is the woman who knew perfectly well where Jaime was that first night with Ryan and still called all of us, claiming she was kidnapped."

"God, why did I have to run into her tonight? It's…it's not really what you think."

"So you're not sleeping with some gorgeous nerdy man with eyes that make women everywhere quiver between the legs?"

"What? Gross."

"Her words, not mine. Let's come back to the fact that your boyfriend makes your grandma's lady parts quiver, okay? Let's go back to the beginning and focus on boyfriend."

"I'm going to need therapy," I grumble, taking another healthy gulp of wine, effectively draining the glass. I could use another refill, but I know the longer I draw out this conversation, the more liquored we'll both become, subsequently, the more dirty details I'm liable to give. "What do you want to know?"

"Everything. Start at the beginning."

Sighing, I do as instructed. "Last summer, the accountant I used retired and turned over my business, along with his other clientele, to a new man. Dean McIntire."

"You're screwing your accountant?" Lexi interrupts, practically shouting it across the room.

"Stop yelling. I don't need the senior citizens in the next county to hear, okay? Anyway, when I met him for the first time, he was…wow. He was gorgeous. Every time I had to take my monthly profits and losses statement, and all of my employment and income tax documents to him, he was always there, waiting. I tried to just drop them off with their secretary, but she always said he wanted to see me."

"I bet he did," she quips quietly.

"One night last fall, I was his last appointment. One thing led to another, and then next thing I knew, we were going at it on top of his desk."

Lexi's eyes are as round as saucers. "Nice."

"He went home with me that night, but was gone before the sun came up. We both determined it was a one-time thing, but then it just kept happening. It didn't matter if it was his office or if he stopped by the flower shop, we couldn't keep our hands off each other, even though we both decided it was wrong."

"I don't get it. What's wrong about it? I mean, you were having great sex, right?"

"Yeah, it was amazing, but he is my accountant. I am his client. There is a professional line that has been crossed, and in a big way."

"Pshhhh. Professional shmessional. It's not against the law, is it? No. I say there's nothing holding you back."

"Wait, there's more. When I went to my trade show last week, they lost my reservation. I tried several different hotels in the area and no one had availability because there were multiple conferences in the same vicinity. I was at the last one before I said forget it and headed home, and Dean was there."

"Where? At the hotel?"

"Yep. I was standing there being told that they had nothing available when he walked up to me and offered me half of his room."

"Shit."

"It was my only option if I wanted to stay in Richmond, so I took him up on it."

"And fell right into his bed." My sister giggles with the assumption.

"Well, not the first night. He slept on the pullout couch, so we didn't sleep together that first night, but the second…" I let my words trail off. There's no need to finish the statement. She knows.

"Nice," she says, drawing out that word as she lifts her wine glass in the air to salute. "And it was…" she eggs on.

"It was…better than nice."

"I bet it was, if that smile on your lips is any indication." I'm smiling? I didn't even realize.

"Anyway, we spent two nights together and, yes, they were amazing. We're talking toe-curling, can't remember my own name, best sex ever kinda nights."

"Damn," Lexi groans, fanning her face with her hand.

"When we got home last week, he kinda convinced me to give this whole dating thing a try. As you can imagine, it wasn't an easy pitch for him, nor easy for me to accept."

Lexi rolls her eyes. "No shit. So, you're dating this guy?"

"Yeah," I whisper so quietly that even I barely hear the answer. Clearing my throat, I turn to look at my sister's matching green eyes. "He has a daughter." Sweat starts to break out under my arms.

"Wow, okay. He's probably, what, in his early to mid-thirties? Most adults that age have kids by now. Was he married before?"

"No, she was his client, which is one of the reasons we've avoided getting intimate since we met. They dated for a short period of time, got pregnant, and left shortly after their daughter, Brielle, was born."

"What a pretty name," Lexi says softly, sadness filling her expressive eyes once more.

"She's a gorgeous little girl. When I stopped by his office today after work, she dropped by with his mom. There was an emergency with her sister so she dropped off Dean's daughter on her way out of town. We ended up going for pizza, and I'm pretty sure I fell in love with that little girl tonight," I say, lifting my glass, only to realize I've already drained it.

"And that's a problem?"

"Well, it's not expected. I've been working at keeping feelings out of this relationship, but then I met his daughter. She pretty much stole my heart with her big brown eyes, and that was before she put her hand inside of mine. What do I do now?" I beg. This is not what I wanted at all, but I don't think I can backtrack at this point, either.

"What do you mean? You don't have to *do* anything. You date Dean. You hang out and spend time with Brielle. You enjoy their time and company. If things progress between you and the hot accountant, then you'll deal with it then. Otherwise, why get yourself all worked up on something that *may* or *may not* happen?"

"When did you get so wise?" I ask, smiling across the room at Lexi.

"I have an amazing older sister. She taught me so much about life, and shared her wisdom and knowledge with us mere young'uns. Her name's Jaime," she coos, deadpanned.

Without thinking, I toss a throw pillow and hit her straight in the face. We both bust up laughing, and together, finish off the rest of the wine. Before I know it, the clock is approaching midnight, and our yawns are nonstop. Lexi stands and walks towards the front door, grabbing her jacket and purse from the table on her way. I meet her at the door and wait for her to get ready to go.

Throwing my arms around her neck, I say, "Thank you for coming over tonight and spending time with me. I love you."

"I love you, too, big sister. I'm very happy that you're having all the great sex with the hot accountant."

"He's going to be there Saturday night, so you can't call him the hot accountant."

"I can call him whatever I want," she smirks and steps outside. Before she gets to the bottom of the steps, she turns back towards me. "So the ass prints on your steel table were yours, right?"

Dammit, Grandma!

20

Dean

I'll admit: I'm the poor sucker who sat beside his phone and waited for it to ring.

After putting Bri to bed and reading a quick bedtime story, I opened a beer and tried to relax. Of course, relaxing came after I started a load of laundry, emptied the dishwasher, picked up what was left of Mom's dinner that she started and left on the stove when she had to run out. Then I sent a quick text to Payton to thank her again for accompanying us to dinner.

And then I didn't hear anything.

My mind went everywhere. She's painting her toenails. She's in danger. She fell asleep watching HGTV. Her phone's dead. Her sister's cat got loose and the entire family is looking for it. She changed her mind and doesn't know how to tell me.

God, what a lovestruck sap I turned out to be.

And that's the truth. I'm falling for her. I can feel it.

I've been staring at the same channel for the last forty-five minutes but have no clue what's actually on the TV. The beer is keeping me company, but it isn't strong enough to numb my mind. If she's looking to end this before it really begins, then I'll let her go. I wasn't looking for a relationship when I met her anyway, so no harm no foul.

Except even I know that's utter bullshit.

There's something about her that demands my complete attention. I couldn't let her go even if I wanted to. She owns a piece of my soul without even really realizing it. I've known her for about eight months, and in that time, I've grown to care a great deal for her. She's feisty, energetic, and passionate. Her curves and those damn green eyes have me firmly by the balls, and I know I'd do just about anything she asked of me.

Taking another swig of my beer, I glance back down at my phone. As if knowing that I need to hear her voice, it lights up with her name displayed on the screen.

"Hello?" I ask, setting the beer bottle down on the coffee table.

"It's late."

"It's very late. Why are you still up?"

"Lexi stopped by tonight and we drank booze and laughed. Next thing I knew it was midnight, and I realized I didn't get to say goodnight."

"I'm glad you called," I tell her honestly.

"Sorry it's so late, but I wanted you to know I got your message."

We're both quiet for several moments, though the silence isn't uncomfortable. I can picture her lying on her bed, wearing nothing but the shirt I left at her place. "Are you wearing my shirt?"

"Yeah."

Getting up, I head into my bedroom and close the door, making sure to lock it behind me. "Thinking of you wearing it right now makes me want to do crazy things to you."

"What kinda crazy things?"

"Dirty, filthy things. Things that I shouldn't even say out loud." My cock thickens to the point of pain in my sweatpants. It takes every ounce of self-control I possess not to grab a hold of it.

"Maybe you should show me then, since you can't say it."

"I would like nothing more than to show you, sweetheart, and if I were there, that's exactly what I'd do. Do you think you can follow my directions? Then it would be like I'm there with you, touching your gorgeous body." I've never done anything like this before, but my blood is pumping to one concentrated area, and the thought of knowing she's about to touch herself on the other end of the phone makes my body flush.

"Tell me."

"Is my shirt buttoned up?"

"Yes." Her words are already raspy. I can feel the desire coursing through the phone.

"Slowly unbutton it. Start at the top and work your way down to the bottom." My words sound stern, demanding, even to my own ears. A smile spreads widely across my lips as I sit back, close my eyes, and picture her fingers toying with the small buttons.

"Okay. It's unbuttoned."

"Spread it open, but don't take it off. I want my shirt to be able to touch your skin, even though I can't. Have you ever had phone sex, Payton?"

"N…no." I can feel her excitement and nerves through the phone.

"Me either. Are your nipples hard for me?"

"Yes."

"Put the phone on speaker, then touch them. I want you to close your eyes and pretend it's my hands caressing your breasts. I want you to picture my fingers pinching them gently. Imagine that my mouth is on them, licking and sucking on each one. Can you feel it?"

Her response is a long groan.

"Good girl. Now keep one hand on your breast but slide the other down your stomach to your panties."

"I'm not wearing any," she whispers, breathing heavily enough that I can hear it through the receiver and it goes straight to my rock-hard erection. I start to throb in a way I only experience with this woman, and the only way I can think to alleviate the ache is to grab my cock and give it a gentle squeeze.

Now it's my turn to groan. I grab my t-shirt and rip it off my head as quickly as possible.

"Touch yourself, Payton. Are you wet for me?"

"I already know the answer to that question without touching myself, but yes. God yes, I'm wet for you. So wet."

"Slide your fingers through the wetness. I want you to touch your pussy for me. Imagine it's my fingers," I instruct, my grip on my dick tightens, my hand starts to move on its own.

"Dean." My name is a moan and the sexiest fucking thing I've ever heard.

"I'm right here, Payton. I want you to fuck yourself with your fingers."

"I am. It feels so good."

"Go slow, sweetheart. I want to savor this moment. If I were there, I'd draw out the pleasure as long as possible."

"I need to come," she pleads.

"You will. I promise. Spread your legs wide for me. I want you to rub your clit with your opposite hand while you slowly fuck yourself with your fingers."

"Dean…"

"Do you know what I'm doing, Payton? I'm stroking my cock while you finger yourself. I'm so fucking hard and ready to explode just listening to you take your pleasure."

"I'm getting so close," she pants between noises.

There's no slowing either of us down now. I'm racing full-speed ahead towards an epic orgasm, and listening to Payton get off is only making the entire experience that much more magnificent.

"Touch your clit. Pretend it's my tongue."

That does it. She erupts, crying out my name over and over again. It's music to my ears as I stroke myself off at the same time. Warmth shoots across my stomach and I damn near drop the phone as my body convulses and shakes in the aftermath.

"You still there?" I ask, panting and trying to regain my composure.

"Wow."

Chuckling, I reach for my shirt and swipe it across my stomach. "I made a mess," I say absently.

"Me too. I need another shower."

"Damn, I wish I were there to help."

"Me too," she whispers, yawning as she grabs the phone and brings it to her ear, turning the speaker off.

"Go to sleep, sweetheart. I'll see you Saturday night."

"Pottery. The Beaver."

Again, I chuckle. "You're lucky I know what you meant by that or I'd think you were ready for round two."

"Class starts at seven. The other guys should arrive around eight. They'll hang out and wait for us. I'll introduce you."

"I look forward to it. Sweet dreams, Payton."

"Good night, Dean," she whispers, the smile on her lips heard through the phone.

Hanging up, I smile at not just what transpired, but also the prospect of meeting her family Saturday night. I'm a bit nervous since I haven't really met someone's family in several years, but I've seen most of the Summer sisters around town and they seem pretty easy-going.

Tossing the soiled shirt in the hamper, I stretch out in bed, anxious for Saturday night.

From the moment I graduated college and started working in the real world, I drifted from the few friends I had made in school. After a few years of hard work and keeping my nose to the grindstone, I met Brooke and our social life revolved around her and her friends.

So when my buddy Greg calls me up Saturday morning, saying he'll be in town for the weekend, I jump at the opportunity to meet up with him. I'm supposed to take Bri to Mom's house mid-afternoon, which means I have plenty of time to get together with Greg, have dinner, and catch up before I need to head to The Beaver to meet Payton.

We decide to meet at Joker's Wild because they serve the best steaks on Saturday nights. When I walk through the front door, I make my way through the bar to the back room, which serves as their restaurant. I spot Greg right away at a back table with a large mug of beer sitting in front of him.

"Hey, man. Good to see you," he says as I approach.

"You too. Having that MD behind your name looks good on you," I quip goodheartedly.

He laughs and takes a drink from his full mug. "It better look good on me for all the sleep and social engagements I sacrificed putting myself through medical school."

"How's life?" I ask, grabbing a menu.

"Good. Busy. I joined a small practice in Virginia Beach two years ago when I completed my residency and met a woman who doesn't complain about my crazy work schedule."

After ordering a beer for myself, I reply, "That's great, man. Congrats. Are we going to be doing the YMCA and the Casper Slide at your wedding soon?"

"Actually, that's why I'm here. I'm hoping you'll make a weekend out of coming to Virginia Beach on August thirty-first and standing up with me while I profess my love to one woman for the rest of my life."

I blink several times, surprised at his request.

"I can tell I've caught you off guard. I wasn't expecting to start off our dinner with this, but that's where it went."

"No, I'm happy for you. I'd be honored to stand up with you."

"Thanks," he says sheepishly. "I'll admit that we haven't stayed in touch as much as I would have liked over the last decade since college, but I've always considered you one of my closest friends. And with my work schedule, I haven't made too many friends who aren't work colleagues, so I made an exception and asked you."

I can't help it, I laugh hard. "Well, even if your options are limited, I'm honored. I'll be there."

"Thanks, man. Let's order so we can catch up."

Greg and I each order the prime rib, baked potato, and vegetables and are on our second beer before we turn the conversation from his upcoming wedding to me. "So, what's new with you? Last time we spoke Bri was getting ready to start school."

"She's in kindergarten and loves it. The geek in me loves it that she wants to read books every night instead of video games or something like that."

"Oh, I get that. Keri loves those dirty romance novels. Reading those things before bed is better than porn," he says with a cocky smile.

"Well, thankfully she's a little young for that, but I get what you're saying. I'm glad you found someone who has the same interests as you." Back in school, Greg was your typical bookworm like me. We spent many weeknights studying together in the campus library. Even though our fields of study were different, it was nice to have a buddy to hang out with, even if the majority of the time was spent on homework.

"What about you? Anyone beating down the door to become Mrs. McIntire?"

My face flushes instantly as Payton's picture comes to mind. "No, not really."

Greg looks at me with a critical eye and must notice my hesitation. "No?"

I give my friend a small smile and wait him out.

He sits back and gives me his own knowing smile. "I've got all night." Apparently, he's going to wait it out too.

Finally, after three or four minutes of both of us just staring at each other with stupid smirks, I concede. "Fine. There's someone. It's new, but I have high hopes."

"This is big," he says as the waitress delivers our food. "I mean, you haven't dated much since Brooke." He makes a face like he bit into something sour when he says her name. Greg wasn't a fan of Brooke's the few times we all hung out. No, it's not something he confessed, but I could see it on his face and read his body language well enough to know that he didn't care for my girlfriend. And I'm certain the feeling was mutual.

"That was a polite way of saying single loser."

"No way. You have been a committed dad for five years, most of them as both mom and dad. You've done something very commendable, my friend. I hope to be half the dad you are someday." He offers me a warm smile that tells me he means every word.

A blush creeps up my neck at the compliment. "Thank you."

"Anyway, back to this woman. Who is she?"

"She owns a business here in town, and I've known her since I moved here. We've…been friendly for a few months now, but recently decided to date more publically. Frankly, she's amazing and I love spending time with her."

"Nice. Sounds like a great woman. You know, you're welcome to bring her to the wedding in August."

"We'll cross that bridge when we get there," I say, finishing off my steak. "She met Bri earlier in the week by accident."

Greg pushes his plate away and tosses his napkin on the table. "By accident? How does that happen?"

Again, I feel myself blush. Thank God the lights are fairly dim in this joint. "She was at my office when Mom stopped by with Bri. I had no choice but to introduce them. Bri fell in love with her right away, which makes me happy, but I'm still a little worried that she'll get too attached. Not that I don't see this going further with Payton, but it's still new, you know?"

"I hear ya, and that makes sense. I'm glad to see you smile again, buddy." As the waitress delivers our check, he continues. "I hope it works out for you. You deserve this more than any man I know."

"Well, thank you. I'm heading over to a local pub tonight to meet up with her and her family. It'll be my first time officially meeting them as the boyfriend."

Greg smiles widely. "Good luck. If you can survive the family, you can survive anything."

I hope he's right. Just hearing a few of Payton's stories about her family, and those from a few residents around town, I know her family is extremely close and maybe a bit whacky. Honestly, that might be the aspect I'm looking forward to the most. I'm an only child so there's a huge thrill at getting to see the camaraderie they share, firsthand.

"You'll bring Keri by soon so I can meet her, right?" I say as we step outside of the bar. The night air is crisp and you can feel the rain coming in.

"Yes. We're going home for my mom's birthday in May so we'll make arrangements to get together. Maybe I'll be able to meet your Payton," he says with a smile.

"Maybe," I agree with my own grin.

We do that customary bro hug that all guys seem to know and agree to be in touch soon. As I quickly make my way to my car, I run through a few pieces of our conversation. It was great to catch up with my friend, but I'm anxious to get to the next part of my night. I shoot a quick text message to my mom and make sure everything is good with Bri, and after receiving her confirmation that everything's great, I jump in my car and head towards The Beaver.

I head towards Payton.

The Beaver isn't crowded as I make my way inside and towards the front bar. There's a handful of stools open, and fortunately one right beside Ryan Elson. I've not officially met him, but I've seen him around town enough to be able to pick him out of a crowd. He's incredibly tall with brown hair and brown eyes and has one of those tans guys get from working outside.

"Hey, is this seat taken?" I ask before sliding on the stool.

"Nope. It's yours," he says with a friendly smile. "You must be Dean. I was told to be nice," he adds as he extends his hand.

I can't help but laugh as we shake hands, instantly feeling at ease with my new situation. "I am Dean, and you must be Ryan."

"That's me. Josh should be here any minute. Actually, I'm surprised he's not here yet. He usually beats me to these things."

"These things?" I ask as I order a beer from the bartender. Payton says these nights last pretty late so I should be okay to have one or two before switching to water. Then I'll be good to go and hopefully can talk her into coming home with me.

"Sister nights. They do them every month. They're supposed to be girls only, but Josh and I always crash them. Some of them complain, but it's all goodheartedly and not meant to offend. Payton used to be the biggest offender actually, which is why I'm loving the shit out of her inviting you tonight."

"I see. Well, since it sounds like a big deal that I'm here, I guess I'll take that as a positive sign."

"You should," he says before taking a drink of his beer. "They're in the back room, but I've seen Payton look out the window no less than a half dozen times."

"Really?" I ask, looking just off to my right and noticing the window for the first time. There's a handful of brunette women all clustered together, staring and smiling. Every once in a while, one of them says something that makes the others cackle.

"We've had an audience since you sat down. I'm surprised one of them hasn't come out to refill drinks." Ryan nods toward his bottle of beer. "This'll be my last one and then I'll switch to non-alcoholic. One thing I've learned about these sisters is when it's time for girls' night, they love to drink."

"I figured as much. I'll have one and then switch to water."

"You can help chauffeur. It'll be like your initiation into sisters' night. But be ready. They love to talk about sex. Like all the time. They get all embarrassed when Grandma and Grandpa talk about it, but they're just the same. The apples definitely didn't fall too far from the tree."

As he looks over at the window where the girls used to be standing and smiles fondly. Even though we can't see them, it's like he knows his woman is on the other side of the wall. My heartbeat picks up at the notion that I could be in the same boat as Ryan. I can picture her standing in front of whatever project they're working on, with paint smeared across her cheek. I give my own involuntary smile, knowing that she's there, and I'm right here thinking about her, waiting for her.

I'm falling in love with her, this I can no longer doubt. Shit, I'm probably already there, and that thought is both scary and exciting. I haven't considered the possibly of falling in love after the mess Brooke left behind, but now? I'm anxious to see what transpires next.

We chat for the next hour, both switched to something other than alcohol long ago. Ryan fills me in on one of the jobs he's working, as well as some of the home improvement projects he's doing in his spare time at the home he purchased last fall with Jaime.

The lights flicker a few times as the storm outside picks up intensity. It's been coming down in buckets for the better part of an hour, but I haven't noticed much. I've enjoyed hanging out and talking with Ryan, though he was a little concerned that Josh hadn't arrived yet. He also filled me in on Lexi's husband, Chris, who rarely attends family functions, let alone sisters' nights.

All and all, it's a pretty good night.

It only gets better when the door opens to the backroom and the woman I've been fantasizing about walks into the bar, a wide smile across her face.

Yep, I'm pretty sure my heart is already gone.

Payton

He's here.

I knew it, felt it, the moment he hit The Beaver. No, that's not a euphemism for something dirty. My body was on high alert and my lady parts started to tingle. When I looked out the window and saw him sit down beside Ryan, I'm pretty sure I started to pant. And that's what drew the attention of my sisters who all ran to the window to gawk at the newest piece of man candy to grace a Summer sisters outing.

My newly glazed, brightly painted vase is drying on the rack. I love paint nights with my sisters. Even though I suck, it's a huge stress reliever to paint. And it does help that the instructor often walks around and helps fix my mistakes. So at least when I leave, I'm not completely embarrassed by the finished product.

Jaime's the first one out the door. She's practically sprinting towards Ryan. "Hey, babe!" she hollers, sliding onto the empty stool on the other side of her man.

"You're gorgeous, and pleasantly tipsy," he says with a huge smile before kissing her soundly.

"Stop that! It's sisters' night! No boys, remember?" AJ chastises.

"Normally, I'd be on your side, AJ, but not tonight," I say as I approach Dean. He looks so handsome in his white button-up shirt and dark blue jeans. He's wearing his glasses, which does weird things to my lady parts.

"I'm not wearing any panties," I confess against his ear, my lips grazing along the shell of his lobe.

He responds with a gasp and a cough that's an attempt to cover his groan. His eyes are dilated already and his smile predatory.

"No having sex at The Beaver, ladies." This from Lexi who's tipsier than normal. "Where's Chris? I told him to have his ass to The Beaver tonight or else he wasn't getting the beaver any more. Not ever. I'm officially cutting off the beaver. He's done."

"Stop saying beaver," Abby requests. "It's gross."

"I told him I was getting hammered. He had strict orders to pick me up and sex me down tonight. It's baby-making night, dammit! I'm ovulating!" Lexi slurs as she props her hip against an occupied barstool. Fortunately, the guy who's sitting there just shuffles over a bit and lets her lean on him.

"Hey, where's Josh?" Meghan asks, looking around to the other side of Ryan.

"Uhhh, we haven't seen him yet tonight," he answers.

"That's weird. He texted me an hour ago and said he was on his way," she says absently while grabbing her phone.

"It's really odd that Josh isn't here yet. He's usually the first one to crash our night, but even when he's running behind, he's always here by the time we're done with our outing," I tell Dean.

"Did you have fun? Your vase looks like it should be displayed in a museum."

"Are you kidding me? How much have you had to drink tonight?" I ask with a laugh. "I suck, I know. You don't have to kiss my ass to get laid tonight. That's a definite," I add with a smirk.

"Can you two hold off longer than Ry and Jaime tonight?" Lexi asks, interrupting us and leaning into my arm. "Because those two will barely make it out of the parking lot before the sexing starts. Since my own husband doesn't care to make sure I get home, I'm going to need a ride and I'm hoping you two are a safer bet."

Dean grins warmly at my drunk little sister. "You can have a ride, but I can't promise you anything on the sexing part."

Lexi groans. "Payton Ann! You're rubbing off on poor Dean. He probably never used the word sexing in his life, but he hangs around you for two minutes and now he's a regular dirty word maker-upper like you!"

"Um, actually, that's your word," I reply to Lexi.

"Oh, yeah, it is. My bad, Dean. I'm rubbing off on you. I like you. I think I'll keep you."

"Actually, I think *I'll* keep him. You already have a man."

"My man sucks donkey balls, Payton!" she practically hollers, drawing the attention of our sisters and others around us. "Oh my God! I didn't mean to say that out loud. I'm such a horrible wife, aren't I? I am. I'm horrible."

"You're not horrible, Lexi, you're just frustrated. That's completely understandable."

"Did you tell Dean you weren't wearing any panties yet? Dean, she's not wearing any panties," Lexi yells to the bar.

He laughs at my sister's antics. "She did tell me. I'm very excited about the no panties bit," he says with a smile.

"Good. Because someone should definitely be sexing tonight since it won't be me. Ryan and Jaime will be sexing, but they always have the sex. Someday my twin and her Levi will be sexing too. I know it. They both want the sex, but won't get off their asses and just have the sex." Yeah, that drew the attention of Abby.

"I'm not going to have sex with Levi. We're friends."

"Friends shmends."

"Stop calling it the sex. You sound like Grandma," Abby retorts.

Lexi gawks at her, wide-eyed and shell-shocked. "What did you say?"

"She's kinda right. Grandma always calls it 'the sex.' She's rubbing off on you," AJ adds.

"Fuck. I sound like Grandma!" Lexi declares with a sour look.

"I'm sorry my family is so crazy. I'd like to say that this isn't normal behavior, but it really is. My sisters are nuts, but they're the best." My mouth is close to Dean's ear so that he can hear me over the excessive noise in the bar.

"You're family's great. I'm an only child so this level of chaos is new and exciting for me."

"You should see us at a dinner where my grandparents are present. They add a level of craziness that's unprecedented."

"Can't wait to officially meet them," he says with a warm smile, and I can't help but grin back.

He's touching my back, running his hand up and down while we talk. His cologne tickles my nose and makes me want to lean further into his embrace. I still haven't ordered a fresh drink so I use my empty hand and snake it around his waist. We're close– and in public, I might add, but I don't care. Maybe it's the alcohol or maybe it's the fact that I'm just okay with a little PDA with Dean.

Crazy, right?

"Guys, I can't get a hold of Josh. He's not answering his phone," Meghan says, pulling my attention away from Dean's brown eyes and towards a pair of very worried green ones.

"I'm sure everything's fine, Meg. He probably got called back to work or something," Abby adds.

"To the bank? What could he possibly be called back to work for on a Saturday night?"

"Maybe he forgot where we were painting the pottery stuff tonight," I say, trying to calm down Meghan. She's definitely getting herself worked up.

"He told me he was on his way here, Pay. And now he's not answering his phone or texts." She gazes down at the phone in her hand, silently begging it to ring.

"I'm sure he's fine, Meggy. Don't get worked up until you have a reason to," Lexi says, sounding a little more sober than she did just moments ago.

The front door of the bar opens up and a couple walks in, shaking the rain off their jackets. The lights have flickered a few times over the course of our pottery night, but we've never lost power. The wind has been howling and the thunder shaking the building, but we've been inside the entire time so haven't dealt with the effects of the storm.

"Holy cow, it's really coming down out there," the woman says to the crowd at large. "We had a hard time getting here. Main Street is shut down at the edge of town because of a big accident. We had to drive around the Perry farm in order to get here."

"How bad of an accident?" a man sitting near Ryan asks.

"Bad. Multiple cars. I heard it was head-on," she says.

I step forward to flag down one of the bartenders when I feel a hand on my forearm. My heart stops beating when I see Meghan's stricken face. "We need to go."

"What's wrong?" I ask, confusion mixing with my panic.

"It's Josh. Something's wrong, Pay, I feel it."

I stare at my sister for several heartbeats, not sure what to do. Josh could walk in the door any moment, and we'll all have a good laugh at Meghan's paranoia. "Meg, maybe he's just stuck somewhere. That other couple said they had a hard time getting here. Plus, it's storming. I'm sure he's just tied up with the accident."

"Payton, he *is* the accident. I can feel it." Her voice drops and I almost don't hear her words. But I do. I hear them, and I'll never forget the way my body shivers. Tears start to fill her eyes and something clenches in my stomach. She's certain, and until we find out differently, there's not going to be any way of convincing her otherwise.

"Okay. Okay." What to do? "Dean?" I start to ask, turning towards my guy for guidance.

"I'm on it," he says to me, worry marring his handsome features. What once was a light and fun gathering has turned stormy and dark, and until we have answers, I know that none of us will be able to enjoy the rest of our evening.

Dean's on the phone with the local hospital, not getting anywhere because he's not family, when Meghan's cell phone rings. Her hand is trembling as she brings it to her ear and whispers a hoarse greeting.

"This is she," she says into the phone. Moments later, I can see it. The color drains from her face and her body practically goes limp. Ryan is there, grabbing a hold of her arm to keep her from going down all the way, and I grab her phone.

"This is Meghan's sister, Payton," I direct into the phone.

"This is Jupiter Bay Hospital. We have a man here named Joshua Harrison who was brought into the emergency room via ambulance. He's in critical condition but asking for Meghan Summer."

"We're on our way," I say as I disconnect the phone.

Dean is standing with Meghan, on the opposite side of Ryan, both of them holding her up while she cries. "Hospital. Now." Those two words cause a flurry of activity. Abby and AJ start grabbing purses and jackets, while Jaime throws cash down on the bar. Dean and Ryan each help guide Meghan towards the exit. I don't even tell the instructor that we'll be back another time to get our finished product. I couldn't care less about those vases right now. Getting to the hospital is more important.

Outside, the storm is blowing, rain pelting us like tiny sledgehammers. "My car is right there," Dean says as they make their way towards his vehicle.

"AJ and Abby, go with Ryan and Jaime. Lexi, get in the front seat with Dean," I instruct. No one questions my orders; everyone just follows suit. Before we all separate, I see the anguish mirrored in the eyes of my sisters. While Ryan helps Meghan buckle her seatbelt, my sisters all plead with their eyes to make this okay. As the oldest, I've always been the fixer.

But, my God, I can't fix this.

"He's going to be okay," I tell them, praying with everything I have that my words are true.

Piling in the back seat beside my sister, I try to console her, but she's crying too hard to pay attention to me right now. So, instead, I hold her. My shirt is soaked from the rain and the tears, but I don't care. Dean is driving as fast as he can to safely get us to the hospital, while I hear Lexi make a call to our dad. After a very short conversation in a hushed voice, our eyes meet across the car and I know she feels it too: gut-clenching fear.

Dean pulls into the circle drive in front of the emergency department. Before he even has it in park, we're piling out of the car, Ryan's truck parked right behind us. The six of us head towards the automatic sliding doors that lead to the entrance of the hospital.

"We'll park the vehicles and be right in," Ryan hollers as he and Dean go to move from the emergency entrance.

"Josh. Joshua Harrison. He was brought in a little while ago from a car accident," Meghan says evenly as we approach the desk just inside the front door.

"And you are?" the older woman asks, glancing up from her computer.

"Meghan Summer. Someone called me."

The woman types on the keyboard in front of her. When she glances up, she says, "There's a private family area right through that doorway. Have a seat for a moment, and I'll go get someone to help you." Then she scurries away quickly through the closed door of the emergency room.

"Come on, Meg. Let's have a seat," Abby says gently, leading us all through the doorway and into the empty room.

"I can't sit. I need to see him," Meghan pleads with angst eyes.

"Someone will be out soon," I add as the guys come rushing in from the parking lot.

Dean's arms are around me instantly, warm and comforting. I lean into his embrace, calling upon every ounce of strength I possess to be strong for my sister. We don't even know anything yet, but I don't have a good feeling about this. My gut tells me something is drastically wrong, and I don't have a clue what to do about it.

A few moments later, Dad comes rushing into the room with Grandma and Grandpa hot on his heels. They all look disheveled, and I'm pretty sure my grandparents are still in their pajamas, but no one seems to care. Dad pulls Meghan into a hug as a man in blue scrubs and a white jacket comes into the room.

"Meghan Summer?"

"That's me," she says, her voice wavering and cracking. We all gather around while the doctor steps forward.

"Would you like to go somewhere to talk?"

"No, whatever you need to say can be said in front of my family."

"All right. Mr. Harrison was in a car accident this evening and has a fractured leg, arm, and lacerations to his face and chest. But our biggest concern is a TBI, or traumatic brain injury. It's caused from his brain jarring against his skull during impact. We know there is blood and a lot of swelling in the frontal lobe. There's also internal bleeding in his chest. He was pinned between the steering wheel and his seat when the vehicle was crushed causing damage to his liver, as well as blood around his heart. I'm afraid we must get him into surgery as soon as possible to see how extensive the damage to both his chest and the brain. We have paged a neurosurgeon along with our chief surgeon, and as soon as they are ready, we'll get him prepped for surgery."

"That sounds bad," Meghan whispers, sniffling, as the tears continue fall.

"His condition is very critical, Miss Summer. You should know that this surgery is both lifesaving, but also very complicated. There are a lot of injuries to major organs, and when you add them all together, well a lot could go wrong with a surgery of this magnitude."

"What are his odds?" my dad asks from his position beside Meghan.

The doctor hesitates. We all see it. "We're going to do everything we can for Mr. Harrison. We're ready to get him to the OR and prepped for surgery. He has been in and out of consciousness, and even though we've tried to sedate him, he refuses until he gets to see you first. It'll have to be a very short visit, but you can come in while we prep Mr. Harrison to be moved."

"Thank you," she replies, latching on to Dad's hand. Together, they walk towards the closed doors. Before they can enter the emergency room, Meghan turns. "Oh, my phone."

"I have it," I say, pulling it from my pocket.

"Someone needs to call his parents."

"I'll do it," Grandma says, stepping forward and reaching for the phone in my hand.

"John and Angie," she says before turning and disappearing behind the doorway.

I don't pay attention to Grandma as she walks across the room to make the call that none of us wants to make. Instead, I head over to one of the hard plastic chairs against the stark-white wall. Dean is there, holding my hand as we wait. There's no conversations, no small talk, no noise except for the ticking of the wall clock. We all sit or stand, anxiously awaiting word of Josh's condition. My hand is warm where he holds it tightly in his own, the silent gesture of support appreciated more than he'll ever know.

It seems like only a matter of minutes before Meghan and Dad are back from the ER. She looks completely stricken, heartbroken and inconsolable. I instantly worry that something happened while they were inside.

"They're taking him into surgery now. They said they'd keep us updated, but they won't know the extent of some of the injuries until they get him opened up," Dad says, steering his daughter towards the floral patterned vinyl covered loveseat. "Someone will be in shortly to move us up to a waiting room by the OR."

Meghan stares at the ground, completely ignoring everyone and everything around her. I suppose if I were in her shoes, I'd be the same way. Just the thought of Dean being on the other side of that wall makes my heart bleed and the lump lodged in my throat suffocating. Sitting here, surrounded by the scent of sterile chemicals and stale coffee, I know I'm completely in love with him.

I just wish I knew what to do about it.

After months of dancing around emotions and each other, we've finally decided to give a relationship a try. And what does it give me? Clarity. Clearly we've been working towards this place for a while now. Everything was fast-tracked in Richmond. The slow dance we partook in led us right here: to the big L.

I'm not certain he feels the same, but he might. I've seen the way he looks at me. I'm not so dense that I haven't felt his eyes on me or swooned at the smile he gives me when he thinks I'm not looking. Something has been brewing for a while now, and I know he feels it too.

His arm wraps around my shoulder, pulling me into his embrace. My head connects with his chest, his heart beating strong against my ear. I try to relax, taking deep cleansing breaths in and out. Unfortunately, the calming effect only lasts a few moments before the reality of the situation rears its ugly head again.

After about twenty minutes, we're moved to another room. This one is larger with old copies of magazines on the tables and a television on mute in the corner that's on some news channel. Not long after that, the door opens and Josh's parents run in. I've met them both on a few occasions where our family gathers with his family and they seem like great people. Like their son.

Angie is hysterical and clings to Meghan as if she were a lifeline. They're both speaking through their sobs, but I'm unable to tell what they're saying. John goes over to my dad and grandparents first. My dad fills him in on the information that the doctor gave before taking Josh to surgery. Once he has all of the details, John settles into the chair beside his wife and holds her.

The minutes crawl by at a snail's pace. Ryan and Jaime are over with AJ and Lexi, while Abby is curled into our father's arms. Meghan still sits in a chair, rocking and praying. Her eyes are glued to the floor, but when they do finally glance around the room, they look so haunted and empty.

Dean has been stationed beside me since we arrived almost one hour ago. His presence is not only comforting, but necessary. He's the very air I breathe, and I'm not sure I'd be able to keep my sanity without him here.

We've made small talk to help pass the time. Five seconds after our conversations, however, I've already forgotten what was discussed. My mind just keeps replaying everything about this night, from hearing about the accident all the way to waiting out the surgery. How can we go from drinking and painting, laughing and have a great time, to this?

It seems like an eternity before the door finally opens. The doctor from earlier, along with another man in scrubs, come in, their faces void of emotions. We all stand up. The room is silent except that stupid ticking of the clock on the wall. No one moves, no one breathes. When their eyes lock on Meghan's, I know.

I know.

And she does too.

The worst cry I've ever heard erupts from my sister, her legs refuse to hold her body up any longer. Mrs. Harrison wails beside her before collapsing on the floor right next to Meghan. They cling to each other tightly, neither of them ready for the words that will haunt them until their dying day.

John and my dad each help the ladies up off the floor and guide them into chairs. Both doctors sit across from them, speaking softly in hushed tones. Finally, Meghan looks up and shakes her head.

"I'm Dr. Lopez, the neurosurgeon for Jupiter Bay Hospital. My team, along with that of Dr. Beck, did everything we could for Mr. Harrison. Unfortunately, the extent of his injuries to his chest, as well as the damage to his brain, was too severe. He passed away in surgery while we were trying to stop the bleeding."

Meghan's head drops, her shoulders shaking from the force of her crying. I tune out the rest of their conversation and everyone around me. The weight of what has happened is too much to bear. I turn into Dean's arms and cry. I cry for my sister, for the beautiful soul that was Josh, for his parents and siblings, as well as our own family, who has grown to love that man as if he had always been a part of it.

There will never be another Josh Harrison.

Ever.

My heart is completely broken.

Dean

22

Coming from a small family, I've never really experienced death like this before. Sure, my grandparents both passed away, but that happened when I was younger. I lost my uncle Frank, Kate's husband, about five years ago, but I don't recall it hitting me as hard as this. Yes, I was close to him, but I was also a new dad at the time of his death, and just remember going through it in a sleep-deprived daze.

I never even met Josh, and I'm affected.

Maybe it's because I see the agony in Payton's face, hear her pain in her voice, and feel it in her touch. And don't get me started on Meghan. I can't even look at her. Just the thought of seeing her so broken leaves me tearing up with a golf ball sized lump in my throat. Two hours ago we were smiling and laughing, and now this.

After the doctors left, a grief counselor came into the room and talked with Meghan and Josh's parents. His brother showed up not long after the doctors exited, and we all had to experience the loss all over again while they told Jason that his brother was gone.

When the coroner came in, Meghan, John, Angie, and Jason all went back to view his body and start to make the final arrangements. There wasn't a dry eye in the room while they were gone, nor a single word spoken. No one knew what to say. So instead, I just held Payton in my arms and offered her as much strength and support as I could.

While I numbly offered cups of lukewarm coffee to Payton's sisters, the door opened. A man I've not met yet walks in, his hair disheveled and his face full of worry. His eyes zero in on Lexi before he makes a beeline for her. I watch as he wraps his arms around her and buries his face in her neck. I also notice that she's tense and doesn't hug him back. I can only assume that's the elusive husband who didn't show up at The Beaver tonight.

Now, we're pulling into my driveway. Payton hasn't said much since leaving the hospital. I didn't offer to take her home, instead making the choice for the both of us to take her to my place. Her dad, whom I spoke to very little, took the rest of the girls home, while Grandma went with Meghan to the place she had shared with Josh.

"I feel like I should be with her, you know? I don't know what I could do, but I feel like she needs all of us right now."

"Your grandparents and dad are staying with her tonight. I'm sure she's going to need all of you over the next few weeks, but your dad was right, you should try to get some sleep tonight."

Unlocking her seatbelt, she says, "I don't think I can."

I reach over and graze my finger across her jaw. "You don't have to sleep if you don't want to, but I think it'll do you some good to rest for a bit."

Payton looks out the window as if seeing where we are for the first time. "This is your place?"

"Yeah," I tell her, unbuckling my own seatbelt. "Bri is away at my mom's tonight, so I thought we'd come here."

"Okay." That one word is full of exhaustion and dejection.

I slip out of my car and head around to help her out. Fortunately, it stopped raining some time while we were at the hospital, so at least we're not getting soaked to the bone once again. Leading her towards the front door, I keep my arm securely around her waist as we step up to the entrance.

Inside, I give the place a quick once-over. It's slightly cluttered with toys and half done craft projects, but it doesn't look too bad. There's no funky odor or dirty socks on the living room floor so that's a plus. Payton glances around, but I don't think she really sees it. Her eyes have a dazed look to them, and I can see the exhaustion settling in.

Making sure the front door is locked securely, I steer her towards the hallway and to my bedroom. It's dark inside, but instead of turning on the overhead light, I opt for the small lamp on my nightstand. Payton is staring down at the bed, her arms wrapped around her chest in a protective manner. No, I don't think she has to protect herself from me; I think she's protecting herself from life, from the hurt and the pain she feels.

"Come on, sweetheart," I say gently, walking towards her.

She doesn't say a word as I grab the hem of her shirt. When she realizes what I'm about to do, she raises her arms and stands still. Together, we slowly undress her. It's not sexual, per se, but comforting, though my wayward cock apparently didn't get the memo. When she stands in just her bra, because dammit if I didn't forget that she's not wearing panties, I grab one of my long sleeved, button-up shirts from the closet. I could probably grab just a tee from the drawer, but something tells me Payton needs the familiarity.

I remove her bra and try to not ogle her amazing breasts. It's hard, and, well, so am I. Of course I sneak a peek before slipping the shirt over her arms. She's giving me the slightest grin when I glance up at her face. Of course she would catch my wandering eye, but I can't help it. I smile back at her.

"Do you need to use the bathroom?"

She shakes her head, her eyelids starting to droop. Grabbing her hand, I lead her towards my bed. With the covers thrown back, my breath catches in my throat at the sight of her lying there. Her warm brown hair fans across my pillow, her soft curves nestled against the bedding. She's a goddess and doesn't even realize it.

It only takes me a few minutes to strip out of my own clothes, down to my boxers, and quickly use the bathroom. When I make my way back into my room, I don't find her sleeping like I expected. I find her crying, and the sight guts me.

Sliding into the bed beside her, I draw her against my chest and let her cry. My skin is wet from her tears, but I don't make a move to wipe them. Instead, I swipe at her lower eyes, but as soon as one tear is swept away, a new one replaces it. There's nothing I can say or do to take away her pain, so I choose to do what I've done all night: hold her.

With her head nestled against my neck, I stroke the top of her hair, brushing it back with my fingers. I love the way the soft strands feel entwined between each finger, the way it tickles my palm when I grasp it in my hand. At another time, this would be the start of something dirty and erotic, but not now. Not tonight.

Soon, her soft cries turn to sniffles. Reaching over, I set my glasses down on the nightstand, grab a Kleenex from behind my alarm clock and hand it to her. Her face is void of makeup and has been for much of the night. Her eyes are swollen and her face blotchy, but something inside my chest bursts with longing and happiness, and it feels a lot like love. My heart palpitates in my chest, jumping around and tapping out a happy little jig. So much I want to tell her, but can't. It's not the right time, and I don't think she's ready.

"When I first met Josh, Meghan brought him to dinner for the twins' birthday. He was so quiet and shy, which you can imagine how that went over with my family. Anyway, Grandpa walked over to him and told him that if he was going to make it in this family, he was going to have to strip naked and dance along to

Prince in the middle of the yard. Of course, he was completely flabbergasted at the thought, and just when he was about to make a mad dash for the highway, Grandpa started laughing and told him that he was joking. And the crazy part is, we still don't know if he really was. Josh rolled with it, though, and was just a part of our family from that moment. He went everywhere Meggy went, would do anything for her. He loved her so fiercely, so infinitely that I don't know how the sun will come up in a few hours in his absence."

"I'm sorry I didn't get to meet him. Ryan told me great things about him," I tell her soothingly, rubbing small circles on her upper back.

"They've become close in the last several months. With Chris's constant absence, they were the only guys. They hung together during every sisters' nights, and even some just because they wanted to watch a football game or some fight on Pay-Per-View. Levi is around a lot too, but not as much as those two were."

"Levi?" I ask, racking my brain to connect the name with a face.

"He's Abby's best friend. They actually live across the hall from each other, but have been best friends since grade school. I'm pretty sure they secretly love each other, but refuse to acknowledge it. He's an EMT and firefighter here in town and plays guitar in a band."

"I'm sure I'll get to meet him soon."

"Yeah. Probably at the funeral," she says, choking on the words.

I pull her closer yet, the front of the shirt she's wearing wet from all of her fallen tears. "I'm sorry you lost him, sweetheart. I'm sorry your entire family has lost someone so loved by each of you."

"Thank you," she whispers, her lips grazing against my neck sending ripples of lust straight to my groin.

"Try to get some sleep."

"I should be with Meghan."

"Let's get some sleep and we'll go be with her tomorrow, okay? Right now, you need some rest."

"Okay," she finally concedes, taking a deep breath.

I feel her relax in my arms, the weight of her worries finally starting to lift. She drifts off to sleep, her warm breath tickling my skin. My own exhaustion starts to set in, my lids too heavy to keep open any longer. We're in for a rough and long few days, that's for sure, but I plan to be by her side every step of the way.

There's no other place I'd rather be.

Three days feel like a lifetime when you're planning a funeral. I wasn't able to take the entire week off from work, but was able to move appointments for three of them. It'll make the end of my week busier than hell, but I wouldn't change it for anything. Being with Payton while she grieves the loss of someone she loved is the most important thing right now.

We made it through the visitation in fairly one piece, but now we have the funeral tomorrow. I, for one, am not looking forward to this in the least. And I didn't even know the guy.

Tonight was brutal. Meghan was overwhelmed for much of the evening, and that was hard for Payton to witness, which, in turn, made it difficult for me. The five Summer sisters sat back, helpless, while Meghan greeted person after person, heard condolence after condolence. Four hours of putting on a brave face and having dozens of people tell you how sorry they were for your loss.

It fucking sucked.

We're pulling back into my driveway now. Payton struggles not to fall asleep in the passenger seat, the result of sleepless nights. I wanted her to stay with me so that I could hold her in my arms, but she wouldn't. Not only did she stay with Meghan one night, but she didn't want to disrupt my daughter's routine.

Well, forget that.

Tonight, she sleeps in my bed.

"Come on, honey," I say as I park my car and get out to help her. She's wearing a black dress that hugs her curves, with that long brown hair that I love twisted up in some sort of fancy knot on her head.

"I should get going," she mumbles as she stands beside me, nodding towards her car parked in the street. I watch as she sways a bit, practically dead on her feet, for lack of a better term.

"Not tonight, sweetheart. You're exhausted. Come inside and you can crash here. After Bri gets off to school, we'll run to your house and you can get ready."

"Ready. For the funeral. I don't think I'll ever be ready."

"I know," I concede, kissing her forehead before steering her towards my front door.

"But Brielle is here."

"She is."

"But don't you think that will confuse her? If she sees me here at night and then again in the morning."

"I think my daughter is going to be too excited to even realize. She asks about you every night."

"She does?" she asks, stopping and turning towards me when we reach the door.

"Every night."

Big green eyes stare at me. She looks nervous, yet pleased at the same time. Before I can formulate a reply, she kisses me. For as much affection as we've shown each other in the last few days, this kiss is different. It's not of security but of desire.

Her lips are soft and warm and mold to mine perfectly. Her body lines up seamlessly. Her hand to my chest is an accelerant to my raging libido. We fit. Click into place like puzzle pieces.

Like she was made for me.

I'm pulled from my thoughts by giggling. Payton realizes it at the same time and together we pull apart and glance at the front door. My daughter is there, smiling like the cat that ate the canary.

"You guys are kissing," she snickers, her hands covering her mouth.

"And you were snooping," I say as I pull the screen door open. My daughter doesn't fly into my arms the way I expect her to. No. She flies into Payton's.

"No snooping, Daddy. I heard you pull in and Mimi said Payton was with you!"

Even though she still looks exhausted, she's smiling at Brielle, holding her against her chest. The image they make steals my breath, making it hard to breathe. Bri's little arms are wrapped around Payton's neck and she's squeezing tightly.

"Careful, Bri. Don't hurt Payton."

"She's okay," she replies before placing a kiss on my daughter's forehead.

"Are you gonna come play?"

"Not tonight, Bri. It's bedtime and Payton's very tired. She had a very long day."

"'Cause your friend went to heaven?" Bri asks innocently.

Payton's eyes fill with tears and she smiles fondly down at the girl in her arms. "Yeah, because my friend went to heaven."

"That makes me sad," Bri whispers.

"Me too."

"You know what makes me feel better when I'm sad?"

"What?" Payton asks, her full attention to my daughter.

"My daddy snuggles with me and rubs my back. Maybe Daddy can snuggle with you and rub your back for you too."

She smiles down at Bri a breathtaking grin. "That sounds like just what I need."

"Can I snuggle with you too?" Her eyes look so hopeful.

"I would love that," Payton confirms.

We finally make our way into the house. Mom is standing there, wearing her own grin. I'm about to ask her what she's smiling at, but I think I already know. Payton puts Bri down, and they instantly lock hands. The movement doesn't go unnoticed by me, nor Mom.

"I'm very sorry to hear of your loss, dear." Mom steps forward and wraps her arms around Payton's neck. "Please let me know if there is anything I can do for you and your family."

"Thank you," she chokes out, stunned by the onslaught of attention and emotion it's creating.

When mom leaves, I send Bri to the bathroom to brush her teeth. Payton, on the other hand, heads to my room to get ready for bed. After a quick sweep of the house, making sure all of the doors are locked and the lights off, I head to find my little girl. She's just finishing up her teeth, so I have a seat on the toilet lid until she's done.

"Can I ask you something?"

"Uh huh!"

"Are you okay if Payton sleeps here tonight?"

She turns those brown eyes on me. I can tell she doesn't understand why I'm asking.

"It's just that I want to make sure you're okay with her staying here. When you wake up in the morning, she might be sleeping in my bed."

"Like married mommies and daddies?"

"Yeah," I reply, choking on air.

"But you're not married." It's not a question.

"No."

"Are you gonna get married?"

"I don't know, sweetheart. It's too soon to know the answer to that."

She looks to be deep in thought, so I let her work it out in her own head. If she has more questions, I know she'll ask. Like most young kids, she's inquisitive and never has a problem vocalizing her curiosity.

"It's okay wiff me. She's really sad and I don't like to see her sad."

"Me either, honey. That's why I'm having her stay here. She's very tired, but if it makes you uncomfortable, then I can take her home."

"She said I can snuggle wiff her."

"She did," I confirm, giving her a slight grin.

"Can I be in the middle?"

"Of course."

"Then let's go. She's sad and needs to snuggle, Daddy."

Together, we walk out of the bathroom and into my room. Payton is standing there, staring out the window, lost in thought. Her hair is brushed out, her face void of what little makeup she wore to the visitation. I notice immediately what she's wearing. She has the button-up shirt that I consider hers now, and a pair of my cotton shorts. They hang on her hips slightly, hugging her thighs in a way that sends blood to my groin.

Not a good time, wayward dick.

Bri walks up to her and hugs her waist, pulling Payton's attention back to us. She glances up at me, the question clear in her eyes. So, I answer her with a smile. *Yes, this is okay.*

The girls walk to my bed and climb on. Payton lies on her side with Bri facing her, their arms linked. I watch for a few minutes as they make small talk, my child telling my woman all about her school day and what my mom made her for dinner. I slip inside the bathroom and get myself ready for bed. Once my teeth are brushed, I throw on a pair of cotton shorts folded up in the laundry basket of clean clothes that I hadn't put away yet.

When I get back to my bedroom from the en-suite bathroom, I flip on the lamp before turning off the overhead light. Then I make my way to my side of the bed and tuck in beside my daughter. As soon as I'm settled, I glance across the bed and into the emerald eyes of Payton. They're laced with humor along with her weariness.

We lie together, my arm across Bri, her arms wrapped around Payton. It's a lovely image, one I've never really allowed myself to envision. But now? Now, that I'm experiencing it, I'll never get it out of my head. I'll remember this moment, this mental photograph, for the rest of my life.

"Do you feel better, Payton?" Bri asks, her voice quiet as sleep starts to take her.

"I feel amazing, Brielle."

Glancing up, I gaze at startling green eyes that reflect my own emotions. It takes every ounce of control I possess to not tell her that I'm in love with her. My heart is beating wildly in my chest, my eyes locked on hers. Her features are soft and relaxed. Content.

Payton's eyes finally grow heavy and start to close. Brielle has gone quiet and still between us. I lie there, watching them both sleep for as long as possible until my own eyes become too heavy to keep open, and then, I finally allow myself to drift off to sleep.

One thing is certain: I feel pretty amazing too.

23

Payton

Will things ever get back to normal? No. A week after we bury my sister's fiancé, the Summer family is having to navigate a new normal. One that still involves tears and a huge void where one person once was. Everything has changed, and none of us really know where to start.

First off, there's Meghan. She's not our Meggy right now. She's grieving something none of us ever hope to experience, and if I could take her place in this traumatic turn of events, I would in a heartbeat! I would do it for any of my sisters, and know they would do the same for me.

Even if it hurts.

I haven't spent the night with Dean since the night of the visitation. Not because he didn't ask, but because I needed space. It would be so easy to get caught up in the magical bubble he wraps around me. You know the one where everything is cozy and comfortable and content. He and his daughter and the way they make me feel like a part of their little family.

And that right there is the problem.

I can't be a part of their little world. Yeah, sure, in theory, when I close my eyes, I can see myself sitting on the couch with both of them, wrapped up in a blanket and watching a Disney movie. Or all of us seated at the dinner table enjoying a meal I cooked. Or what about bedtime where Dean and I tuck Bri into bed before slipping into his room, where we fall into our own and make love until we're both sweaty and exhausted.

Those are dreams.

No long reality.

Reality for me is lonely, and while I might be able to gloss over it with time with him and his daughter, it won't hide the truth forever. He'll want more kids.

And that's where I would come in.

But I can't give them to him.

One thing I've learned in the last week is that love hurts, painfully so. And while I'd gladly take the place of my sister so she doesn't have to feel an ounce of this heartache, it's also made it brutally clear that there is no happy ending in store for Dean and me. As much as I'd love to see it happen, it can't. It won't. He'll be disappointed in me just the way Cole was all those years ago when we finally broke up.

I know what I have to do, and it hurts.

I don't sleep because when I close my eyes, I see their faces. I don't eat because my stomach can't handle it. I can't breathe because the ache of knowing he won't be there when I want to talk makes it too painful to do something as simple as moving oxygen in and out of my body.

The agony is coming and there's nothing I can do to stop it.

It's Friday night and the shop closed a little over an hour ago. I'm in my office, working on an order to be delivered next Wednesday when I hear a knock on the back door. My phone has been in my purse much of the day, and I'm sure it has texts and messages that have remained unseen.

Reluctantly, I get up and head to the door. My gut tells me it's Dean, which wouldn't surprise me since I haven't seen him much in the last week. With taking much of last week off for Josh's funeral, I've been playing catch-up like crazy at the shop. Rachel helped keep it running, but not the behind the scenes stuff. The office and clerical part, as well as the inventory and ordering is all me.

So when I open the door and Abby is there, I'm a little surprised.

"Hey," I say, holding it open so she can enter.

"Am I interrupting much?"

"No, no. Just going over some of the order forms that need to be sent in. My next shipment is coming Wednesday, and it couldn't be soon enough. Since I wasn't here last week, I didn't get anything this week. I'm dangerously low on my staples."

She follows me into my office and glances around at the stacks of papers on my desk.

"Have you eaten?" she asks before turning those mirroring green eyes on me.

"No," I say, just as my stomach growls.

We laugh together while she digs out her cell phone. "I'll order pizza."

"Sounds good," I sit down behind my desk and shuffle the papers that need to be filed.

"Oh, wait. You don't have plans with Dean tonight, do you? Am I messing something up?"

"No, no plans." I avoid eye contact and keep moving papers around on my desk.

I notice right away that she's quiet and can feel her eyes on me. Instead of looking up and confronting her inquisitive eyes, I keep my head down, piling the papers. It only takes a few moments before I feel the weight of her stare and know that I'm avoiding the situation, not her.

"I haven't talked to him much this week," I confess.

"Why?" she asks, sitting down in the seat in front of my desk.

"It's not going to work." Saying those words aloud is almost gut-wrenching.

"I know how you feel," she whispers. My eyes fly to her. She looks so defeated with her hands twisting together in her lap.

"What's the matter?"

"I don't think I can be friends with Levi anymore," she confesses, her eyes shining with unshed tears.

"Why not? You two have been friends for as long as I can remember."

"I know. He's great, really. But lately, things have been...different."

"Different how?"

"I don't know, really." She's quiet for several moments, and even though I want to press her for more info, I sit back and wait. "He still wants to hang out, but I don't think I can." She averts her eyes. "I...I, well, I like him."

"Duh." The word is out of my mouth before I can rein it in, and if the way she looks at me, full of surprise, she wasn't expecting me to say it either. "Sorry."

"I know you all think I'm in love with him, and well, maybe I am a little, but he's my friend. That's it."

"That doesn't have to be it," I encourage her.

"Yes it does. He's made it very clear that he sees me as a friend and nothing more."

"Things change."

"No they don't. Don't take this the wrong way, but it's a Friday night, you have a boyfriend, and you're choosing to work instead. Even though you have a reason to go home, you're here."

"I'm here because I'm a chicken too." Again, I surprise even myself with my bluntness.

"What do you mean?" she asks.

"Things aren't working out with Dean and I'm hiding out here and working instead of talking to him and just ending it."

"Why do you have to end it?"

I want to tell her, dammit I want to confide in her so bad. "It's complicated."

"Life is complicated. I want my best friend. I'm the poster child for complicated, Pay."

"Touché."

"So tell me about your problem with Dean."

"He's great, Abs. He's caring and doting with his daughter, he's sexy in that geeky way, and he's fabulous in bed. He's picture perfect in the relationship department, and will make some woman very happy in the future."

"But not you?"

"No, not me," I tell her with a sigh. "He's not going to want me."

"Why would he not? I see the way he looks at you. Not to mention how supportive and amazing he was all through the funeral. He went above and beyond the typical boyfriend, Pay. If it wasn't so sweet it would have been nauseating."

"I know. But there's something that I haven't told him. Something that'll change the way he feels about me."

That has her attention. "What's going on?"

And before I realize what's happening, I'm spilling everything. I tell her everything about the demise of my relationship with Cole and the reason it won't work with Dean. When I glance up, I see tears in her eyes and realize they match the ones sliding down my cheeks.

"You've been sitting on this for the last, what, six years? Why wouldn't you tell us about this?"

"I wasn't ready. It's too painful. I had to give up a dream, and I mourned the loss for a while. Honestly, I don't think I've ever really been ready to talk about it."

After our pizza arrives, we eat in silence for a few moments before she speaks again. "You know, I think you're making a mistake with Dean. I think you should tell him and let him be the judge of the state of your future. If he can't handle it, then fine. Walk away. But what if that doesn't matter to him?"

"It matters to everyone."

"You don't know that. You assume, and you know what Grandpa says about assume, right?" I give her *the look* as I wait for the line I already know is coming next. "You make an ass out of you and me."

"Why are you being such a pain in the ass?"

"Because I'm your little sister and that's my job. And you only think I'm a pain because you know I'm right, and you can't stand that because *you're* always right."

"I am always right. I must be rubbing off on you."

We laugh as we finish up our pizza, chatting about her work and making small talk. When I glance up at the clock, I realize it's already almost nine. It always surprises me how fast time can fly when I'm with my sisters.

"I should go."

"Heading home?"

"Yeah. I was invited to The Shed tonight to see Levi play, but I'm not feeling it," she says with a shrug.

"Abs, don't give up on him. I really think that you guys have something special, more than just a friendship. Don't be afraid to explore that side, okay?"

She shrugs casually without committing. "Don't be afraid to tell Dean your secret. Let him decide if it's too much for him or not, okay?"

I can't help but grin back at her. "You're still a pain in my ass."

"Ditto, big sister. D-i-t-t-o."

"I love you," I tell her as I pull her into a big hug.

"I love you too. I'll talk to you soon," she says before slipping out the back door. I watch as she walks to her car and heads out of the lot.

Knowing that my night is complete, that no work will be finished now, I flip off the lights and grab my stuff. I don't even take home the folder with tomorrow's order forms; I'm pretty sure I won't get to them later either. Right now, all I want is my couch, comfy jammies, and a bottle of something hard.

Making sure all of the doors are secure, I head to my own car and climb inside. My phone vibrates in my purse, but I leave it there until I get home. Needing to concentrate on driving and not on the pending conversation I'm going to have with Dean, I forgo the phone and head home.

It's been a long, exhausting, and emotional day, and the booze is calling.

Dean

She's still not picking up.

I know she said she had tons of work to catch up on during the last few weeks, but I can tell something is different. She's pulling away from me, and there's not a damn thing I can do about it. Hell, I can't even get her to answer her phone. The only thing I can think of now is to just show up at her door and wait until she speaks to me. Payton's stubborn and feisty on top of being gorgeous and loyal.

I can imagine that going over well.

But that doesn't stop me from driving to her flower shop on Saturday morning. Even after she texted me last night after nine and said she just got home and was exhausted from her day and yada, yada, yada. I can feel the coolness that has settled between us.

And I don't like it.

Not one fucking bit.

Bri is dying to see the flower shop and has not stopped asking questions since we got in the car to come here. Now, pulling up in front of the building and getting out of the car, I'm not so sure this is the best approach. If she hasn't wanted to spend time with me before, showing up at her place of business, with my daughter in tow as some sort of buffer, probably isn't going to go over well either.

Oh, well. There's no turning back now. Bri is already at the door, pulling with all of her might, so I jump into action and help her get it the rest of the way open. As soon as I step over the threshold, I'm instantly assaulted with the scent of fresh flowers. Roses, daisies, hydrangeas, and more, every color under the sun. Not to mention the potted plants and other gifty items like vases and figurines.

I feel bad for not taking it all in the last time I was here, but the last time I kinda only had one thing in mind, and that was relieving the ache in my pants. We didn't even make it past her workspace. The lights were off so no one could see, but I took her three ways to Sunday on top of that steel table. My balls start to ache as the memory starts to play out. Well, until I hear my daughter yell out that one word that makes my heart beat faster in my chest. "Payton!"

She comes out of the back room, a hesitant smile on her face. But as soon as her eyes land on Bri, the smile is wide and genuine. My daughter launches herself across the shop and straight into her arms. Again with the damn heartbeat thing.

"What are you guys doing here?" she asks Brielle and then glances over at me. Her smile is still real, but I see worry. Something has happened to my spirited girl, and I need to know what. I can't fix it until I get to the bottom of this.

"We came to see you! I want to see some flowers," Bri instructs.

"Rachel, can you watch everything? I'm going to give this little lady a tour of the shop," Payton says to the younger woman at the counter.

"Come over here," she says to Bri, putting her down and taking her hand. "This is one of my favorite parts of the shop."

I follow as she leads Bri towards the glass case filled with bright arrangements. "When I first opened the shop, I would come over here and just stare at all the vibrant colors and smell all the gloriously fragrant scents. If the day was particularly stressful, which a lot of them were in the beginning, I would come over here and play with some of the blooms. It always seemed to ground me."

"Pretty."

"Yes, they are."

"Which one is your favorite?" I ask.

She offers me a warm smile. "That would be like asking me to choose a favorite child."

"I like this one," Bri says, pointing to an arrangement in the front.

"Oh, me too! If I was forced to pick a flower, I would probably pick those. They're called forget-me-nots, and most of the time we see them in this pretty blue. But I grow them at my house during the summer and my favorite is these pink ones. I had some brought in earlier this week for a special order. These are the majority of what's left."

"I want to see more!"

Payton crouches down in front of Bri. "I have a better idea. How about we make you your own bouquet that you can take home with you?"

"Really?"

"Absolutely. You can help me pick the flowers and everything."

"Yay! Daddy, I'm gonna work at the flower shop with Payton!"

"Sounds like fun, princess."

Again, I follow behind as Payton leads Bri to the back room. Together, they pick out a vase, which isn't surprising at all to be a deep purple color. Then, they head into a walk-in cooler where my daughter picks out bloom after bloom of bright purple, pink, and yellow.

Payton explains the process as she starts snipping the ends off the flowers, compiling them into groups by length. Bri is hanging on every word she says, nodding her head every so often in understanding. Then, they get to work.

I stand off to the side so that I don't interrupt them. Payton explains how she's using the blooms with longer stems for the center and works her way out with the shorter ones. The colors are a mix, but seem to make my daughter happy as she helps arrange them in the vase. When the flowers are in position, they walk over to the sink and add water. Then to finish off the project, Bri chooses a polka dot white and pink ribbon for the bow. Even though Payton makes it, she takes her time, explaining each twist and loop of the ribbon. When it's completed, Bri places it around the lip of the vase and Payton ties it into place.

It's complete.

And so is my heart.

When Payton glances up at me, there's a moment of pure joy and excitement radiating from her. Unfortunately, it's quickly squashed when something else takes over her features. Not wanting to lose what we've been slowly building, I head over to where she's standing.

"That was amazing. Bri will never forget it."

"It was fun. I enjoyed getting to show her this side of my passion."

"You love your work. It's evident in how you spoke about it and how detailed you were in your teaching."

"I do love it." She nods and gazes fondly back over to her little helper.

"Thank you," I say without hesitation.

She looks back over at me, confusion written on her face. "For what?"

"For spending time with her, for teaching her something I couldn't, for loving her." I take a stab in the dark that my comment will hit its mark. I know she loves my daughter, I see it in the way she interacts with her. I just don't know if she's ready to acknowledge it. She's so gun shy when it comes to relationships, and even though one with my daughter is on a different scale, it's still a big step for her.

"That's easy to do," she whispers. I don't miss the tears filling her eyes. "She's a very special, amazing, lovable little girl."

"She is. I don't know how I got so lucky."

"She's you." Her words hit me like a sledgehammer, right in the chest. My love for her is boiling over and I want to say it. Hell, I want to scream it! I want to tell her that she's it for me, *the one*.

"Daddy, can Payton come have dinner with us?" she asks, moving her floral arrangement from the table to the front counter.

"I'm not sure, honey. Why are you taking your flowers up front?" I ask, following her through the doorway.

"So dat the other people can see how pretty they are. Payton says flowers make you smile and I want to make everyone smile."

Pride spreads through my chest. It's warm and familiar and something I've experienced several times over the course of this life journey as a father. "Those will make everyone smile, I'm sure."

"Do you wanna have mac and cheese with us, Payton? Daddy is gonna take me to dinner and I get mac and cheese."

"No, you don't get mac and cheese. If we're going to a restaurant, you have to pick something you don't eat almost daily at home."

"Daddy," she groans, clearly unhappy with my rebuttal. "Payton, can you come to dinner wiff us?"

"Oh, I'm not sure, sweetie." I can tell she's trying to figure out how to get out of it.

"Puh-lease? I promise to eat all my dinner. And I'll get something besides mac and cheese."

She smiles down at the little brunette giving her the big doe eyes in front of her. Her resolve is clearly cracking and crumbling around her. "I might be able to have dinner tonight," she concedes with a small smile.

"Don't feel obligated," I say, feeling a little annoyed. "If you have other plans, that's fine."

"No," she defends quickly. "I don't have other plans."

I give her a few moments to change her mind or back out, but it doesn't come. I give her a quick nod. "We'll pick you up at six, if that works for you."

"That's fine. I'll be ready."

"Yay!" Payton exclaims.

"We should get out of your hair," I finally say, nodding towards the customer that Rachel is helping over by the fresh flower bouquet case. "How much do I owe you?"

"For what?" she asks.

"The flowers. I didn't bring her here for you to give her flowers. I can pay for them."

"I could never take your money. Those are for Bri."

We stare at each other for a few tense seconds.

"Thank you," I finally concede.

"I'm glad you stopped in." Her words are quiet, almost a confession that she's trying to wrap her head around.

"We'll see you tonight?"

"Yes."

"Come on, Bri. It's time to let Payton work. The shop is gonna be closing soon."

My daughter groans, but doesn't complain too much. Instead, she goes over and gives Payton a big hug. "Can I come work with you someday? I can help make the pretty flowers."

"I would love that," Payton replies with a smile.

As I steer my child towards the door, Payton calls out behind us. "Here. Don't forget your flowers," she says, passing the pink and purple bouquet to my daughter."

"I can take them home?"

"Of course you can. I want you to put them on your table so you can see them every day."

"And smile every day," she adds with a brightly toothy grin.

"Yes. Every day because you have a gorgeous smile that lights up the room," Payton says with a wink and a smile.

Bri giggles. "My smile isn't a light bulb, Payton."

They hug once more before I finally drag my daughter out of the shop. Payton's going to dinner with us tonight, which makes me happy, even if Bri had to coax her into it. It's a step, even if the smallest of baby steps. At least we're not heading backwards, right?

For now, I'll just hang out and wait until tonight. There are some things we need to talk about and I'm hoping we'll get those cleared up this evening. I'm a patient man, but when it comes to Payton, I find myself running out of tolerance. I want her. Plain and simple.

Now it's time to make it reality.

She's quiet as we walk into the café, but only because she's unable to get a word in edge-wise. Bri has been talking non-stop since we picked Payton up ten minutes ago. Glancing around, I spy an open booth in the corner, but before I can lead the girls towards the space, our attention is pulled in the opposite direction.

"Yoohoo! Payton! Come sit with us," I hear over my shoulder. When I turn, I spy her grandma and grandpa, as well as one of the twins.

"We don't have to sit with them, but let's at least say hi."

"We can sit with them," I respond as we walk in their direction, my hand finding a comfortable spot on her lower back.

"We don't have to," she whispers as we approach the table.

Before I can reply, Brielle slides into the chair beside Emma, who is helping her take her jacket off. "I guess the decision is already made," Payton whispers again.

"I don't mind," I say, grabbing an extra chair from a nearby table so that we have enough seats. It's a tight fit, but all six of us make it work.

"Dean, it's so good to see you again. I'll give you a hug when we're done eating," Emma says as she magically pulls crayons out of her purse.

"You just want to grab his ass," the twin says, letting me know it's Lexi and not Abby.

"That's just a bonus. I like hugging," Emma says brightly.

"Oh, she's a very good...hugger," Orval adds with a mischievous grin on his face. I'm pretty sure we're no longer talking about the same thing.

"Yes, I do enjoy our...hugs," Emma coos with a wink.

"Anyway," Payton interrupts, doing her best to steer the conversation away from the inappropriate direction it was clearly heading.

"I like hugs!" Bri adds. "Daddy hugs me good, but Payton's hugs are the best."

My throat closes as I look across the table at my daughter. She's casually coloring, not even remotely aware that her simple words caused cardiac arrest on her dear ol' dad.

"Payton learned to give hugs from the master. Isn't that right, Dean?" Grandma asks with another wink. Again, I'm pretty sure we're not talking about the same type of hugs.

"Uh, okay. Although I'm starting to wonder if there is a right or wrong answer to that question."

"Grandma, leave him alone. We don't need to discuss my abilities to hug at the dinner table."

"Oh, Payters. It's always the right time to talk about hugging! And what better time than at the dinner table with family." Emma has an ornery glean in her aged eyes.

"No, you should never talk about hugging at the dinner table, nor with family, especially your grandparents," Lexi says, a horrified look on her face.

"Are we back to that again? Must I explain to you how hugging is a natural part of life? I thought we went over this when you girls were younger."

"Yes, we did. I'm pretty sure I was the only person who learned about the birds and the bees from her grandma who brought multimedia resources to help during show and tell," Payton chides.

"Show and tell?" I whisper, leaning in to her side.

"*Penthouse* and *Playboy* magazines. Plus, she left Grandpa's copy of some cheesy 1970's disco porno and told me to knock myself out."

"That was educational," Emma defends.

"It was not. It was disgusting and vulgar. Not to mention the fact that I was never able to look at a roller skating rink the same."

"That was my favorite scene," Orval says with a fond grin. "This girl was bent over, her rump in the air, while her partner held on to her hips for leverage, all while skating around the rink. It was a true test of her flexibility and his stamina. I could never get my Emma to reenact that scene with me."

"Please stop," Payton and Lexi both beg at the same time.

"I want to skate! I'll go skating with you!" Bri exclaims innocently, making me choke on the ice tea the waitress just delivered.

"Yes! Let's go skating. Orval, let's plan to take Miss Brielle skating soon."

"You guys can't go skating. You'll break your hips," Payton cries, outraged at their carefree, blasé outlook on something as dangerous as roller skating.

"We'll be fine. If we were at risk of breaking a hip, it would have happened by now. Your grandfather is a fan of my nimbleness."

"Jesus, kill me now. Are you sure you don't want to get our own table?" Payton mumbles.

"Can I go with you?" Lexi asks.

Fortunately, the rest of dinner progresses without any more talk about sex. Bri ordered the chicken fingers and ate all but one. Plus, she had some peaches and a bunch of Payton's fries. Considering it wasn't mac and cheese, I was happy with her meal choice. Payton seemed to relax through dinner, offering me a few genuine smiles as she shared stories of her childhood and the antics of her and her sisters.

When dinner is done and dessert nothing but empty plates and bowls, we get up to leave. I try to pay for our dinners, but Orval won't hear of it. He wouldn't even accept cash to put towards the bill or the tip.

"Thank you for dinner," I tell them as we all stand up and gather jackets.

"It was my pleasure. I'm glad we ran into you," Orval says, sticking his hand out for me to shake.

"I'm sure we'll see you and Brielle again very soon. We have dinner together every few weeks, so I'll be sure Payton mentions it to you when we plan the next gathering," Emma adds as she steps in and wraps her arms around my waist.

Glancing over at Payton, her eyes are sad again, which tells me there's a good chance I won't actually be invited to the next family dinner. "Thank you for the invite, Emma," I reply, not really knowing what else to say.

Suddenly, her frail arms tighten around my waist and I feel hands grip my ass. This little sprite of a woman has two handfuls of my ass and a broad smile across her face. "Oh, Dean, the pleasure is all mine."

"Grandma, let go of my man's ass," Payton chastises from behind. Lexi dies laughing when she finally lets go, but not without a quick squeeze for good measure.

"What can I say, she's an ass man," Orval whispers as he leads his wife towards the door.

"Keep your wife under control," Payton reprimands.

"There's no controlling her, my dear. She's as wild as the wind."

"And you love it," Grandma adds before he leads her out the door. "Come on, Lex. We'll take you back home."

"I'm wishing I had driven myself," Lexi whispers as she crosses in front of us and follows behind her grandparents.

After final goodbyes and promises to take Bri roller skating, they head off to their car parked on the side of the street. I go to take my daughter's hand, but find she's already in Payton's arms. They're ahead of me now, walking towards my car, discussing the upcoming trip to the skating rink.

I'll be honest, I'm confused. She has been pushing me away for the last few weeks, but calls me her man in front of her family. She's planning a trip with my daughter, but makes me wonder if she'll actually be around long enough to go on said trip. I'm confused as hell, and there's only one way to find out what's going on.

Or one person who can explain it to me.

We get in my car and pull out, but I have no intention of heading towards Payton's house. We're talking tonight, and I've got my daughter. Therefore, the only way to achieve this is to head to my house.

"Where are we going?" Payton asks from the passenger seat as I pass her street and head towards mine.

"My place."

"Why?"

"I have to get Bri home and in bed, and I think we need to talk." I glance over and see her staring at me. Her throat bobs as she swallows, but gives me a quick nod.

"You could have dropped me off so I could get my car."

"True," I concede, keeping my eyes on the road, "but this way you can't sneak out without me knowing." I offer her a quick smile and a wink, but honestly, it's the truth. I hide my smirk knowing that she won't be able to leave without a ride back to her place, and therefore, will be forced to stay with me. All night. All weekend. Forever.

Yeah, let's go with that.

Back at my place, I'm second fiddle as Bri asks Payton to help her with her bath and get ready for bed. If she was uncomfortable with helping my daughter with her nightly routine, she didn't show it. In fact, it was as natural as if it were an actual mother/daughter relationship. Again, my heart pounds in my chest.

I read a book, followed by one from Payton. Even though there's a bit of begging and pleading, we finally get Bri into bed and the lights off. She gives dozens of hugs and kisses to each of us, asking tons of questions and trying to prolong bedtime as long as humanly possible. You gotta give her props for trying, right?

Finally, Payton and I are alone in the living room. "Would you like something to drink?"

"Just water," she says quietly after taking a seat on the couch.

Heading into the kitchen gives me a few minutes to get my thoughts together. I know we need to talk, but there's a nagging fear inside of me that reminds me that this could be the last time she's sitting on my couch after putting my daughter to bed. After a few calming, cleansing breaths, I head back into the living room with two glasses of water.

"Thank you." Our fingers touch as she grabs the glass, causing those pesky, familiar lightning bolts of lust to strike my cock. Apparently, the wayward appendage doesn't care that we're about to break-up.

I take a seat across from the couch on the loveseat. As much as I'd love to sit beside her and pull her into my arms, I need to keep my head about myself, and therefore, keep my hands off her. We stare at each other, neither of us really knowing what to say. She looks sad and resolved, her green eyes dim.

"How have you been? I haven't seen you much lately," I start.

"Okay. I've spent some time with Meghan. She wants to move, says it's too hard to stay in the house that they just got, but then when she picks up the paper to actually look for something, she feels guilty and cries herself to sleep."

"I couldn't imagine. It must be very hard for her. And you."

"It's the worst. I want to help, to make it all better, but I can't. I think that's the worst of it all. I've always been the one to make it all better, you know? As the oldest, they've come to me with everything from boy troubles to homework help. But this? I can't fix this."

"No, you can't."

We're both quiet again. She stares down at her water, turning the glass in her hand as if it were the most interesting glass of water in the world.

"There are other things I can't fix either," she finally whispers. When her eyes find mine, they have tears in them. Tears that practically reach into my chest and squeeze my heart.

"What kinda things?"

Silence again. I can tell she's gathering the courage she needs to say her piece.

"Do you remember when I told you there were things I wasn't ready to tell you?" Her voice is shaky, but she's trying so hard to be brave. She squares her shoulders and looks me in the eyes. Instead of answering her question, I nod.

"Well, there's something I've known for some time now, and I'm not sure I've ever really dealt with it."

"Okay," I encourage.

"Can I ask you something first?" Again, I nod. "Do you want more kids?"

Her question throws me. It's definitely not what I expected her to ask, that's for sure. But she's nervously awaiting my answer, so I give it to her. "Honestly, I've never really thought much about it? I mean, when I found out about Brielle, it was a bit of a surprise. She wasn't planned, but that doesn't mean I wouldn't change it for anything.

"I guess the best way to answer the question is to say maybe. If the right woman came along, and she wanted kids, then yes. Would I be upset having more? Hell no. Brielle was a dream, even though it was tough parenting by myself. But if I didn't have more, I'd be just fine."

"What if you couldn't have more?" she asks, her voice barely above a whisper.

"What do you mean? Me personally or me as in me and the woman I love?" It seems so easy to say the words, even though I haven't actually said them to her yet.

"You and the woman you...love." She looks pained to repeat my words.

"Well, if it couldn't happen, I guess then the decision is made for us, right?"

"What if you wanted them and the woman you loved wanted them, but she couldn't have them?" The tears start to fall, and I'm unable to stay seated any longer. She looks so defeated, so dejected, and so fucking heartbroken.

"Tell me," I whisper as I wrap my arms around her and pull her into my lap. Her hands shake as she grips my shirt, clinging to me for strength.

"I can't have kids. I was diagnosed with PCOS when I was in my early twenties." I try to wipe the tears from her cheeks, but more fall just as quickly.

"What's PCOS?"

She pulls back, her hands still locked on the front of my shirt. Swallowing hard, she tells me. "It stands for polycystic ovary syndrome. I have irregular periods, which causes abnormal ovarian function, or so the doctor said. Basically, I don't ovulate right. Because of this, the chances of me actually getting pregnant on my own are slim to none."

"On your own?"

"Well, there are injections of drugs that could help, but it's not guaranteed. There's also IVF, but I'd have to go to a bigger city for that. It's not offered in Jupiter Bay, not to mention that it's not covered by insurance. Plus, there's the fact that I'm approaching thirty-five which is practically a death sentence for women with PCOS and their ability to conceive on their own."

She continues to cry, and I finally see it. She's not just saddened by the news, she's mourning her ability to have kids. My beautiful, strong Payton has been sitting on this piece of information for years, and if I had to guess, hasn't shared it with anyone. She has let it continue to eat away at her until she was drowning in it. That thought breaks my damn heart.

"Does this PCOS thing affect anything else?"

"Well, it can cause hormonal issues, things like facial hair or hair in other gross places, stuff like that. And cysts on my ovaries and uterus, but the ones I've had thus far haven't been much of an issue."

"Okay," I say, taking in everything she's told me. "So your big hang-up is…" I leave it open-ended, so she can clarify and just say the words she needs to say.

"I can't have kids!" she proclaims, louder than I think she realizes. "And who wants to be with a woman who can't give him an heir?" Again, the tears start to fall ripping at my heart.

"So this is why you've distanced yourself from me? This is why you didn't want to get close to me or anyone else? You think I won't want to be with you because you can't provide me with an heir?"

"Of course I think that! Cole didn't want to be with me, so why would anyone else?"

My blood runs cold. "What?"

Taking a deep breath, she tells me about her ex. "Cole and I had dated for a while. I had always had irregular periods, and when I mentioned it to my doctor, he wanted to do a pelvic exam and scheduled an ultrasound and some blood work. After, he explained what he found and told me it would be very difficult, if not impossible for me to get pregnant. Okay, he didn't say impossible, because even with PCOS, there is a rare chance, but it was basically like being told I'd never have kids.

"I was really upset when I found out. I mean, I had always wanted kids. I saw myself as a mother, you know? When my doctor told me that, it felt like it was stripped away from me. I was devastated. Cole was upset, too. He wanted kids. Hell, we'd talked about it, but after everything was said and done, there was nothing left for him with me."

"That's bullshit," I tell her with a vengeance I wasn't expecting. "That's complete, utter, unacceptable bullshit."

She looks at me with shock in her gorgeous green eyes, but I'm not going to stop now.

She needs to hear what I have to say.

Payton

"What?" I ask. Well, choke out is more like it.

"That's bullshit." He turns me in his lap so that I'm practically facing him. "There is so much more to you than your ability to have a baby, Payton. You are the most loving, fiercely loyal, gorgeous woman I've ever known. You've proven how smart you are by successfully running your own business. You've shown me more patience and love when you interact with my daughter than anyone else who is around her. The fact that you may not be able to have a baby has nothing to do with you as a woman. You're still an incredible person."

I try to swallow, but it gets caught in the golf ball lodged in my throat.

"Do you hear me?" he asks. Something warm and comforting wraps around me as he slides his hands up the sides of my face and into my hair. His grip tightens, not enough to hurt, but enough to let me know that he's here, beside me, with me. If I weren't able to feel it in his touch, I can see it plain as day in his eyes.

"I hear you," I whisper, sniffling and probably looking all gross and shit.

"If you were, someday, able to give me a baby, it would make me the happiest man alive. But do you know what? That doesn't define you. That doesn't define us. The truth is, I love you, with or without a baby in our future."

There's no controlling the stream of emotions falling down my face. Closing my eyes, I hold tightly to his words, reliving them each time he repeats them. And he does. He tells me over and over that he loves me as he pulls me against his lips and claims mine with his own.

My heart breaks wide open, a new euphoria that I've never known filling my entire being. His lips are soft but urgent, his tongue coaxing my mouth open. The kiss is so much more than a kiss. It's a declaration.

Gripping the front of his shirt again, I let myself get swept away by the moment. He tilts my head slightly, lining himself up perfectly to deepen the kiss. I finally feel myself letting go of everything: the past, the questions of the future, everything. It's just him and me, together.

Well, us and an adorable little girl who will forever hold my heart.

Eventually, when we're both breathless and delirious, he slowly pulls back, licking and nipping at my swollen lips. "Let's take a moment to recap, shall we?" Kiss. "You might not be able to have a baby." Kiss. "You were going to break-up with me tonight so that you could spare me the agony of saddling myself to a baby-less life with you." Kiss. "I'm in love with you, so all of that doesn't fucking matter." Kiss. "Because." Kiss. "I." Kiss. "Love." Kiss. "You."

Best. Kiss. Ever.

"I'm not letting you end this, Payton. I don't know where this is going to end up, but I know where I hope it'll go. I knew the first time you walked into my conference room that you were different. So I plan to spend the rest of my life proving to you that you can be happy and that I can be happy, even without a baby. Because, as long as I have you, I'm happy."

"You love me?" I ask, pleading with him to confirm once more what I already know.

"I do. I fell in love with you when we were in Richmond, sharing a hotel room."

Closing my eyes, I savor the words. Sure, my sisters say it, my dad says it, and my grandparents say it. But hearing Dean tell me he loves me? Trumps everything. Cole used to tell me all the time, but over the years, it became more out of routine and with less feeling. Now that I look back, it got to the point where neither of us really said it at all in the end.

"Do you know what?" I ask, wrapping my arms around his neck.

"What?" he whispers, his breath fanning across my chin.

"That actually works out really well for me because I love you too."

His eyes light up with excitement as he offers me the biggest grin ever. "Yeah?"

"Oh yeah. I'm pretty sure I started to fall for you in Richmond too," I confirm.

"Those were two amazing nights." He pulls me in and nuzzles my nose.

"I loved waking up beside you in the morning."

"I loved falling asleep with you in my arms."

"No interruptions."

"No time restraints."

"Just you and me and a whole lot of nakedness."

"Those were my kinda nights."

"What about tonight?" I ask, hopeful and eager.

"You notice your lack of a car, right? Well, I'm not taking you home. The only place you're going is to my bed. Preferably without any clothes covering up this sinful body."

With his hands sliding up my side and resting on my breasts, his lips find mine once more. This kiss has a little more passion, a little more intensity. As if I weigh nothing, Dean picks me up and moves me towards the hallway. Without breaking the kiss, he leads me into his bedroom and only stops when I feel his bed hit behind my knees.

"Just so you know, I expect you to be in my bed as much as humanly possible. I know you have your own place, but I like it better when you're beside me."

"I like that too." Gazing up at him, I grip his shirt and lift it over his head. He doesn't move as I run my hands up his chest, feeling the way the light dusting of hair tickles my palms. "Dean?"

"Yeah, babe?"

"I'm sorry about how I've acted lately. I was going to tell you everything tonight about the PCOS. I actually told Abby the other night, and it helped. She was very understanding and listened, asking questions when she felt the need. But she's also the one who told me to tell you the truth and let you decide for yourself if a future with me was possible or not."

"Smart woman. I should send her flowers. I know this great little shop."

"She is, yes, but I would probably avoid sending another woman flowers. Especially ones you purchase from your current woman's shop." I give him a slight grin before sobering a little. "I was planning on breaking it off with you. I knew I was falling in love with you and knew it would be too hard to deal with you leaving when you found out about the PCOS."

"You thought that I'd walk away when I found out about it, so it would be easier for you to do that now on your own terms." It wasn't a question, but a statement. Even after only knowing each other for a short time, less than a year on the calendar, and he already has me pegged.

"Yeah. I'm sorry."

Reaching down, he grabs a hold of the hem of my shirt and gives it a lift. Without saying a word, he reaches around and unsnaps my bra clasp. With my breasts free, he palms them both and eagerly sucks one nipple into his warm mouth. I gasp at the instant flood of sensations racing through my body. My core is immediately wet and throbbing with desire.

"Silly, silly, Payton. Haven't you figured it out yet? There's no getting rid of me now. You were made for me," he says before latching on to the other nipple and giving it equal attention.

"Please," I beg, reaching for his belt buckle.

"I love it when you beg," he quips, a wicked gleam in his dark eyes.

"I can tell," I reply, palming his large erection. His hips flex into my hand as he grinds against me.

"Keep that up and we won't be able to get to the good stuff."

"I like the good stuff," I murmur, stroking him through the denim.

"And I love you." His whispered words are a statement, the punctuation, and everything in between.

Together, we strip off the rest of our clothes, taking our time and savoring the feel of each other's bodies. When we're finally skin-on-skin, Dean leads me back to the bed. His eyes are intense and dark with desire as he covers my body with his own. We're both flushed to the core, his lips soft and gentle as he glides them over my neck.

"Do you trust me?" he whispers against the place my pulse is pounding.

"Yes."

Pulling away just slightly so he can look down at me, he says, "No more condoms. You know we're both clean. I want to feel your body wrapped around me, feel your pussy gripping my bare cock again."

A shiver races through my body. "No more condoms," I confirm.

His lips have a little more urgency in them, as he lifts my left leg and hitches it high on his hip. He explores my mouth with his tongue as I feel him slowly pushing forward and sliding into my pussy. Gasping, I open my eyes and find his locked on me. It's always amazing with Dean, but this time there's something else there.

Love.

When he's buried to the root, he groans. "God, you feel so fucking good." He holds perfectly still as if savoring the feel of our bodies joined together.

"Mmmmm," I purr, blood zinging through my body.

And then he moves. Pinning my hands over my head, he uses them for leverage as he thrusts into me. He's completely relentless, raw with desire, as he pushes us both higher and higher. Together, we're climbing towards a blockbuster orgasm, one that will change us forever. Because there will no longer be a Dean and a Payton. We will be one. One heart beating together, one soul sharing a future.

I know it.

I can feel it.

When I'm unable to hold off the pending orgasm any longer, I give in to the rush of sensations. The way his chest hairs tickle my nipples. The way he holds me down as if staking an ownership in my pleasure. The way his pelvic bone grinds against my clit, creating the most epic flood of desire.

My orgasm washes over me, sending me flying and soaring above the clouds. Dean is right there with me. He tenses above me, thrusting with more force than ever before, as my internal muscles grip him with everything they have. A loud groan slips from his lips, and it's immediately followed up with my name.

As he starts to still above me, his lips find mine once more. Our labored breath is mixed as we pant and kiss, shutters and aftershocks racing jointly through our bodies. He keeps touching me, as if he can't get enough. Eventually, he starts to peter out, no pun intended, and lies on top of me. The heaviness of his weight doesn't feel restricting, as I would have usually thought, but instead feels comforting and grounding.

"Wow," he says, nuzzling his nose against my ear.

"Yeah," I pant, loving the feel of his body against mine. "Let's do it again."

Dean laughs in my ear, making me smile widely. "I'm not the spring chicken I used to be, sweetheart. Give me a few more minutes to collect my thoughts and I'll be ready to go again."

He carefully rolls off me, leaving a trail of warmth and wetness behind. That's definitely something you don't think about when you're used to using condoms. Without a word, he jumps up and goes to the bathroom. I take a moment to ogle his muscular backside as he walks into the room and flips on the light. He doesn't cover up or hide, just grabs a washcloth and wets it with warm water. After taking care of himself, he rinses it well and comes back into the bedroom. Again, he doesn't say a word as he washes off my thighs and between my legs.

"Why are you smiling?" he asks as he tosses the cloth into his hamper and climbs back into bed.

"I've never had someone do that before."

"What? Take care of you?" He turns on his side and scoots against my back, spooning me against his body.

"Well, yeah."

"Get used to it, sweetheart. I know you don't want someone to step in and take control, and I have absolutely no intention of doing that. I just want to help share the burden. My job is to help shoulder some of the weight when things get too heavy for you to carry, okay?"

"Okay." What else can I say?

He gets me.

I find myself dozing off to sleep, feeling better and lighter than I ever have in my life. Even though our family is dealing with a great loss, I find myself happy. Dean has done that. He has offered me something I never thought I'd have.

Hope.

"I love you," he whispers, his voice gravelly with sleep.

"I love you," I reply as he places a kiss on my shoulder.

Together, we fall asleep.

Dean

26

THREE MONTHS LATER

It's a beautiful May day. The sun is shining brightly in the sky, and the entire Summer family is gathered in the back yard of Brian's home. I've come to really enjoy spending time with Payton's entire family, but none more so than her father. As a boy who was raised without one, it's an indulgence I find myself enjoying as much as possible.

In fact, he invited my mom along on this gorgeous Sunday afternoon cookout. Mom has taken to Payton like a fish to water. They've done shopping trips with Bri and lunches whenever they can squeeze them in. It's heartwarming to see, especially since Payton lost her mother as a teenager.

"Daddy, watch!" Brielle exclaims as she swings the little plastic bat and hits the little wiffleball on her first attempt.

She runs towards the makeshift first base, where Lexi is waiting. Bri fakes left and runs right. Lexi pretends to be caught off guard and lets my daughter make it safely on base.

Ryan comes over with two beers and sits in the folding chair beside me. "You should be thankful they let Brielle play. They're usually very competitive. So much so that I hate playing sports with them," he says with laugh. "But since Brielle begged and with Meghan still not herself, they're bending their rules a little bit."

"Yeah, even with my five-year-old out there, I'm glad I'm not playing."

"Yeah, most of them cheat," he adds, holding out his beer bottle for me to clink.

"You're not telling me anything I don't know. Payton is horrible at Uno."

"Cheaters. All of them. That is their grandma's fault. She's a sneaky little woman, but I love the stuffin' out of her," Grandpa says, taking a seat on the other side of Ryan. Then he leans in and whispers conspiratorially, "Plus, she's dynamite in the sack." And then to add to my mortification as I choke on the beer I just took a swallow of, he adds a wink. Glancing over, we find Emma with her head close to my mom's. Why does that worry me?

Before long, Levi joins the party, dropping something off at the food table before grabbing a beer and heading our way. "Hey, man," Levi says as he pulls up a chair beside me.

"Working?" I ask the young man I've met only a handful of times. I know he's Abby's best friend, but according to Payton, there's something else going on there. Even if neither of them acknowledges it.

"Yeah, last night. I caught five hours of sleep before heading over," he says through a yawn. Levi's a fireman and EMT, but spends a lot of his free weekends playing guitar for a popular local band.

"Come on, Levi! Abby's team is behind. She needs your strong, fine ass to knock one out of the park," Lexi exclaims from the outfield.

Glancing over, Abby's face flames bright red as she stands at the plate with the bat. Levi stands up, and even from my position off to the side behind him, I can tell his eyes are on the youngest Summer daughter. There's almost this poetic, erotic exchange that happens when he steps up beside her and takes the bat from her hand. I can feel the sexual tension all the way over here.

Levi steps up to the plate, the tiny little bat so small in his hands. He turns and says something to her that I can't hear, but if I were reading her body language, I'd say it was something of the teasing variety. Abby laughs and takes a step back out of the way. Jaime lets the ball fly and Levi creams it into the field behind the house. Payton and Lexi take off running towards the ball, but Levi is too quick, rounding the bases with his long strides.

When he rounds second, he catches up to my daughter. It's hilarious as he bends down and swoops her up into his arms. Brielle's laughter can be heard all the way to the front lawn, and there's no missing the smile on her face as Levi carries her around third and over home plate. He sets her down and lets her stomp on the floor mat, jumping up and down in victory. AJ and Abby give her high-fives before Levi swoops in and grabs Abby in his arms. He holds her against his chest for a moment, swinging her around, but quickly changes his hold and throws her over his shoulder like you see firemen do in movies. Abby screams for her release, which only earns her a swat on the ass from Levi.

"Those two. One of these days, they're gonna find themselves unable to deny their feelings," Orval says as we all watch the girls tease each other about the last minute victory.

"Agreed," Ryan adds as Jaime walks our way. His eyes are glued to her as she sashays a little extra for his benefit. There's no missing the smile on his face as she struts up and takes a seat in his lap. "Close game," he says, giving Jaime a drink of his beer.

"They cheated. Again."

"You all cheat," Orval adds.

"Grandpa!"

"What? It's true. Remember Candyland when you were kids? I always had to keep one eye on each of you and my own gingerbread man. They always moved."

"I don't know what you're talking about," Jaime mumbles before taking another drink of beer.

"Hey," Payton says as she walks over to me. I pat my leg in invitation. Before she takes a seat, she glances around nervously. My girl still gets a little shy showing affection in front of her family. When she sees Jaime perched on Ryan's leg next to me, she slowly lowers herself onto me.

"Hi. Good game."

"They cheated, as always. They pulled in a ringer from the bullpen."

"Bri seemed to have fun, though."

"She had a blast. She's very competitive. Fits in nicely," she adds with a small smile.

I agree. My daughter fits in beautifully with Payton and her family. And they've all taken to her instantly, including her in everything they can. Bri eats it up like ice cream. She's never had so much doting attention from so many women and men in her life. And that's not including the extra devotion she gets from Payton. Those two are two peas in a pod when they're together, which is often.

Abby and Levi join us as new drinks are passed around. The conversation quickly turns towards the one thing I've learned it always does around this family: sex.

"Ryan, how's the pussy treating you?" Orval asks with a straight face. Unfortunately, for poor Ryan, who was taking a drink of beer, he wasn't quite so lucky.

"Excuse me?" he stutters, his jaw practically dragging on the lawn.

"The pussy. Last I heard, she was tearing you up."

"The cat," Jaime whispers loudly through laughter and tears.

"Oh, yeah. That pussy. She's...great." The sarcasm rolls off Ryan in waves.

"Boots still doesn't like Ryan much," Jaime says, running her hand across his chest. "She gets mad when he touches me."

"She bites me."

"Yes, she bites him a little, but she's just so cute," Jaime coos.

"And how's the pussy for you, Dean?" Orval asks, catching me off guard.

"Ummm, I don't have a cat, sir."

Everyone looks between Orval and me when he smiles widely and says, "I know."

I walked right into that one, didn't I? The entire group bursts into laughter, and even though it might be at my expense, I join in. When the laughter dies down, he glances back over to me, one eyebrow raised as if waiting for my answer. "It's...great, sir."

Orval laughs before turning his attention to Abby and Levi.

"Great?" Payton asks discreetly, the slightest of smiles playing on the corner of her lips.

"Well, what was I supposed to say? That his granddaughter rocks my world almost nightly?"

"Gorgeous, brilliant, and fabulous granddaughter," she corrects.

My laughter draws attention, but I ignore them. "You are correct. You are gorgeous," I start, kissing her bare shoulder. "Brilliant," I add with a kiss to the back of her neck. "And fabulous." This time, I go for the gold, turning her towards me and placing a kiss on those lush, full lips that taste like strawberries and beer.

I'm just starting to coax her mouth open with my tongue, completely oblivious to our surroundings, when a throat clearing interrupts us. "The toy room is available upstairs, you two." Emma is there, a mischievous and flirty little smile splayed across her face.

"I wanna go play in the toy room!" Bri exclaims, walking with Emma.

Before I can say anything, Payton and all of her sisters yell, "No!"

"Is it messy? Is that why I can't go in there? Daddy always makes me pick up all my toys at the end of the day or I can't have my friends over to play." The way everyone is laughing at Bri's sweet innocence, I can tell there's a story here.

"Toy room?" I whisper, inhaling the scent of her shampoo.

"Think Fifty Shades. Not Sesame Street."

"Really?" I ask, pulling away to gauge if she's telling me the truth or not.

"Dead serious."

"Can I see it?"

"No! I don't even want to know what's in there. My *grandparents* use that room, Dean."

"All right, all right." I turn her and tuck her against my chest. Together, we watch as Levi and Abby play with Bri by the swing set. "Maybe we should build our own red room of pain."

She tenses against me and slowly turns her head. "You know about the red room of pain?"

"I've seen the movie."

"Really?"

"And read the book," I confess.

"Shut. Up."

I shrug. "I wanted to see what all the hype was about."

"And?" she asks, eyes wide with excitement.

"Had to jerk off every night for a week while I read it."

The glorious sound of her laughter fills the air. "I'm sure that was a terrible hardship."

"It was. Maybe you can read it to me sometime soon. It could be mutually beneficial to both of us," I tell her, a sly grin on my face.

"I have a feeling it would take us forever to read the book," she quips.

"Probably, but damn, won't it be fun working our way to the end?"

"You're bad," she says, snuggling into my embrace a little deeper.

"Only with you."

"How's work going, Dean?" Emma asks, her eyes twinkling with humor.

"Fine," I reply, clearing my throat.

"Actually, *Grandma*, I've been meaning to talk to you about your little *stunt* you pulled a while ago?"

"Oh? And which stunt might you be referring to?" she asks sweetly. Of course, I notice her use of the term *which*, which tells me she's a regular with the stunts.

"Oh, you know, the one where you added a bunch of zeros to the end of my profit sheet, essentially setting me up for tax fraud." Everyone around us gasps.

Instead of the sheepish, guilty look I would expect to see on Emma's face, I see her eyes gleam with something naughty, her smile one of victory. Shrugging her shoulders, she replies, "It worked, didn't it?"

"What?" Payton and I both say at the same time.

"You two. I knew that hot young man would check everything over before submitting it, and I knew he would call you," she says to Payton.

"So you set us up?"

"Of course I did! My granddaughter was in the market for a good car mechanic, and by God, I found her one," Emma proclaims.

"A what?" Ryan asks, as confused as I am.

"I'm not a mechanic," I say as Payton's face flushes forty shades a pink.

"I'm not so sure about that. Aren't I right, Payters?" Grandma asks. All eyes turn to the woman on my lap, whose eyes are wide and her mouth hanging open.

"You're a sneaky little ol' woman," she finally says when she regains her composure.

"But I was right, wasn't I?"

"How did you know?" Payton asks.

"What in the world are they talking about?" Jaime leans over and asks me.

"No clue," I tell her honestly.

"Grandma knows everything, Payters," she says with a coy little smile. "Everything." They share a look, and even though I have no idea what they're really talking about, understanding and love passes across their faces.

"Yeah," Payton whispers sweetly.

"Everything," Emma says loudly. "I even know about Lexi's motorcycle ride, Abby's trip to the preacher's house, AJ's extra innings in the dugout, Meghan sneaking in through the bathroom window when I locked her out of the house, and Jaime's stargazing down by the Bay."

Gasps are heard from all directions, as the girls' eyes all bounce from person to person. Shock is written all over their faces, as Grandma just grins and gazes down lovingly at my daughter beside her.

"What is she talking about? What stargazing?" Ryan asks.

"We'll discuss it later," Jaime mutters, glaring back at the elder woman.

I'm sure they will. By the way all of the girls are casting their eyes downward, I imagine those instances are probably pretty juicy. And Grandma with juicy details probably isn't the best situation for all involved.

Catching movement out of the corner of my eye, I glance over and see Meghan arriving to the gathering. Even though we've all been here for three hours, she's just now getting here.

"She went back to work this week," Jaime says, still sitting on Ryan's lap beside us.

"Dr. Adams has been wonderful through this whole ordeal," Abby adds.

Everyone watches Meghan, trying their best not to be noticed, as she busies herself at the food table, getting things ready to go once Brian takes the burgers off the grill. The sisters all glance at each other, their worry and heartbreak written all over their faces.

I found out from Payton that Meghan works as a dental assistant at a small practice in town. Dr. Adams gave her as much time off as she needed after Josh's death, and has been very supportive and sensitive to her situation. She took just over three months off, and according to Payton, is bored at home and tired of staring at the walls. She's still in the house that she and Josh rented before he passed away, and I'm not sure she'll ever be ready to relocate.

Time will tell.

At the end of the evening, Payton, Bri, and I set out to head home. Those that are left at the gathering all give hugs, and before we can make it to my car, Grandma Emma stops me.

"Here," she says, stuffing a white gift bag into my hands.

"What's this?" I ask, moving the tissue paper aside.

"Not yet," she chastises, smacking my hand. "Wait until you get home and can open it with Payters. Alone," she adds with a wink.

Why am I afraid of this gift bag?

Before I can turn away, I'm engulfed in a bear hug from a pint sized little ol' lady. She's freakishly strong. And in true Emma fashion, it's only a few seconds later when I feel her hand on my ass. She gives it a quick little squeeze before releasing me. I get another wink before she walks over to Payton to say goodbye.

Not giving it anymore thought, I help Bri get loaded into my car and head towards my place. There are not many cars on the road, even though it's barely eight o'clock. Unless you're down at the beach or in downtown, the rest of the town seems to close up when the sun goes down.

Reaching over, I grab Payton's hand. "You staying with us tonight?" I ask, bringing her hand to my lips.

"Mmmmm," she purrs like a kitten.

"Yeah, stay with us tonight, Payton. Daddy can make us cheesy eggs and toast for breakfast," Bri chimes in from the backseat.

"Who am I to pass up cheesy eggs and toast?" she asks, giving my daughter a smile over her shoulder, which makes Bri cheer.

"You know," I say casually, though my throat is lodged in my throat. "You could just stay with us. All the time."

I'm testing the Payton waters right now, not really sure how this is going to play out. Sure we've mentioned forever in conversation, but never really sat down and talked about moving in together or anything beyond that. I wasn't planning on broaching the subject tonight, however. It just kinda slipped out, and now there's no way I'm taking it back.

But if she doesn't want to move in yet, I'll respect that. We've come a long way in the last few months, and I don't want to do anything to jeopardize that. Not that this would, but the idea of *us* is still a new concept for my fiery brunette.

"Like *all the time*, all the time?" There's a hint of panic in her voice.

"That is what all the time means. But if you're not ready, that's okay. I just thought that since you're at my place most nights anyway, we could just make it easier on you. You know, save on gas and stuff."

"Save on gas."

"Are you going to repeat everything I say?" I ask, smiling across the front seat at her.

"Yes." She's quiet for a few minutes, and I decide to let her think. When Payton needs to work something out in her head, I've discovered it's best to give her time to digest before I push her to talk. So I sit back, not letting go of her hand, and drive home.

Inside, she helps me get Bri into the tub and cleaned up for bed, while I throw in a load of laundry. I've also learned to let the girls be during bath time. I've always loved helping my daughter with her bath, but there's some sort of bonding between those two, and it always happens at bath time. I'll admit, I got a little jealous the first few times Bri requested Payton help her with her bath, but after seeing both of their smiles when they were done, I decided to step aside and let them have their moment together.

When I'm almost done emptying the dishwasher, I hear the familiar footfalls of the woman I love. There's already a smile on my face when I feel her arms wrap around my waist, her cheek pressed against my upper back. "The princess in bed?"

"Waiting on her daddy to come kiss her goodnight."

Turning in her arms, I wrap my own around her shoulders and pull her in tight. "I should go in there," I say, my lips finding her forehead all on their own.

"Mmhmmm."

I give her another kiss before heading off to tuck my daughter into bed.

After a quick story, I make my way to my bedroom. Payton's already in there, naked, except for this sexy lace negligee. The sight of her makes me stop in my tracks in the doorway. It's a rich purple color that makes her tits look ten degrees of amazing. My cock is already hardening and I haven't even entered the room.

"What about my shoes?" she asks, slowly walking my way with a hypnotizing swing in her hips.

"What about them?"

"I have a lot of them. I would need ample space to store them," she says as she places my hands on her luscious mounds.

"Yes, very ample," I stutter, my eyes riveted to her breasts as if they held state secrets.

"And what about my makeup? I might need more than one drawer in the bathroom vanity to keep all of my products," she continues, sliding her hands up my chest, pushing my shirt up as she goes.

"You can take every damn drawer in the bathroom. Hell, I'll build you a bigger bathroom."

She offers me a victorious little smile before helping rid me of my shirt. As soon as it's gone, my hands return to the gorgeous lace-covered tits in front of me.

"And what about HGTV? Are you willing to lose the remote every night so I can have my fix of home improvement shows?" she asks, reaching down and unbuttoning my shorts.

"You can watch whatever you want. I'll be too busy watching you."

This smile is award winning. "Such a charmer," she says before leaning in for a kiss. Her lips are soft and plush and taste like berries. This seems to be her show, so I stand there and let her lead. Her kiss is almost exploratory, slow and tentative, and her hands continue to roam across my bare chest and shoulders.

"Okay," she whispers against my lips, her little tongue snaking out and licking across the seam.

"Okay?" I repeat, my brain short-circuited with lust.

"Are you going to repeat everything I say?" she mimics from early on the ride home, and I can't help but laugh. Payton pulls back so I can see the brightness in her emerald eyes. "Yes, I'll move in with you. It'll probably take me a little time to sort through things, and my lease isn't up until July."

"Well, I think I've waited this long for you, I could survive another two months."

"And I'll still be over here all the time. Not only do I love your daughter as much as I love you, your French toast skills are killer," she says with a saucy grin.

As I move her towards the bed, much happier and lighter than I've felt in a long-damn time, she sees the white gift bag on top of the mattress. I threw it on there when we got home while the girls were having girl-time in the bathroom.

"What's that?" she asks, sliding on the bed and reaching for the bag. "Is it for me?"

"It's for both of us, I believe. Your grandma gave it to me before we left."

"My grandma?" she asks, her hands stalling on the bag. I can't tell if she wants to throw it across the room or dive into the blue tissue paper. "Last time she gave a gift, Jaime and Ryan got a cat."

I join her on the bed. She gives me a look before slowly pulling the tissue paper out and looking inside. I can see a few things, but nothing I can really tell what it is. When she reaches inside the bag, she pulls out a notecard. Removing it from the envelope, she reads it aloud.

> When the time is right, I know there's a baby in your future. Until then, enjoy each other. And enjoy a little extra assistance for makin' the baby. According to the old wives' tales, these can all be used to help boost fertility. Good luck and enjoy! And if you ever have any questions about the sex, just call your dear ol' grandma. I'm very knowledgeable. ;)
>
> Love Grandma & Grandpa
>
> PS: The honey is not actually inserted into the vagina.

I stare down at the card, almost deathly afraid of what is inside the bag. Payton seems just as nervous as I am.

We told her family about her PCOS last month, and everyone was extremely supportive, as I knew they would be. Lexi cried, and Payton told me afterwards that she's been trying to have a baby with Chris for a few years now. With Payton's diagnosis, Lexi's ready to go back to the doc and have herself checked again.

"Honey? Why in the world would she think you would put honey in your…place?"

"Why would she ever think I would call her for sex advice?"

We stare at each other for a few moments before bursting into laughter. "Come on, let's see what the ol' woman got us."

She pulls out a baggy containing a small, shiny rock in a dark grey color. There's another notecard taped to the bag, and she reads it out loud. "This is a moonstone, used to increase fertility. The tale is that you wash it with cold water, picturing all of your worries washing away. Then place it on a windowsill during a full moon to recharge it. After it's charged, carry it in your pocket. That's it. Oh, and sex. Have lots of sex."

I offer her a small smile as I reach into the bag, pulling out a small jar of organic honey. Of course, there's a note attached to the jar as well. "Honey is believed to boost fertility. The old wives' tale says eating honey mixed with a bit of cinnamon will increase blood to our reproductive organs, preparing them for conception. That's code for sex."

Payton glances in and pulls out a white porcelain figurine of a woman. "Of course," she says to me, smiling as she reaches for the attached notecard.

"What?"

"I already know what this is. She gave something similar to Jaime and Ryan for a housewarming present. It's a fertility goddess statue. You're supposed to touch it for fertility luck. Though, the one she gave Jaime wasn't porcelain." Payton rubs on the statue before setting it aside.

Together, we glance down and find one last item in the bag.

I pull out a notecard, but it's not attached to anything. Glancing at her, I read. "According to the old wives' tale, the best way to ensure fertility is to conduct the ritual baby dance under the full moon. Now, I've been practicing this dance on your behalf, even though the full moon is actually tomorrow night. Practice makes perfect, Payters. Remember that. Anyway, head outside and let the music of the night sway you into a dance. You can do it naked, which is how I've preferred thus far. Let your body naturally move, letting yourself go, your mind clear. And if that doesn't work, follow it up with the sex. Now, go! Be free! Sex it up and make the babies. We love you, Grandma and Grandpa."

She's silent for a few moments, pulling my attention towards her. "Don't you find it weird that your grandma was practicing the baby dance?" When I glance down, I see she's holding the stone in her palm, the faintest smile on her lips.

"I can't believe her," she mumbles.

"It's all pretty wild, right?"

"You should have grown up with them," she quips goodheartedly.

"So, honey on our toast tomorrow, right?" I ask with my own smile.

"Definitely. But you know what I think?" she asks, setting the bag and all of the stuff down on the nightstand.

"What's that, sweetheart?"

"We should dance."

"Dance?"

"You know, together. Because practice makes perfect." Payton throws herself against me, knocking me down onto the mattress.

"This is my kinda dance," I say as she straddles me, my arms sliding up her outer thighs.

She's a goddess as she stares down at me, her hair hanging over her shoulders and almost touching my chest. Her breasts almost spilling from the top of her lace negligee, she's the vision of perfection. My woman. The woman I love.

"This is my favorite dance, too," I say reaching the junction of her legs.

"Best. Dance. Ever."

I pull her down to meet my lips, hungrily and full of love. She's everything I didn't even realize I wanted in a woman, in a friend, in a partner. Eventually, I'll make it official, but right now, I think we'll just enjoy the hell out of fertility dancing in my bedroom. Even if we never conceive a baby, I'll be happy as long as she's by my side. She's all I need: her and my daughter.

Before she can say a word, I roll us over so that she's flat on her back. I'm nestled between her thighs, my erection clawing through my pants. She looks up at me with a look of lust mixed with love. It's my favorite look on my favorite woman.

She's panting beneath me and we're just getting started. Started on making love, but also starting something much bigger, much greater in the universe. There's no need to dissect it right now, because as long as she's in my arms, I know I've got all I need.

Tonight, yes.

Tomorrow, definitely.

Forever, God I hope so.

"This is my kinda night."

Epilogue

Payton

It's a Summer sister tradition that on the first Saturday of each month, the six of us get together. We take turns picking the location or activity, anything from margaritas and a movie to wine and painting classes at the small gallery uptown. One thing, though, is as certain as the sun rising over the Chesapeake Bay every morning; there will be alcohol involved.

Always.

Tonight, we're enjoying the glorious June night by playing bags in the garden at The Beaver. Jaime voted for putt-putt golf, but we all vetoed her choice as soon as we saw a set of beanbags boards open. We are three teams of two, and the drinks are flowing like the salty water of the Chesapeake Bay. Laughter rings out over the sounds of the beanbags hitting the boards at our feet.

But the best part about tonight? Meghan is here, and Meghan is smiling.

After only a bit of begging, pleading, borrowing, and then even more begging, which may or may not have included siccing Grandma on her, she finally agreed to join us for our monthly sisters' night out. We felt it important to change up the routine, so I stopped by and picked her and Abby up.

We all cried when we first got here. I'm not gonna lie, it was hard to look at the bar and know that Josh wasn't going to show up well before closing time to drive her, and any of us, home. I've caught her many times staring off at nothing, the look of sadness and longing so clearly prominent on her beautiful face, traces of tears in her eyes.

We've all kept a close eye on her, especially since she hit the drinks pretty heavily at first. She's still grieving, and probably always will be, so who are we to stop her? As long as we make sure she's safe, I say let her let her hair down. It sure beats sitting at home, surrounded by his things and his memory, like she has been for more than three months now.

"Throw, Payton," my evil opponent, AKA AJ, hollers from across the yard, her nose practically dropped into a glass of some frothy girly drink.

"You know, for a teacher, you have no patience," I retort, taking a bag in my hand and getting into position to throw.

"I have tons of patience, believe me. Last week, I caught two eighth graders making out beneath the bleachers, and I politely escorted them back to class without going into the syphilis and genital herpes lecture," she says.

"In junior high? We didn't even think of doing that stuff until high school," Jaime says beside me. She's AJ's partner.

"Well, you may not have, but ol' Lexi was always sneaking off with that guy who ended up leaving town on a motorcycle the day of graduation and never coming back," Abby, my partner, says from across the game.

"Whatever," Lexi chimes in from the picnic table, where she's sitting with her partner, Meghan, awaiting for their turn to play the winner. "That motorcycle was hot."

"Didn't he wear leather pants?" AJ asks before throwing her bag and sinking it in the hole.

"Mmmhmmmmmmm," Lexi coos, a lustful grin barely concealed behind her drink.

"Remind me how you ended up with Chris again," I joke. But glancing over, I see a look on her face that tells me my comment might have hit a little too close to home for Lexi. She was always the most ornery sister, giving our dad and grandparents many sleepless nights.

I watch her look inside the bar, her eyes resting on the place where Ryan and Dean sit and talk. Chris isn't there, but he never is. If the look on her face is any indication, I'd say Lexi is about at the end of her rope with her husband's constant disappearing routine.

"Anyway," she says, drawing out that word, instead of answering my question. "His name was Blaze, and yes, he had that old Harley. Lost the V-card on that bad boy."

"You lost your virginity on a motorcycle? That's what Grandma meant! How did we not know this?" Jaime asks, her face showing the same shock I'm sure we all feel.

"Ehh, everyone assumed it was with Chris because I started dating him shortly after, and I didn't say anything to dissuade you."

"But a bike? How does that even work?" I ask, glancing back at my sexy, nerdy accountant, and wondering if he'd be willing to get a motorcycle. Or rent one? Maybe we can borrow one for a night or two.

"It's definitely possible. A few ways, actually," she says without adding anymore. And the rest of us are all left wondering and imagining the possibilities.

"Hey, doesn't Levi have a bike? You could do some research and report back next month," I say to my little sister across the yard.

Abby makes a face and stutters. "What? I'm not...doing that...sleeping and stuff...with Levi! He's my friend," she adds with as much conviction as she can muster.

"Friends to lovers, Abby. That tale is as old as time," I remind her.

"Actually, that tale was enemies to lovers," AJ adds.

"Whatever," I say, pointing my finger at the shyer of the twins. "You should go for it. I think Levi likes you."

"Not happening," she mumbles, glancing over to where her best friend is chatting it up in the bar. He's surrounded by females, all smiling widely and hanging on his every word. Some, even hanging on him.

My heart goes out to her. I know she has feelings for him, even if she refuses to acknowledge it. Jaime and I share a look, having our own conversation without even uttering a word. We've been able to do it since we were little. *Yes, I see the look she gives him. Yes, I've caught the way he watches her when she's not looking. Yes, I think they need a little nudge towards each other.*

Smiling, I glance over and see my own man watching me from the window. Yeah, I might have needed a little nudge myself. I'm so thankful he took a chance on me and wouldn't let me push him away. Lord knows I was going to, but he held his ground, and the result is a relationship that is heading towards Foreverville. For as much teasing as I've given Jaime for her coupledom with Ryan, I'm all giggly and giddy at the prospect of a long-term future with Dean.

When our game is complete, Abby and I crowned victors by, well, ourselves, Ryan and Dean make their way out to the garden. He's at my side, his arms wrapped around my waist, and pulling me close into his embrace.

"Ready to go home?" he whispers, his warm breath tickling my ear.

"Yeah," I answer, glancing over at Meghan. Abby and AJ are right there, talking and engaging with her, but I can tell she's reached the end of her night. "We need to take Meggy home."

"Okay. My car is out front. Leave yours here and we'll run over and get it in the morning."

"I brought Abby too," I tell him.

"I can take Abs home." The comment comes from behind me, and a moment later, Levi steps up beside me.

"You sure you don't have *entertaining* to do tonight?" I ask with a smile, glancing over his shoulder to see a slew of women staring, grinning, and waving at him.

"Naw, I'm good," he says, heading over to where Abby is standing. She's laughing at something AJ said, but sobers as soon as Levi walks up. I don't miss the way he touches her back as he steps up to her side, nor the way her slight smile appears to be filled with nerves.

"Let's grab Meg and we'll head back to your place."

"It'll be your place soon," Dean says, guiding me towards my other sisters.

"It will."

"Do you guys want a cat? I know one that you can have as a housewarming gift," Ryan says, stepping up beside us.

"Don't you dare give away my Boots! I would cut you off so fast, you would remember what it was like to lose a tooth before you'd remember what it was like to have sex with me."

Dean whistles beside me, but it's drowned out over my laughter.

"You know I wouldn't do that, babe. As much as I'd love to pawn Satan's cat off on sweet little Bri, I would never do that to them. Boots is our pain in the ass. I love you too much to hurt you like that." Ryan pulls Jaime into his arms and kisses her square on the lips.

"Let's go. I can't wait to play with your joystick. Maybe even road-head for being so awesome," she whispers very loudly.

"Time to go," Ryan hollers, practically dragging Jaime to the door. She waves over her shoulder, a bright smile on her face as they head home for the night.

"Do you think they'll make it home in time or will one of us be bailing them out again for indecent exposure?" Lexi asks.

"Oh, leave them alone. They're young and in love."

"Speak for yourself. She was my ride," AJ chimes in.

"We've got you," I tell my sisters.

With Abby heading home with Levi, that leaves Meghan, Lexi, and AJ to pile in the back seat. As we make our way through the bar and towards the parking lot, some swaying a little more than others, I revel in the fact that I'm so close to my sisters. We've always been tight, but as we grew older as adults, we've formed an inseparable bond. We're sisters, sure, but we're so much more than that. We're best friends. We're confidants. We're the lifelines that get us through the hard times when all we want to do is call it quits.

We've got each other's backs, and won't let them go at it alone.

We're doing it for Meghan, and we'll do it for anyone else if the need ever arises.

After dropping them off at their homes, Dean and I make our way to his place since it's closer. Brielle is spending the night with Gretchen, so we have the place to ourselves. Stepping inside the front door, I instantly feel the difference.

"It's so quiet without her here," I say aloud.

"Always has been that way for me too," Dean replies, taking my purse out of my hand and depositing it on the table. "We'll just have to come up with our own ways to fill the silence."

Turning, I find his eyes dark with desire, and they are locked on me. "I can think of a few ways to make some noise."

His lips are soft but urgent as he takes the kiss straight to scorching. There's a trail of clothes from the living room to the kitchen where I'm perched on top of the kitchen table. "I thought I'd have a little snack before bed." His grin is wicked as he squats between my legs.

When he goes to remove his glasses, I stop his arm. "Leave them on."

"You have a thing for geeks, Miss Summer?"

"Only you."

He gives me another killer smile, his hands running up the insides of my thighs, before settling in for his midnight snack. Sighing happily, I rejoice in the feel of his touch. And I'm not just talking about with his hands. He has a firm grasp on my heart and my soul. His grip is so deep, so strong that I'm sure I'll always feel it. He's a part of me.

Yep. Only him.

Another Epilogue

Abby

The truck is quiet as we make our way towards our shared building. Why do I feel so antsy? I'm practically dancing in the seat, while he's sitting there, all cool and collected, his arm casually resting on the window ledge, one hand on the steering wheel.

But Levi's always cool as a cucumber. That's one of the things I always envied about him. His laid back, go with the flow attitude.

That's also what draws every other woman with a pulse towards him.

"Did you have fun tonight?" he asks, drawing my attention back towards him.

"Yeah. I'm glad Meg came out for the night. It wouldn't have been a sisters' night without her."

"It was good to see her out," he adds, keeping his attention on the road.

We're silent the rest of the way to our apartment building. Levi parks his truck in the back lot, and asks me to wait before I get out. The truck is big and tall, with meaty tires and an engine that'll pull about anything. He's always been a gentleman when it comes to his truck, which is why I wait for him to come around and help me down.

"Thanks," I tell him as I slide out. His hands are warm against my waist, and even when my feet are both firmly on the ground, he still holds my hips.

I'm unable to move, unable to think, unable to breathe. I've been close to him more times than I could possibly count. We've slept in the same bed (clothes on, of course), ate off of the same plate, and given massages after horribly long shifts at the firehouse. But this? This feels different. It's almost intimate.

Which is how I know I'm reading this completely wrong. No way does Levi think of me in any way other than a friend, a sister almost. We've been close since we met, but lately I feel things are shifting. My feelings for him have been changing, and I just don't know how to handle that.

Slowly, I take a step back, losing his touch. He locks up his truck and, together, we make our way into the building. We take the stairs up to the third floor. Since Levi told me about what he learned about elevators in firefighting school, I've avoided them, if possible. If there's ever a fire, it's quite easier to get out via stairs than it is to get out of a stuck elevator, and then down and out of the building.

When we get to the third floor, I head towards my apartment, which happens to be directly across the hall from his. No, that wasn't planned. Levi was already here, and when this one became available, and I was looking to get out of my dad's house, he put in a good word for me with the superintendent.

"Well, good night," I say, placing my key into the knob and giving it a turn.

I don't get a response, so I glance over my shoulder to see if he's still there. He is, and he's close. His chest is practically pressed against my arm, which makes the hairs on my arm stand on end. My breath hitches in my throat, and it's suddenly hard to swallow.

He reaches forward and gives the knob a turn. When he does, his hand wraps around mine, encompassing it in heat that shoots straight up my arm and spreads through my entire body. Levi gives the door a little push, which moves his head very close to mine. I'm paralyzed with nerves, fear, lust, everything. It's all there, fighting to be the front-runner in the Drive Abby Crazy race.

"Night," he finally whispers, his breath fanning across my cheek.

And before I realize what's happening, he places a kiss on my forehead. Sure, he's done it before, but this time, his lips linger there, as if there's a permanent connection between his lips and my skin.

Oh God, how I would like to know what his lips feel like against my skin. *Other* skin.

That thought startles me and I jump back. I quickly put distance between us, stepping into my apartment so that I can no longer smell his delicious cologne. He seems casual as he gives me a little smile and wave before turning and heading across the hall.

My heart is hammering in my chest as I wait for him to unlock his door. When he does, I get another wave before I close and lock my door. Only then does he close and lock his own. It's the same every time.

But this time, I feel like I'm about to have some sort of coronary episode. This is the worst scenario that I could ever imagine. I think about him day, night, and every waking moment in between. I try to fight it, but the more I do, the harder it seems to make it through the easiest of situations. Like dinner or a simple phone conversation.

I want my best friend.

But I know that'll never happen.

THE END

Dear Reader

If you've read my books prior to this one, then you know I did something in this book I've never done before.

Josh.

When I started plotting this series last summer, I knew I was going to lose a character. It was something I wanted to do as an author, but I was so very nervous. Death isn't easy, but it's a part of life. That's why I did it. If you were one of the readers who fell in love with Josh in the first book, I truly am sorry for your loss. And I do believe that, as readers, we love, hate, laugh, and cry right along with these characters and their stories. We live them. So his death was part of all of us. It wasn't easy. Believe me, I second-guessed myself several times, sent text messages to my friends, and questioned if this was the right step. But it was.

I promise you this: It will be okay. I would never leave you without a happily ever after. Ever. So while you may want to throw your e-reader at my head right now, please promise me you'll see this ride through the end. Meghan will be okay. She will heal. She will get her happily ever after.

I promise.

All my love,
Lacey

About the Author

USA Today Bestselling Author Lacey Black is a Midwestern girl with a passion for reading, writing, and shopping. She carries her e-reader with her everywhere she goes so she never misses an opportunity to read a few pages. Always looking for a happily ever after, Lacey is passionate about contemporary romance novels and enjoys it further when you mix in a little suspense. She resides in a small town in Illinois with her husband and two children.

Website: laceyblackbooks.com
Email: laceyblackwrites@gmail.com

Sign up for my newsletter so you don't miss a single sale, reveal or release!
www.laceyblackbooks.com/newsletter